Ben drove the six miles dad's house convinced h furniture, punched-out walls, and But he had to see for himself what happened.

Turned out, the desert scape yard was no different than when his folks had it laid out five years earlier. If he hadn't known better, he would've figured his dad was home pulling together another piece for the website. He walked up the driveway, swung a leg over the crime scene tape and, with no patrol cars in sight, unlocked the front door and stepped in.

His dad had been gone over seven hours.

The house smelled like the day after a week-long frat party. Maybe his dad still had a glass or two of wine when Ben wasn't there. But his dad had never liked beer. And after the trouble in Seattle, his dad refused to have it around.

Ben shut the front door, headed down the hall and bumped the air system on high to blow the place out: house, garage, even the attic. Once he'd hit the lights and scanned the place, he realized what he'd missed when he'd first walked in. Tagging, thick as a railroad yard full of freight cars. Could kids do that to his dad? And where were the signs of a fight? And—hold it— the front door lock had worked just fine. Would it, if somebody'd forced it? He checked. Not a scratch on the front doors, nothing on the French doors, meaning his dad must've let his killer in. And he wouldn't have let in a stranger, not his dad, not a stranger.

Trap Play

by

B. Davis Kroon

The Ben Leit Series

Trap Play

Cover Art by *Jennifer Greeff*

The Wild Rose Press, Inc.
PO Box 708
Adams Basin, NY 14410-0708
Visit us at www.thewildrosepress.com

Publishing History
First Mainstream Thriller Edition, 2020
Print ISBN 978-1-5092-3008-2
Digital ISBN 978-1-5092-3009-9

The Ben Leit Series

Published in the United States of America

death. He knocked it aside and nearly stumbled over his own feet getting up. He didn't give a damn about CTE or their study. He was out of there.

Once they'd piled their bags in the Town Car and were halfway to Logan Airport, his dad spoke up. "Could you hear her at all?"

Ben kept his focus out the window, his headache was still killing him. "Hear her? Just at the end, the thing about attitude."

"But it's better now. The noise."

He could feel his dad's gaze. He shrugged a *Yeah, better.*

"You had a good run, you know—"

He shut his eyes. Like maybe that would shut his dad up. "I'm thirty-five years old, remember? What the hell am I gonna—"

His dad pushed the button that closed the window between the back seat and the driver, then cleared his throat. "You're making a mistake."

Ben glanced over. His dad looked exhausted.

"They can't tell," his dad said. "That's what she was going on about. You couldn't hear her, could you? They won't be able to tell for years. She said you had a concussion. And we knew *that.*"

His dad, just trying to make it better.

"I'm not saying get over it. I'm just telling you, she said it's fifty-fifty whether you'll ever develop CTE, okay? And even if you do, it's years away. Meantime, who knows what they come up with." His dad settled back in the seat and stared into their reflection in the smoky glass.

Ben picked at a skinned-up place on his left hand.

Then, and he would think about this later maybe a

thousand times, his dad said, "You know that thing I've been working on. I could sure use your help on it. Once that story hits the fan, it'll blow the place apart. You should come down to Arizona, work on it with me. You could take the college angle. Think about it, okay?"

****

Three weeks later, Ben moved into temporary digs in Seattle. The noise in his head had mostly disappeared. But not the headaches. He got a couple of names from Boston Med and followed up about his headaches with doctors at the UW Medical Center. His dad flew back to Arizona but kept in touch by phone. Ben always said he was doing fine.

He was fine. If he sounded a little touchy sometimes with his dad's questions, it was just he was usually hung over and that no, he didn't want to jump into his dad's big-time sports thing. And finding a job was not on his list. Finding the right watering hole was. A good one. With a smart bartender and not too much noise, so he could drink and not be hassled. Preferably it would have one of those old wood bars that stretched from the front door to the back and looked like somebody had built the place around it.

Henley's was the closest he could come up with. For one thing, it wasn't a sports bar, for another, nobody made a thing about who he used to be.

By the end of his third week in Seattle, he'd extended his drinking to match Henley's pouring hours. A week after that, he cut back on shaving. He stopped going anywhere but Henley's, went to wearing the same clothes and discovered that if he stayed loaded, his head didn't hurt all the time.

He still talked to his dad Monday mornings at 8:30.

She'd tracked Leit herself, pirated his emails, and when she discovered he was about to meet with a U.S. Attorney—well that meeting would not be happening.

Time for Mr. Frank Leit of Scottsdale, Arizona to have a fire. One in which the copies of whatever-it-was he kept referring to—but not publishing—would go up in smoke.

Without proof Rex had broken the law, Frank Leit could howl at the moon. Rex would cement its control of the market, its current CEO could make his run for the U.S. Senate, and she, Anna Lise Thorsen, would step into the Number One spot at Rex. There'd be no billion-dollar fine to pay, no jail time and no risk of prosecution for a fire that killed a few dozen people in Indonesia.

That's what you call safe.

****

She caught up with Frank Leit as he left his gated compound outside Scottsdale. She tracked him down the winding streets to an upscale shopping center where she slipped into the grocer's check-out line ahead of him. Wearing jeans, trainers, a little T-shirt and jacket, she was a blonde, six-foot-two-inch goddess running errands. As she waited to pay, she stepped back, bumping into him, her hip snug against him, and she turned to apologize.

His eyes widened. "Didn't I see you at Guidon's last week?"

An orange escaped from her bag, arching, spinning... Their hands bumped mid-grab and there was that snick of an electric charge. He blinked. Then he shot her that famous smile and handed her back the orange. "I'm Frank. You were looking at maps at

9

Guidon's."

"And you remembered that?"

He looked away a second, then back. His ears pinked. Was he embarrassed?

"Sorry," he said. "Not a stalker. Honest. It's just— You interested in hiking?"

Thorsen considered sticking with her original strategy of being not too interested. But then, what the hell? She let a tentative smile play across her face. She leaned forward and looked straight into his steely gray eyes.

"I do remember." She shook her head, ran a hand through her ultra-short hair and did her best to look chastened. Had he noticed she'd delayed leaving in order to pop in line just ahead of him?

He followed her out, talking about his usual local trails, then recommended Oak Creek Canyon. When his talk shifted from hiking to local politics to sports, she let him win her over. She sat her bag down, fished out a card from her jeans and said "I'm free most evenings and I'd love to. Just give me a call."

At 7:00 that evening, Thorsen strolled across the lobby of the Phoenician and out to the hotel lounge. The jazz was good and not intrusive. Frank Leit had already staked out a table near enough to the fireplace for her to spot him and far enough from the room's traffic that they could have an intimate conversation.

She paused for effect in the bar's entryway. Her whole look—bare legged, pale cropped hair still damp—suggested she'd barely had time to change after a swim. Her blue silk dress had a tendency to cling to her thighs and breasts. Even from across the room, it was obvious, she had nothing else on...except for a rabbiting—her father had called it that—slow and close on her neck. He was standing behind her, not quite touching her. His breath pulsed against her hairline.

She had to stop what she was doing. It reached so far into her past, she might have cut herself. She placed her knife on the countertop and reminded herself: *wine glass, knife, counter, cutting board.* Her fingers found the fluted edge of the marble and she waited, utterly still, as he traced the curve of her shoulder. Almost imperceptibly, she stretched, making room for his face to press into her neck below her ear.

He reached around her, his hand between her breasts. Then spread his fingers and slowly pulled her back, tight against him. As he held her, his free hand stroked the length of her arm.

She watched it all from the furthest part of the ceiling, how this man touched her and what he did. Sex had been like that ever since her tenth birthday. She'd discovered then how to go away.

He took his time. And she had to admit, the guy was good. Her pulse drummed away. If he picked up on it, he'd think it was him.

His voice brought her back. "Tell me what you want."

Was he onto her? This wasn't about what she wanted. The point was, what *he* wanted.

He turned her around to face him, pressing her hips back against the kitchen island, then lightly stroked the side of her face with his fingertips. The promise of a smile played across her face. "Yes," she said, and reached her hand, initially to his waist, then up and across his chest.

They carried the wine, their glasses and her bag

down the long hall to the master suite. He set the glasses on a dresser, opened the new bottle and poured for each of them. Then, as if he'd changed his mind, he abandoned the glasses and walked over to where she was standing on a Navajo rug. He took her face in his hands and kissed her as if he meant it.

She waited through his kiss the way a cat waits. Utterly still as he stroked her body, sure of the pleasure he felt touching her, sure it had nothing to do with her, certain that when she wanted, she would get away. She curled her face into his neck and breathed against him, pushing at her breath to make it real for him. She gave it a moment. And another. Then lightly cleared her throat. "Trust me, I don't mean to stop you," she said. "But could I talk you out of a glass of water?"

He returned with a tumbler of ice water. She drank and set it down on the chest, next to her purse.

He smiled. "As I recall, we were having some more wine." He offered her a wineglass. The one with a smudge of lip gloss. In his own glass, the roofies had dissolved completely. He gave her a boyish, slightly drunken grin and toasted her.

She watched as he drained the glass. Nothing to do now but wait for the roofies to kick in.

He smoothed a little tuft of hair that always wanted to pop away from her temple. His gaze traveled to the hollow of her throat. As though he were memorizing her, he traced his fingers over her skin so lightly she shivered. Finally, he dropped on one knee in front of her and laid his face in the soft hollow between her thighs. She held him there until she felt him sigh. As he stood, he caught the hem of her dress and lifted it up, away from her, and tossed the blue silk next to her bag.

16

sports program in Minnesota and the feds wouldn't give a damn.

The next five boxes though—real trouble: the Indonesia transactions, all of it confidential. How had Leit come up with this shit? It had to be a board member, or somebody from when Rex downsized its contract management group. She definitely had to make finding the insider a priority once she'd wrapped this up.

More boxes—a load of stuff on pricing, sales, market share reports. She found one entire box of calculations comparing cost of manufacture to cost of sales. Jesus. Of course Rex was price fixing, how else were they going to corner the market? The feds would see it as a slam dunk winner of an anti-trust case if they got hold of it.

Well she was there to prevent that, wasn't she? But if they did, she'd blame the whole scheme on Fitzroy. Her hands were shaking, fumbling with the papers. And she was just getting to the real dirt. Up too long, too much stress.

And there it was, on a bottom shelf: all her memos. They tied her directly to the take-down of two competitors and the fire in Jakarta. Her heart pounded and inside her latex gloves, her palms were sweating. On the one hand, *YES!* She'd found what she'd been hunting. But, Christ, how had he come up with so much of it.

She set the box by the garage door and kept going. She checked her watch. Christ, nearly 8:45, and here was another box with her name, no, two of them—they even covered her work reframing their marketing program. Those definitely would not be staying.

Hands on hips, she surveyed the mess—lids tossed, documents half-pulled out. She ripped through the last dozen or so key boxes and decided she had to call it done. To thoroughly check everything would take weeks. Spending another two hours on it wasn't worth the risk.

Out of the corner of her eye—smoke detector. A couple of minutes with a ladder and screwdriver and she popped out the lithium battery, pulled the alarm away from its connections, and stowed it in one of the boxes she was taking.

It took no time to link the incendiary packet to the prepaid phone and set it among the boxes she was leaving behind. She quashed the ringer on the phone— all she wanted was a little pop, then fire in one box. It would spread in no time. It'd gone down like clockwork in Jakarta, so why not in Scottsdale?

If she'd learned anything from her man in Indonesia, it was that it takes time for a fire to spread if a device is stowed in something as dense as boxed papers. The fire smolders as much as it burns. It's much better in silk or raffia... But you work with what you have, so loose paper. She wadded up enough paper the fire would get going, then loosely stacked the boxes around her device. For insurance, she sprayed the contents of a can of WD-40 on the burnables. Sooner or later, all the boxes would take off and eventually the heat would get to the gas tank of the Buick.

At 9:10 a.m., she was set. Would opening the garage door wake Leit? If it did, he'd be too confused to do anything but go back to sleep. Besides, nothing was risk-free. She pushed a switch by the door into the house and the big door behind the Buick climbed. She checked the street. All clear. She piled her bag and the boxes she couldn't leave behind into the back of the Wrangler and dumped her car keys on the front seat.

Once she made it a few blocks away, she would set off the fire. But an open garage door would draw attention. She headed back inside to hit the button and was taking one last look when she noticed a handful of files she'd missed. She stopped to toss them onto the burn pile and heard the garage door stop. She glanced over...it had stopped before it closed. And Frank Leit was staring at her. No, he was coming for her, weaving a little. And she saw the light go on for him.

"Rex," he spat. "That son-of-a-bitch Fitzroy." Leit stumbled forward, made a grab for her. She spun, fired with her left foot and connected with his knee.

If he hadn't grabbed hold of the metal shelves, her strike might have dropped him. Amazing, he only staggered back against the Buick. By the time he'd recovered his balance, though, she'd planted herself in the wide space in front of the cars.

Leit hobbled toward her, barel... injured leg. She spun on he... jack-hammered the k... earlier. He w... much...

She ... another thresh... down and onto the poo... forward and she'd end up ha... anyway. Less than eight yards to the ... hoist him out of the chair and go for it.

She pushed both doors open, and a neighbor's dog started barking. Immediately, somewhere the other side of Leit's privacy wall, a man yelled at the dog to shut up. And when nobody appeared, she squatted and brought Frank Leit out of his chair, again into a fireman's carry. She hefted him once to settle him on her shoulder—he felt heavier this time—then she carefully crossed the patio to the edge of the pool, lowered the body to the rounded lip and slid him into the water.

For a moment, she watched him floating face down. She stretched her back, then sprinted into the house, pulled the desk chair back from the French doors, wiped it down and left it in the shadows.

ribs. He fell back all the way to the Lexus. His f...
streaming with sweat and tears. He set his jaw ...
once more, charged her.

That was the trouble with athletes—too d...

As he reached for the hood of the Buick t...
used to pain. The only ...

himself, she landed a last blow to the side of ...
And Frank Leit slid to the floor. The only ...
she could detect was some shallow breathing ...

"Well, shit," she said and closed the gar...
the way.

Frank Leit lay sprawled on the gara...
could leave him there. That would poin...
his work and that would lead them strai...
took a swim first thing, hit his head, for...

Quickly, she stepped over his b...
the garage for anything she might u...
nothing. In her competitive days...
...but that was a trick. She tu...

Chapter 3

Ben woke at 6:30 a.m., clear-headed, with his
energy back and his body better than it'd been since
he'd stopped playing football. Yes, he'd spent six-
month in mandatory rehab. But he had made a new
start, moved and come up with a new routine—an hour
run around the south side of Lake Union, a coffee from
Starbucks, followed by an alcohol-free project.

By 8:24 he was making real strides putting together
a California Closet for his new digs on Queen Anne
Hill. The phone rang. It was Peggy Ford, his dad's
across-the-street neighbor. Her voice grim, his dad had
been assaulted, she said. She was calling from her car,
following the ambulance. How soon could Ben get
there?

Flights to Phoenix not leaving for hours, he called
his lawyer—his dad's closest friend—Paul Kaufman.

"Grab your passport," Paul said, "and get to
Boeing Field, I'll line up a private jet."

Two minutes later, Ben hit the road. He called
Peggy back from his car saying he was on his way.

"Oh Ben…" She was crying. "He's gone."

Gone. He sank back in the driver's seat, his hand
dragging at the steering wheel. He couldn't breathe. A
blast from the truck in the next lane over brought him
around and he stayed on task until, past the I-90 exit, he
checked his side mirrors and called Kaufman back.

"I just talked with Peggy. Dad didn't make it."
Silence. Had he lost Kaufman? "Paul? I'm still headed
down there…"

Then he heard background noises and Kaufman
came back on the line. "If Frank was assaulted, the
body will be off-limits, part of the crime scene."

Jesus. Like he should wait for the police to be in
touch? Like that made sense with his dad lying there.
"Damn it, Paul. It's not *the body*. It's Dad. I'm going
down there. And I am gonna see him. Now MAKE IT
HAPPEN."

Phone off, he took the Albro Place Exit, did the
loop over to Boeing Field and minutes later, the
Learjet's cabin attendant asked what she could bring
him…champagne, a mimosa, bloody mary?

He was tempted to say whatever she had back there
and keep 'em coming. But what good would that do?
"A water," he said. "And maybe something to write
on?" He started a list, just point-by-point bullets to
begin with. But in no time, he was fighting his breath
and his goddammed shakes were back. He'd been
counting on his Dad. Because once he couldn't take
care of himself, who else would be there?

He tossed the writing pad across the aisle. What
kind of a self-absorbed jackass was he?

The cabin attendant rushed forward. Was he okay,
did he need help?

He couldn't look at her. He shook his head no, he
was fine. But he wasn't.

****

The hospital's director was waiting for him—a
little woman, dark, very soft spoken. He said his
attorney had called about seeing his dad. She nodded,

but not like *okay*. "As I told your attorney, hospital policy prevents us—"

He got it she was telling him no. But she was walking him down the hall, staff dodging out of their way. She steered him onto an elevator—down. It was a labyrinth of connecting hallways; through most of the walk, she talked about the Frank Leit she knew from the newspapers. "A truly great man," she said. "Working for the people the way he did. It's terrible to think he was assaulted. What kind of a person would do that?" She turned and motioned Ben into a cul-de-sac. They stopped outside a door labeled Pathology.

"You understand the exception we are making in permitting you to see your father." She regarded Ben a moment and touched his forearm. "Mr. Leit...you don't have to do this."

Didn't he? Didn't he? He cleared his throat. "Thank you."

She nodded. "One more thing before we go in. No questions of Dr. Berger unless he invites them. Understand?" She pressed the door open and the cold hit him, then the chemical stink—antiseptic, chlorine. Funny that it didn't seem to affect the director.

She introduced Ben to Berger and made a production of how important Ben's dad was to the nation's health care community; what a leader Frank Leit had been. Then she nodded to Ben and took off.

Except for the step-in rubber shoes, Berger looked more like a crew-cut Marine in scrubs than a doctor. And no getting around it, the guy was pissed off. He scrutinized his fingertips, worked his jaw a couple of times and finally turned to Ben.

"Mr. Leit," Berger said. "This is not a place for

family. Your father's body is part of a crime scene. If you remain here, you must touch nothing. Understand? Not the body, not the table, nothing. Is that clear? If you think you might be sick, there is a metal sink. Or, if you prefer, the men's room is in the hallway on your right."

Without waiting for Ben to agree to his rules, Berger pulled together a pile of linen and jammed it at Ben. "Put this on. We're down the hall on your left."

Gowned, masked, and with his head covered in what looked like a shower cap, Ben headed into a little operating room. Berger was standing at the far end.

It felt like a different universe to Ben, one with a heavy-duty fan going. The overhead light was so intense, anybody looking could see the finest hair. For a second, he couldn't feel his feet and he had to keep fighting off the urge to hit something just to stay inside himself—*anxiety*, the people at rehab would've said. But Christ, this felt as bad as the day he'd sat with his dad to get the news he was likely a dead man. He took a breath and waited.

The doctor turned and stepped aside.

His dad lay on a steel table, stripped, covered by a modesty towel.

He'd thought he was prepared. But he wasn't.

He would say later that it was like watching a movie with the sound turned so low you couldn't take it in. And the longer he stood there, the more hiss and roar and thrum filled his head. In the end, he was working just to keep his breath even and his knees from buckling.

He stepped closer, careful to show Dr. Berger that he was not trying to touch his father, only trying to get a handle on what happened. They'd beat his dad to death. A gang, it had to be. For what? If they broke in, if they'd wanted the car, money, his dad would have handed it over, no problem. But they'd killed him. It didn't make sense.

He went for the breathing exercises he'd learned in rehab, gave himself a minute to settle down, then looked again. It was his dad's strong jaw. There was the little scar on his forehead. The cleft in his chin. It was his dad. But everything about the man that had raised him, taught him, the man he loved...that was all missing and the truth was, the body on the table didn't look like his dad at all. It looked more like a broken waxy replica.

He locked his eyes on Dr. Berger's. "Nobody could've taken Dad out without help. Just look at him. He's—he was a big man, strong, you can see how fit he was. One man could never have taken him down. Not without a gun, accomplices, something."

"I thought your father was a congressman."

"Retired," Ben said. "But before that, he played ten years in the NFL. The thing that made him so good—he was big, way more rugged than your average wide receiver."

He tried to explain about football players, the pain they get used to. It mattered, somehow, that Berger understood how, in a fight, his dad would've hung in there. Berger asked about his dad's football injuries. Only one, really. The scar on his dad's back at the left shoulder was from a surgery when he was still playing. The hair had never grown back.

For a moment they stood side by side, looking at his dad. Finally, Ben said, "What the hell happened?"

Berger grimaced. *What happened exactly* would be

up to the police and the Medical Examiner. Unofficially, "Your father was struck violently in the arm, ribs, the back of his head, and the knee. As you see." Berger pulled a stool over to the right side of the table, retrieved a small mirror and adjusted it to show a spot behind the right ear. He motioned for Ben to sit, to follow where he was pointing with a pencil.

Ben leaned in to get a better look. At first, it seemed like just a big bruise. But then Berger adjusted the mirror, and Ben got it. The bruise was huge. It spread out, back of his dad's ear, into the hairline and down as far as he could see across his dad's neck.

"Bruises like this tell the story. In medical school, they called this Battle's sign."

Ben looked up. "Battle sign? As in war?"

Berger glanced down. "Named for William Henry Battle, who described the injury as one where the victim has been struck in such a way as to fracture the skull at the base, behind the ear." He glanced at Ben and then slid the mirror down to an area near the bottom of the ribs, adjusting it so it reflected his dad's right side where his love handles would've been if he'd had any.

"Also...here, do you see? In the shadow? They struck him in the side at the ribs."

Berger had glanced up, was watching Ben, then back to the mirror.

"Either of these blows," Berger said, "either to your father's head or his side, could have been fatal. The mastoid blow, that is what I called the Battle's sign, would mean there likely was bleeding on the brain. The other—and I will tell you the deep bruising extends across much of his back—suggests something punctured the liver. I would think broken ribs." He pocketed his pencil and briefly turned away.

Ben swiped his hand across his face. It didn't seem possible. How does anyone do that to a man as strong as his dad? He was quick, agile, even at fifty-eight he still pressed over two hundred pounds.

A bone was sticking out of his dad's right forearm...the break had ripped open the skin. *What the hell had they hit him with?*

He must've said it aloud.

Berger nodded and made a quick gesture, swinging his left arm up as if he were fending off an attacker. "This is another sign of the assault, you see. As for the knee..." The tip of the pencil trembled just above his dad's knee. It looked more like a crumpled purple bag than anything. "This likely would have disabled him, the other injuries coming later."

As Berger pointed and talked, Ben kept trying to see the injuries as if they'd happened to someone else's body. Anything to keep from thinking what his father had gone through. Then it hit him, "Could they have drugged Dad? He didn't drink much, I mean..."

"The Medical Examiner's office will test for drugs and alcohol as part of their autopsy." Berger cleared his throat. "As I said before, you must think of your father's body as a crime scene—everything we have discussed is evidence of a crime. The Medical Examiner's Office will prepare a formal report which the police will use in their investigation." Berger seemed to consider whether to say something more but instead turned to Ben as if to ask *What else?*

"What kind of a weapon could do this? A pipe? A baseball bat?"

"A bat perhaps, but—"

"Or what about martial arts?"

"Identifying a weapon would be outside my field. The M.E. would address that in his report. But obviously your father was struck with something. The results, as you see, were catastrophic. For my own opinion, the weapon did not have sharp edges. But it may have had a pattern—one or two of the bruises have faint variations in them that lead me to think this is so. But I am not an expert."

Berger shook open a green drape, covered the body, then stripped off his gloves, hat and gown, and tossed them in a bin. "What you should remember, Mr. Leit: This assault would have been over very quickly. Certainly, once your father suffered the blow to his head, he would lose consciousness. He would not have been aware of any pain. Take the time you need," he said, then headed over to a counter and set to work at a computer terminal.

Ben wanted to shout at Berger. *No pain? Jesus. Look at Dad's knee, look at his arm.* Instead, he rubbed the orbit of his left eye where it throbbed. None of it would've happened if he'd been with his dad, if he hadn't fucked things up so royally.

He turned back to the table. Berger wasn't watching him. He could lift that green drape and take his dad's hand. But whatever his dad had been, his humor, his passion for football and life, all that was gone. There was nothing left but this husk of the man and the sough of the air-conditioning.

Chapter 4

Minneapolis had been freezing for more than a week. The forecast for November nineteenth had been *temporary overnight warming.* The result was four more inches of snow.

Ted Halliday straightened the blotter on his desk and checked his day planner. Satisfied that everything was exactly where it should be, he took in the view out the guesthouse window. The cedars in the backyard of the main house were bent low.

After twenty years living in Minneapolis, he should have been used to Minnesota winters. But this year, the weather was getting to him. And the more he'd buried himself in his work with Frank Leit, the touchier he was.

Not that he was depressed. He just couldn't shake loose from caring about Rex Sports even though he hated everything the company had become.

Rex had been the Fitzroy family's closely held corporation for almost twenty years before Ted and Madge Fitzroy married. And once their vows were solemnized, the family began to compare David Fitzroy—the presumed corporate heir—to newcomer Ted Halliday.

More than one cousin predicted that Pop Fitzroy would force his son David to take a back seat to Ted because the old man thought Ted was hot stuff.

Aunt Ellie said that wasn't why, "Pop just thought Ted was a better bet because David is a good-looking no-account." But Aunt Bitsy always took the other side with some version of "But David's such fun." Inevitably, Uncle Bart put an end to the discussion. "David is a Good-Time Charlie. Always was, always will be. A slick opportunist. That's it."

What the geriatric set did agree on was that Ted was a solid citizen and smart as a whip.

Within months of marrying Madge, Ted became a key player in the family. And though he was a mere son-in-law, just one year after the Fitzroy/Halliday nuptials, Ted was named as Rex Sports' new General Counsel. Ted was happy. Business was exciting. Even business law was fun. Because Rex made a great product and people respected the company.

But by the time Pop Fitzroy died—the same winter as Bart, Ellie and a couple of others who never took an interest in the company—it was David Fitzroy who stepped in as *pro tem* CEO.

A week after Pop's funeral, Ted challenged his brother-in-law for the top job. He came up with a solid plan for growing Rex's all-American business. He maintained that some corporate growth abroad was good, but Rex should keep faith with the company's regular employees before the Board engaged in any international expansion.

The trouble was, as *pro tem* CEO, David had the soapbox and the Fitzroy name. Every board meeting, David pushed his ideas. "It's cost of manufacture that's killing our profits. For every dollar we spend here, we'd spend pennies in Asia. Export our manufacturing and we'll quadruple our profits in no time."

When the votes were counted, family loyalty and the promise of quick money trumped Ted's responsible business plan. And Rex insiders quickly put out the word. Ted Halliday was business poison and *persona non grata* at Rex.

Within forty-eight hours of losing his bid to unseat David, Ted resigned from the Board of Directors and as General Counsel. The whole thing hurt his pride. It devastated Madge. They both said it felt like everything they'd worked for was gone.

A week after he lost the proxy fight, Ted told Madge they couldn't go on, not together.

"If we stay married," he said, "you'll be financially ruined. That's the bottom line and you know it. And you'll be a social outcast if that matters. But if you divorce me, if we make it big, public, and ugly, you'll be okay. Paint me as an S-O-B, honey, I'm good with it. But *you* have to do it. And you'll have to take everything."

Ted didn't mention the fact he was convinced Rex would try to ruin him. He thought it was likely they were already working on it.

Nor did he mention he wasn't done with Rex. Call it revenge if you want, but he was determined to keep the company honest. And once he put that plan in motion, Rex would sue.

Which meant Madge needed to be innocent of what he was doing. It was the only way he could protect her from what might be coming at them.

At first, she refused to go along with the divorce. She pleaded. She argued. Time and again she told him she loved him. "Don't you love me anymore?" She said it as if, somehow, the way they felt about each other would be enough to keep her from being hurt.

"What will our friends think?" she said.

He said, "Your real friends will stick by you."

When she asked how she was supposed to face their priest, he'd said, "With your head held high," and he promised to talk with Father Keeling privately.

Of course he loved her. That was exactly why they had to divorce. Divorce was the only way she'd be secure.

In the end, Madge took Ted's place on the Rex board. She also took the Minneapolis mansion, their Mercedes, their getaway on Maui, all of their other investments and half his 401K. Ted got the Camry, his personal belongings, and a 99-year non-transferable lease to the guest house at the back of the Minneapolis property.

Privately they agreed, no matter what the courts said, they were married in their hearts and before God. That was what mattered. The rest of it—all water under the bridge.

At 10:45 a.m., with his pens lined up, his notepad ready, and the outdoor temp a toasty twenty-eight degrees, Ted commenced his usual tour of the financial news sites. He was reading an opinion piece about the Asian markets when CNN's news banner flickered across the bottom of his computer screen.

Had it said "Leit?"

The bulletin vanished before the content registered.

He scrubbed his stubby fingers across his bald spot, dived into the Internet and accessed a video link on ESPN:

Unconfirmed Report: Frank Leit—former NFL wide-receiver, man-behind-the-scenes for much of collegiate football, former US Congressman and long-time advisor to Washington governors of both parties—dead in Scottsdale, Arizona. Initial reports mention a home invasion.

Ted's blood pressure stalled, then skyrocketed. He couldn't get his breath. Right under his sternum, his chest was killing him. He buckled forward into his desk, pressing himself against the pain, he barely managed to hit 01 on the speed dial.

Less than fifty yards away, in the kitchen of the main house, Madge Halliday was busy at the stove putting together Ted's usual late-morning farm breakfast of fried potatoes, bacon, toast and jam, orange juice and two eggs over-easy. He always called when he was ready for a break from his first check-in at the computer.

So, Madge knew the call must be Ted.

"Honey," he croaked, "I need help. Now."

They spent three hours at the ER. The staff tested everything but Ted's hearing and gave him an injection.

"Ted, your heart's sound as a bell. What you had was a panic attack." The doctor rattled off a canned speech about relaxation classes and stress management and handed Ted some pills to take for a few days.

At thirty degrees, in four inches of new snow, with his lovely ex-wife behind the wheel, Ted wasn't sure they would make it home in one piece. Madge drove cautiously at first, with her full attention on the road. At least it looked that way. But after going several blocks in silence, almost as a whisper she said, "You scared me. I was so afraid I'd lose you."

She switched to driving one-handed and struggled to work her free hand under her seatbelt to fish a tissue out of her pocket. As a tear traced the plane of her cheek, the car began sashaying sideways.

And that doctor had said to relax. That doctor had never seen what happened when Madge got behind the wheel of a car. Ted tightened his grip on the passenger door's overhead handle and sucked in a breath.

As if she were wrestling with disaster, Madge clasped the steering wheel. Her jaw tightened. Those aging cords in her neck—the ones she hated so much—stood rigid under her pale skin.

"Um—"

In spite of her efforts, the car slowly slipped diagonally across icy ridges in the road and headed toward the curb.

Ted hardly dared to look at her—her teeth clenched, chin jutting forward. He knew that look. Damned if she wasn't piloting them clear into a landscaped bed of evergreens and trees separating some doctors' offices from the roadway. Her gaze remained frozen to the street. The more she stared, the more the car fishtailed, eventually bumping against a low hedge and, shifting the other way, back over the center line. Madge jammed her right foot down in the general direction of the brake and ended up frantically pumping the accelerator which only made the front tires lose what traction they'd had.

Relax, buddy, relax.

But he couldn't. Not even with the mega-dose of whatever they'd given him at the hospital. His chest felt like it was ready to explode. They had to get home in one piece. And he had to get Madge away from the house, the phone, from anything that would allow Frank Leit's killer to come after them because, pretty damned clearly, they'd be next.

The trouble was, Madge was full-out crying and trying to drive.

What had she said? *What's upset you?*

How in the name of heaven was he going to tell her what he'd done?

With one hand braced against the dashboard and the other still clenched around the grab handle over the door, "Okay," he blurted. "I'll tell you what it is. I'll tell you. But only if you stop the car."

She was trembling. But she somehow managed to angle the Mercedes over to the curb and turned off the engine.

"Frank Leit's been murdered," he said and waited for her to say something.

Ever so slightly her lips pressed tight together. She sniffed but kept staring past her hands gripping the wheel and out at the still-falling snow.

"Frank Leit who's been trying to ruin Rex Sports?" she said. "We've discussed his blog at every board meeting for the past two years."

"It was on ESPN this morning," Ted said.

She shifted her grip on the wheel and turned in her seat. The look on her face, the tone of her voice, were a mish-mash of worry and regret, frustration and, he supposed, fear.

She said, "I suppose you think I couldn't guess it was you. You gave him what he was using."

If she knew, then why had she let him keep reading the stuff Rex forwarded to her? There was that look again, her eyes brimming with tears.

Another tissue. She cleared her throat. "So, what do we do now?"

We. What an amazing girl he'd married. "If they can get to Frank, they can get to us. Maggie, I'm sorry for all this. I meant to keep you clear of what I was doing."

A delivery van swept by the Mercedes, startling them with a blast of ice and slush.

Ted managed a cough. "Somebody must have discovered Frank was ready to meet with the US Attorney and decided to shut him up." He reached across the console between their seats to take her hand.

"I didn't say anything to anyone." Madge dabbed at her eyes. "And no one's ever said anything about it. About you."

"Of course you didn't." He tried to think through how best to put it to her.

"I need you to trust me on this, Madge. Believe me when I say, we need to leave. To disappear. No more Minneapolis, not any of our old haunts. No announcements, no contact. Tell your brother's secretary you've been called away. Don't tell her anything else. Just you'll be gone for a while and you don't know how long."

Her voice bumped up half an octave and the waterworks took off full blast. "Are you saying that someone…David…that my family…that somebody from Rex had Frank Leit murdered? Is that what you think?"

"What I know is, we aren't safe," he said.

"You think it's the family." She pulled her hand away.

"I never," he said. "I never said it was family."

"That's certainly what it sounds like."

"That's not it at all," he said. "You know very well

41

Rex has shareholders now who aren't family, it's been that way for ten years. And there are at least another dozen people—besides the shareholders—with enough at stake. Any one of them could have arranged for Frank's murder. And your brother wouldn't know anything about it. My point is, we could be next."

She was shaking her head in that way he knew meant nothing would be getting through to her for a while.

"You do remember what happened in Indonesia?" he said. "More than a hundred people died in that factory fire."

"David didn't know anything about it," she said. "If you'd seen his face—"

"Just think for a minute." He'd mentioned Indonesia to make the point that *someone* was capable of violence—he knew better than to accuse her brother. "After Jakarta, whenever Rex made a buy-out offer, the deal went through without a hitch."

"It wasn't David," she said.

"I agree it wasn't David. Your brother's a jerk and a phony, and I think he's missed out completely on his daughter. But—"

"You don't really believe he had anything to do with Frank Leit?" she said.

He gave her a look intended to say David wasn't responsible, that he didn't think that at all. At least for her sake he hoped not.

Finally, and very quietly, Madge said, "I can't leave right now. Not before David's dinner."

He should have remembered. Baird State University's fundraiser, aka the Man of the Year dinner. Who else could Baird pick but David Fitzroy, the

Warren Buffett of Rex Sports International? David Fitzroy had donated half of Fort Knox to his old alma mater. *David's Dinner* made the event sound like a party at a local restaurant. When in fact, every politician in the state plus the state's business big-wigs and more than a few celebrities would be there.

"No one expects you to be there," she said, "but if I don't show up, people would be looking for me. And if they couldn't reach me by phone—"

Not before David's Dinner. Much as he disliked the idea of sticking around for four or five days, what else could they do? "Point taken," he said. "I just want you to be safe. You know that don't you?"

After a moment, she returned his gaze. "Yes. I do."

"We'll take off right afterward then, okay?"

"Make it Monday," she said and started the car.

Monday then.

Alerting their security service, setting things up with his lawyer, an identity change—that would be essential. But he could handle it all without her being involved. Six days to go.

Chapter 5

Thorsen beat it from Frank Leit's place back to her hotel and headed to the airport. On the way, she pulled into Scottsdale Towne Center where she waited for a shredding service to pulverize the papers she'd taken from Frank Leit's garage. The instant the last of her memos hit the waste pile, she paid cash, yanked up her sweatshirt hood and vanished into a crowd of mall shoppers.

She gave herself ten minutes to check out the surveillance cameras. Nobody seemed to notice the contributions she made to the trash cans: a dead smoke alarm unit, Leit's wallet, ID, and Rolex. Then, last but not least, and with a certain regret, she stuffed the blue silk dress, her phony designer bag and the shoes she'd worn to dinner into a couple of restroom trash bins.

She was still congratulating herself twenty minutes later as she rolled into Sky Harbor Airport. One day to go in Houston and no big deal there. Only two meetings on behalf of Rex Sports with a couple of would-be board members and wouldn't that be fun? Once she got back to Minneapolis on Friday though, her life would get complicated. First off, she'd be shepherding David Fitzroy through his Man of the Year dinner and seeing to it that his campaign for the U.S. Senate was officially and successfully launched. The payoff for her—a junior senator Fitzroy would be learning the ropes in

Washington, D.C. As in too far away from Rex Sports to get in her way.

Besides seeing to Fitzroy, she still needed to cram the Seattle Triathlon setup into her usual corporate load—meaning her days would be a little longer for the foreseeable future.

Of course, chasing down Frank Leit's insider had to be priority one.

Through airport security, Thorsen took off down Concourse A—the same time as a man plowed through a herd of passengers and headed right for her. At first, he was just a vague figure, taller than she was, head down, shouldering his way through a swarm of businessmen. As he passed her, he broke into a trot. And she got a good look at his face. Ben Leit, hot-shot quarterback for the New York Giants. No-o-o-o, *former* hot-shot quarterback. And—she couldn't help but smile—*recent* orphan.

When she was fifty yards from her gate, a geriatric herd blundered into her path, forcing her to refocus. She waved them away, glanced at the disappearing shape of Ben Leit, then turned and upped her pace.

Definitely Ben Leit. But, so what? She'd been reading Frank Leit's stuff long enough she'd put money on it, Ben Leit wasn't part of that website. And without *somebody* named Leit at the helm, Leit's blog would be just one of more than a hundred sports gossip sites. *Relax and focus, Annie.* With Leit's war against Rex in the weeds and his proof up in smoke, there was absolutely no reason to fixate on Ben. The only threat to her was that insider. Exactly who was slipping dirt on Rex Sports to Frank Leit? And so much of it confidential. Who was Leit's man on the inside?

By the time Thorsen stretched out in first class, the ends of her fingers were tingling. Even the thought of running the insider to ground jacked up her adrenalin. She could use the flight to think.

A little woman settled into the seat next to her and fussed a book out of her handbag. Then grandma unbuckled her seatbelt and stood, flailed off her jacket, sat again and arranged it over her lap. Ten seconds later the old lady's hand, with a half-dozen gold rings and a fifty-pound charm bracelet, snaked onto the cabin attendant and instructed him about her water. Another ten seconds, chit-chat. Obviously, the old woman was under the misapprehension that the entire first-class cabin would be fascinated by her cultural adventures.

Well, Thorsen wasn't. She made her point by pulling a pen and little pad out of her bag. She would use the flight to pull together a list of insider candidates. Once she arrived at her Houston hotel, she could get down to business using the full power of the Rex system. There'd be the IT people, of course. That Indian head of Technical Security for one—she'd never trusted him. Who else?

She didn't know the names, but it wouldn't be that difficult to recollect the positions on the IT chart. Too bad she'd left her phone and laptop going in her Houston hotel. Inconvenient but they'd provide the necessary proof—if she ever needed it—that she'd been working in Texas on November 19. She twiddled the pen in her left hand and stared at the page. Too obvious to be IT. Possible of course, but in her experience those people lacked the imagination.

What was the insider's angle? Business? Or was it personal?

Getting in on Frank Leit's campaign to ruin Rex would have been damned attractive to any one of a long string of victims David Fitzroy had left in his wake. And that included family. David Fitzroy had screwed the lot of his relatives and gloated about it afterward.

If what Leit's insider wanted was revenge, whoever he was... Well she wasn't opposed to revenge against David Fitzroy, not in the least. She could use it as part of her take-over.

Family alone gave her four or five prospective insiders. Beginning with Fitzroy's own brother-in-law, Ted Halliday. *But let's not forget the two snake-eyed cousins and their revolting father.* She still had a memory of the father, at some corporate thing, eyeing her like she was the cherry in one of his sticky-sweet cocktails.

A cloth napkin fluttered into her lap.

"A beverage, Ms. Dawson?"

Thorsen flicked her head *no,* pushed the cloth aside and pointedly returned her focus to her list.

If revenge was the deal...then, slam dunk, Ted Halliday would be her first choice for Insider. Smart, efficient, cagey, with five or six axes to grind. But Halliday had been locked out of Rex ten years ago. As in, *if you see the bastard coming, call Security*—straight from the mouth of Fitzroy himself.

The snake-eyed cousins, though...they were another matter. She'd be following up on them from Houston.

It could be political, of course—somebody, or a cabal, with plenty of computer skill and invective. She'd have to touch base with Senator Mueller, or at least somebody inside the party, and get their take. And that would require some discretion.

A political pro going after Fitzroy made sense in terms of the timing.

Either way, an exposé of Rex that tied a bundle of white-collar crimes to David Fitzroy just as he announced he was running for the U.S. Senate? The stink from a load of press focused on antitrust violations would kill Fitzroy's campaign.

It would be fun to watch Fitzroy scramble while his campaign sank. But counterproductive. She may have sanitized most of the files, but burning his ticket to D.C. would leave everything at Rex right where it had been for the past two years, with her as Chief Operating Officer and Fitzroy still calling the shots. And she had no intention of playing kiss-up to David-the-narcissist until he dropped dead.

She leaned back in her seat and stared out the window. The first-class cabin attendant strolled by and hesitated.

Thorsen waved off the attention. Suddenly the idea of coming up with a list of people who had a grudge against Fitzroy felt like a gigantic waste of time. Too damned many possibilities. The real question was, how many of them had access to her memos? Ten? Twelve? Once she got back to her Houston hotel, she could check the Rex system history for who besides JR had accessed files containing her confidential memos.

Flight descending, and she was on fire. She scanned back through her notes. By the time they landed, she could barely make sense of the pages, but a smile played at the corners of her lips. Something told her the guy she wanted was right there in her hand.

Chapter 6

Ben drove the six miles from the hospital to his dad's house convinced he'd find blood, busted furniture, punched-out walls, and who knew what else. But he had to see for himself what happened.

Turned out, the desert scape yard was no different than when his folks had it laid out five years earlier. If he hadn't known better, he would've figured his dad was home pulling together another piece for the website. He walked up the driveway, swung a leg over the crime scene tape and, with no patrol cars in sight, unlocked the front door and stepped in.

His dad had been gone over seven hours.

The house smelled like the day after a week-long frat party. Maybe his dad still had a glass or two of wine when Ben wasn't there. But his dad had never liked beer. And after the trouble in Seattle, his dad refused to have it around.

Ben shut the front door, headed down the hall and bumped the air system on high to blow the place out: house, garage, even the attic. Once he'd hit the lights and scanned the place, he realized what he'd missed when he'd first walked in. Tagging, thick as a railroad yard full of freight cars. Could kids do that to his dad? And where were the signs of a fight? And—hold it— the front door lock had worked just fine. Would it, if somebody'd forced it? He checked. Not a scratch on the front doors, nothing on the French doors, meaning his dad must've let his killer in. And he wouldn't have let in a stranger, not his dad, not a stranger.

Not unless the guy had a gun. But if there'd been a gun, his dad would've hit the alarm. That's why it was right next to the front door for God's sake.

So, his dad knew his killer.

Ben caught a breath and wiped his eyes. He needed to get a grip. He was there to find out what happened. Forget about why. Why was for later. He surveyed the huge great room, trying to look past the black and purple spray paint for signs of a fight. He took it slow going over his dad's chair, checking the magazines, squinting, straining to spot something. His dad's arm had to leave blood somewhere for chrissake.

But no sign of a fight at all. Just tagging, tagging and more tagging, even the Matisse over the fireplace. And why hadn't they taken the Matisse? They'd spot it as valuable, wouldn't they? Even if they didn't know exactly what it was worth.

His mother had wrapped her arms around him, held him tight against her, and told him about the painting. He was nine or ten. A wedding present from her parents, she'd said. She'd been wearing a dress the same color as the robe of the woman in the painting. She'd tucked her hair behind one ear and it kept coming loose. Suddenly she'd laughed and said he mustn't think it was a naughty picture, that it was beautiful. A great artist had made it.

A blink brought him back to the miserable great room. It's what you don't see that can take you out.

Moving on, he inspected the rest of the house the same way he'd gone through the great room: the art gallery his mom had set up in the big room next to the entry, the long hallway, the kitchen. Just like the great room, tagging on everything you could reach without a ladder. He stopped where the kitchen and great room narrowed into the long hallway leading to the rest of the house. He hadn't come up with a single blood spot. In fact, except for the fingerprint powder around the doors, and the tagging, the only thing wrong was a couple of ripped up pillows. The tagging was bullshit. He ought to know. He'd seen plenty in New York.

He leaned a hand on the kitchen counter... He could smell beer. Where were the bottles? In fact, where was the mess? He squatted. Low enough to look the length of the marble. Not one ring from a bottle, not one empty? The only smudges on that counter were the ones he'd just put there.

It felt like nettles running up his back, his hands and arms. Fake. The whole thing. He'd bet money on it. The spray paint, the stink of stale beer, a few screwed-up pillows. They might as well have taken out an ad in the newspaper—home invasion.

Suddenly his gut dropped to the floor. He knew where his dad had been attacked.

He bolted the rest of the way down the long hall, past the guest rooms and workout room, knowing how it would be—the bloody sheets, the smashed lamps and mirrors. He skidded to a stop, snatched open the door to the master bedroom. For a nanosecond, all he could feel was the thud of his heart and pure relief.

It took his pulse settling back to normal before he could take it all in. First of all, no blood. Nothing broken. No tag marks either. His dad never left the bed un-made. Otherwise, the room looked so ordinary. The duvet folded and pushed to the foot of the bed; the Navajo rug he'd given his folks for their first Christmas in the house, not a wrinkle in it. He checked the bathroom—nothing out of place but a discarded towel, and his dad would never have done that.

One by one he checked guest rooms, guest baths, the home gym—no fight, not even tagging. That left his dad's office. And plenty of tagging and beer there. The safe was scratched up, but still locked. The desk chair was missing. Then, he remembered it was in the kitchen and why was that? And his dad's computer was gone. The screen was there but a beater laptop in place of the CPU. For sure, a piddling laptop wasn't going to handle his dad's big-time e-traffic.

He booted it up anyway. It felt like a toy. Checking the system directory... What the hell? Nothing but an operating system? Not one document? He shut the laptop down, scrubbed off any fingerprints he left with a tissue and spotted a loaner label, with a phone number only two digits off from the starting center and guards he'd lined up behind for years. He definitely could remember a series of numbers like that.

The other thing—he hardly could've missed it—a ton of papers, plus his dad's collection of DVDs, had been dumped in the middle of the floor, dumped but not trampled. Maybe they didn't find what they were looking for in the computer? Or making double-sure they got everything? What were they looking for? No way to tell and no way to know what they'd taken.

He was stepping over the papers thinking *garage,* when two cops roared in, guns drawn, radios crackling.

"POLICE! Stop right there."

Right. At first, all he could focus on were the guns

trained on him. Stay calm, keep eye contact, do what they say and you'll be okay. But then he got it: these guys were ready for a fight. Full body armor and packing enough shit they looked like they were armed for a war.

Very slowly he lifted his arms away from his body, his hands up and up until they were as high as his head. The shorter, stocky cop who blocked the door, motioned for Ben to move out into the hall. Ben nodded that he understood and, hands still up, slowly started toward them.

Oh shit. Neither one of them was more than twenty. He knew it. They knew he knew it. Both of them beyond nervous, he could hear them breathing like they'd been running. Which had to mean they were edgy. He could even see it around the mouth of the darker one, who'd stationed himself to block the back way out past his dad's bedroom. The shorter one, the thick hands, the one who had done all th... was blocking the way to the front door one ...

The noise from their radi... squirrely and he kept think... situation.

"My nam...

"St...

side of u...
bigger cop an...
blinded. They scram...
door, and the three of them b...
and out.

****

Three hours later, the fire crew had almost ... with mopping up, the neighbors had gone back inside, and Ben was left standing across the street, staring at something he couldn't explain even to himself.

Two years earlier, his mother had died in that house.

And now his dad.

And it sure as hell looked like his dad's work was gone too.

The fire captain promised he'd forward a copy of his report and left.

Nothing much left inside the garage. The firemen helped wrestle the doors closed, and Ben caught up with the detective on the case, a guy named Baldwin. Ben laid out everything he could think of about his dad: habits, contacts, the website and his dad's blog. Baldwin delivered a lecture about letting the police do their job, that Ben was no investigator, and that he'd almost gotten himself killed. "And now," Baldwin marched up to the front door and motioned Ben inside. "You're gonna set the alarm. We're gonna lock up and you're gonna stay out of the house until I give you the okay. Got it?"

Once everybody'd left, Ben walked over to his car and stood there looking. Thirty minutes earlier there'd been a load of people on the street—the fire crew, neighbors, cops—and that quick, he was alone with a

had understood. But Shorty moved away, went for th
phone again, and after maybe a minute said, "Your
Put it on the counter. But slow."

Ben nodded. He kept his left-hand up in full
Slower than slow he reached his right hand ba
with two fingers and a thumb he extracted hi
and laid it on the kitchen counter.

Shorty examined Ben's ID, passed it to h
and after another phone conference, the gun
in their holsters. But there was no apology.

"Okay, you're Ben Leit. You still c
house."

These guys weren't working on
But they could relay information to th
tried to explain why he was in his da
he could help with the investigati
was the key to everything. If they
in the garage, that's where mos
was.

The fact he was trying to
them off, he got that, but he
out there? Not even to verify

The cops eyed him like *are you*
thought maybe, just maybe. Because
Shorty looked ready to hit the road, the dark
wanted to see the garage. After a little back and forth,
Shorty rolled his eyes and made another call. Clearly he
didn't like the answer he got. "Two minutes in the
garage," he said. "And it'll be the three of us."

Ben opened the door to a pitch-black garage.
Hotter than hell. He turned to the cops right behind him.
"There's one step down," he said. And just as he
reached for the light switch, a fireball shot up the far

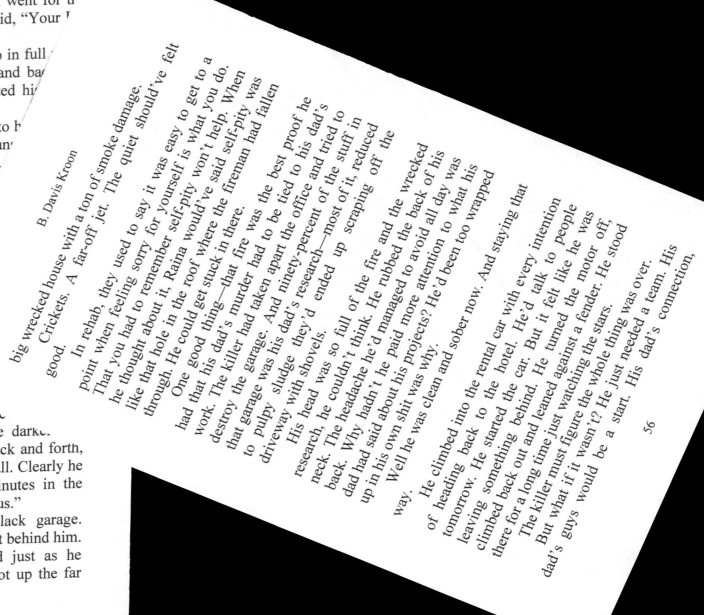

big wrecked house with a ton of smoke damage.
Crickets. A far-off jet. The quiet should've felt
good.

In rehab, they used to say it was easy to get to a
point when feeling sorry for yourself is what you do.
That you had to remember self-pity won't help. When
he thought about it, Raina would've said self-pity was
like that hole in the roof where the fireman had fallen
through. He could get stuck in there.

One good thing—that fire was the best proof he
had that his dad's murder had to be tied to his dad's
work. The killer had taken apart the office and tried to
destroy the garage. And ninety-percent of the stuff in
that garage was his dad's research—most of it, reduced
to pulpy sludge they'd ended up scraping off the
driveway with shovels.

His head was so full of the fire and the wrecked
research, he couldn't think. He rubbed the back of his
neck. The headache he'd managed to avoid all day was
back. Why hadn't he paid more attention to what his
dad had said about his projects? He'd been too wrapped
up in his own shit was why.

Well he was clean and sober now. And staying that
way.

He climbed into the rental car with every intention
of heading back to the hotel. He'd talk to people
tomorrow. He started the car. But it felt like he was
leaving something behind. He turned the motor off,
climbed back out and leaned against a fender. He stood
there for a long time just watching the stars.

The killer must figure the whole thing was over.
But what if it wasn't? He just needed a start. His
dad's guys would be a team. His dad's connection,

whoever was giving him dirt on college ball, that'd be another part of it. Those names had to be somewhere.

Chapter 7

Ben leaned against the hood of the rental car. Too full of everything that happened to really think, his gaze pinged from his dad's empty house to the Phoenix basin below him. The sun was nearly gone and the cold was getting to him. But the stars were everywhere. The stars were what he'd been waiting for, and the only good thing about being at the Scottsdale house. He fished his cell phone out of his jeans, closed his eyes a second, then keyed in the number for *Computer Rescue*. He landed in voicemail.

He was not about to sit around and wait for a call back. His dad's missing computer would have the names and numbers he needed to get moving. So getting hold of his dad's computer guy had to be step one.

Thirty minutes later, *Computer Rescue* turned out to be a one-man shop in a neighborhood on the down slide. The target house sat on a corner lot with the usual yard—forty years ago, some cyclone fence salesman had a big day. The front gate was locked. A yard light came on the second Ben vaulted the fence. But no lights inside and all the ground floor windows and the front door had bars.

He bounded up on the porch anyway, knocked, rang the bell, then hollered. Nada. Back to the sidewalk, he headed around the corner. Vowing if he had to, he'd stay there all night. He followed the cyclone fence past the side of the house and what do you know, found a tidy crushed gravel walk leading to a side door in what used to be a garage. There was frosted glass and bars on the windows and two signs by the door. The big red one read *Guard Dog* *** *Beware*; the other, *Computer Rescue by appointment only*.

Right, he was gonna call for an appointment and wait around while what happened to his dad turned into another subparagraph in the local papers' stories about a home invasion.

He banged on the door.

Behind the frosted glass, somebody said, "Can't you read?"

"It's an emergency," Ben said.

"We're closed."

Ben got as far as I'm Ben Leit when the inside door opened. True, the steel-bar safety door was still lo... but at least somebody'd opened the solid do...

The guy was maybe five-foot-eight ... Asian version of a Mr. Po... shoulders and arms but li... with stubby legs. A ...

The good news ...

Ben

Lo...

up som...
hookup, bu...
him up with an o...
what was wrong. He'd ...
never seen before."

Spyware? "You mean like just c...
could...?"

"No. This was way more sophisticated. Som... was stalking your dad. My guess, they'd been doing it for a long time. Documents, emails, texts, anything in or out of his computer, the spyware sent a copy to an Indonesia address. I should've called him yesterday but..." Park shook his head. "You have to figure Indonesia was just a pit-stop. Deals like this, they forward what they've copied, wash it four or five times before it lands where the stalker is located."

Ben muttered something he'd heard about antivirus security and Park said even the best security software won't catch everything.

"Your dad's system missed the spyware because it came in in pieces, strings of programming sent as invisible attachments to harmless-looking emails. Once all the pieces linked together on Frank's hard drive, the last piece of programming turned the spyware on."

The sting on Ben's arms was back.

His dad would never see something like that coming. And it'd be such an easy way to get to him, given how he'd been living on his computer. It was like the stalker had been standing in the hall, in the dark, watching his every move

A stalker made sense. You play ball, make a name for yourself, get a few TV interviews, there's always a nut around. Probably every guy writing for that website

Ben stepped through the door and stopped—t[oo]
late if he wasn't. This dog was big as a pony. It sho[w]
up out of nowhere and stood right behind Park[.]
growl, no bared teeth, just wary yellow eyes[.]
string of drool out the side of its mouth. The e[ars had]
been cropped close to its head and you could s[ee]
one of them had been mauled. Ben cou[ldn't help]
thinking it didn't much matter that he was[.]
that he weighed two-forty. This dog coul[d]
his thighbone in one bite. The only thing[.]
he'd played ball with a couple of gu[ys]
mastiffs. So the thing to do was keep[.]
and his voice low and friendly. He[.]
chair Park had pointed to. "I nee[d]
computer," he said. The dog di[d]
cough and walked over to a big[.]
showed up with a ball which it d[.]

"Leave it," Mike said to th[e]
Ben. "Where's Frank?" The[.]
floor.

Ben started to explain[.]
wouldn't come. Park waited.

Once he got it together, he lai[d]
at the hospital, how his dad had look[.]
somebody'd beat him, what the doctor said.

Park slid out of his chair, grabbed a box of Kleene[x]
and sat it between them. Then cleared his throat. "Right
after he moved down from Seattle, Frank hired me to
set up his system. And every once in a while, he'd call.
Usually it was nothing." Behind his glasses, Park's eyes
watered. "So when Frank called…he said any big
download about killed his system. Once we got straight
how big the downloads, I told him probably he'd picked

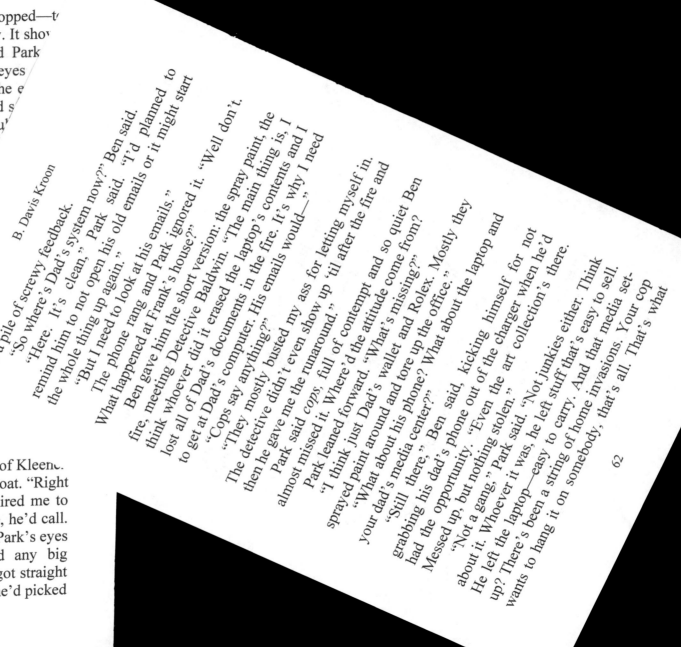

had a pile of screwy feedback.

"So where's Dad's system now?" Ben said.

"Here. It's clean," Park said. "I'd planned to
remind him to not open his old emails or it might start
the whole thing up again."

"But I need to look at his emails."

The phone rang and Park ignored it. "Well don't.
What happened at Frank's house?"

Ben gave him the short version: the spray paint, the
fire, meeting Detective Baldwin. "The main thing is, I
think whoever did it erased the laptop's contents and I
lost all of Dad's documents in the fire. It's why I need
to get at Dad's computer. His emails would—",

"Cops say anything?"

"They mostly busted my ass for letting myself in.
The detective didn't even show up 'til after the fire and
then he gave me the runaround." Park said cops, full of contempt and so quiet Ben
almost missed it. Where'd the attitude come from?

Park leaned forward. "What's missing?"

"I think just Dad's wallet and Rolex. Mostly they
sprayed paint around and tore up the office."

"What about his phone? What about the laptop and
your dad's media center?"

"Still there," Ben said, kicking himself for not
grabbing his dad's phone? What about the art collection's there.
had the opportunity. "Even the charger when he'd
Messed up, but nothing stolen."

"Not a gang," Park said. "Not junkies either. Think
about it. Whoever it was, he left stuff that's easy to sell.
He left the laptop—easy to carry. And that media setup? There's been a string of home invasions. Your cop
wants to hang it on somebody, that's all. That's what

they do."

The dog was lying on Ben's shoe. It'd started to snore. To give himself time to think, Ben reached down and stroked the dog's good ear. Finally, he said, "I really need Dad's computer. It's the only way I can get to this guy, you know? If I can get into Dad's email."

"Do not mess with his emails yourself," Park said. "Get an expert who works with lawyers. He'll make you a copy you *can* look at safely. If you open the emails on your own, it changes them. Do not fuck up the emails, get yourself an expert."

Ben leaned back in his chair. "Why can't you do it?"

"Wish I could. But what you need is outside my… See, I'm a computer geek. I hook stuff up, do hardware and a little teaching. What you want is somebody who works in software. It's a specialized software." Park went on about how the software worked while he pulled a huge box of stuff together.

Ben hardly listened. Instead, his brain went into one of those overload spins. He didn't have time to hunt down an expert, and what else was there to get from his dad's computer, and who else could he ask for help.

Eventually Park set the big box of stuff on a chair. "I'm handing off your dad's CPU, and here's a clean backup set for you, and a I've loaded this laptop you can have—I figure you didn't bring one with you. When you walk out the door, I'll have nothing for the cops. You understand?"

Loud and clear. "Okay if I call you with questions?"

"You? Sure. But don't call for your cop. Do that, we don't talk again." Park pulled a binder off a shelf and began fanning through the pages.

Ben stood, fingering the box. "You know, in a day or two, they'll be onto you as Dad's computer guy. Don't wait for them to find you, okay?" And when Park didn't respond, Ben kept going: "You know I'm right. This isn't a time to stonewall the cops. Give it the night. Call tomorrow. What you say won't change the cops' thinking. But you know sooner or later they will get around to the computer. That'll lead them to you. Whatever your own story is, you'll be ahead of the game. Trust me. I got your back, same as Dad." He fished out his wallet.

Park waved off the money. "This—" he poked a business card at Ben, "—this guy taught me everything I know. Now he's a full-time consultant." Park tucked the card into the box next to the CPU. "Just find a way to get the bastard."

At his rental car, Ben pulled out his smart phone. He googled Mike Park and court cases in the state of Washington. No criminal actions naming Mike Park. *But you can't get rid of news stories.* And there it was, in the Tacoma News Trib. Michael Park, age eighteen, drove the getaway car.

Ben couldn't help the smile—his dad again. Who else could get a conviction wiped off Park's record? Who else could help get Park's life turned around? Mike Park was another one of his dad's projects. Seeing how Mike had turned out, his dad must've been proud.

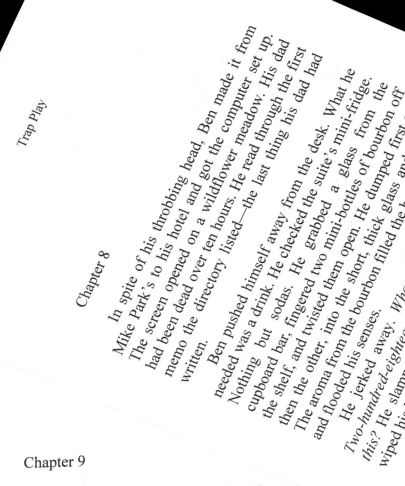

Chapter 8

In spite of his throbbing head, Ben made it from Mike Park's to his hotel and got the computer set up. The screen opened on a wildflower meadow. His dad had been dead over ten hours. He read through the first memo the directory listed—the last thing his dad had written.

Ben pushed himself away from the desk. What he needed was a drink. He checked the suite's mini-fridge. Nothing but sodas. He grabbed a glass from the cupboard bar, fingered two mini-bottles of bourbon off the shelf, and twisted them open. He dumped first one, then the other, into the short, thick glass and The aroma from the bourbon filled the and flooded his senses. He jerked away. Wh

Two-hundred-eighte this? He slamm wiped his

Chapter 9

"Time to go red," Thorsen said to Houston's highly-recommended hair colorist. It'd been less than a week since she'd traded her power broker's dusty-gold bob for a slicked-back platinum look. But after Phoenix and two flights posing as Lee Dawson, she was finished as a blonde.

The rail-thin beautician ran his fingers through Thorsen's nearly white hair and arched one eyebrow. "Any specific shade of red?"

"You pick. But something spectacular," she said.

The salon's air, the colorist, the stylist, the gently probing fingers, the hushed gossip, the stink of the thick hair dye, the touch of the brush—it had been part of her life since her first beauty pageant at age five. Almost out of habit, she gave herself up to the familiar process.

The colorist sectioned Thorsen's hair and asked about her week.

She couldn't help but smile. The point of the trip to Phoenix had been to eliminate the proof Frank Leit kept hinting at. Well it was toast now. And there was nothing to tie Anna Thorsen to Phoenix. Or to Frank Leit. Except that file of emails she'd pirated; but they were buried so deep in the Rex system they'd never be spotted. They were…a ghost file.

So how was her week? She'd give it a nine and a half. But only because she still had that insider to track

said he should've told them before, but please,
liquor. Then he dragged his own phone out of his je
He ignored the screenful of messages and calle
sponsor.

Bobby Joe picked up. But all Ben hea
chairs scraping, then voices in the backgrour
on, okay?" Bobby Joe said. "My group's jus
Finally, the thunk of a heavy door closi
could hear the big man breathing into his
man, I'm so sorry about Frank. You oka
do?"

Ben said, "I'm just—I guess I'm l
tell me how to…uh…"

"Stick with the program? Am
you now? What city?" Ten seco
gave Ben an address.

Twenty minutes later Ber
door of a Unitarian Church r
he felt a lot better when th
shimmer of the fluorescent '
a folding chair, joined the ?

When the time came, he
I'm an alcoholic."

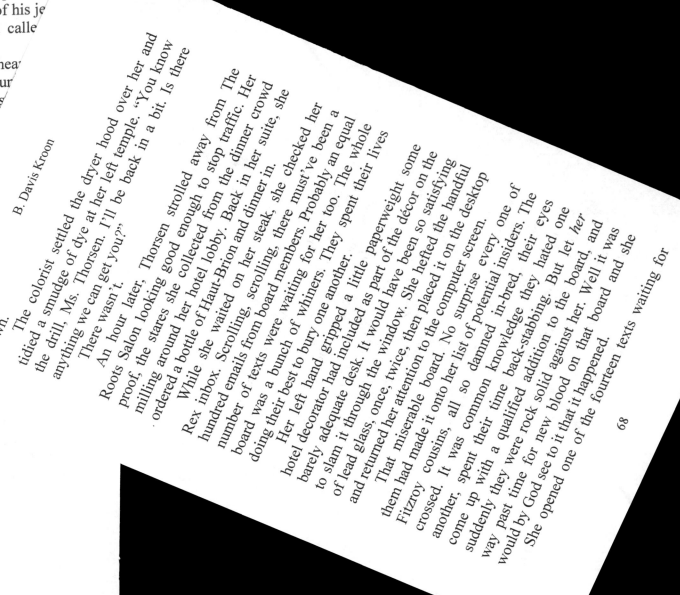

down.

The colorist settled the dryer hood over her and
tidied a smudge of dye at her left temple. "You know
the drill, Ms. Thorsen. I'll be back in a bit. Is there
anything we can get you?"

There wasn't.

An hour later, Thorsen strolled away from The
Roots Salon looking good enough to stop traffic. Her
proof, the stares she collected from the dinner crowd
milling around her hotel lobby. Back in her suite, she
ordered a bottle of Haut-Brion and dinner in.

While she waited on her steak, she checked her
Rex inbox. Scrolling, scrolling, there must've been a
hundred emails from board members. Probably an equal
number of texts were waiting for her too. The whole
board was a bunch of whiners. They spent their lives
doing their best to bury one another.

Her left hand gripped a little paperweight some
hotel decorator had included as part of the décor on the
barely adequate desk. It would have been so satisfying
to slam it through the window. She hefted the handful
of lead glass, once, twice, then placed it on the desktop
and returned her attention to the computer screen.

That miserable board. No surprise every one of
them had made it onto her list of potential insiders. The
Fitzroy cousins, all so damned in-bred, their eyes
crossed. It was common knowledge they hated one
another, spent their time back-stabbing. But let her
come up with a qualified addition to the board, and
suddenly they were rock solid against her. Well it was
way past time for new blood on that board and she
would by God see to it that it happened.

She opened one of the fourteen texts waiting for

her from her assistant.

—*We need to talk*—

She texted back —*What's going on, be specific.* And got: —*Ms. Thorsen is away on business and I am out sick*—

—*Sorry for the inconvenience. If this is urgent,* blah, blah, blah—

She called JR's cell and immediately landed in voicemail.

"JR, call me ASAP," she said. "If I'm in a meeting, I'll get back to you. And JR, you know better than to turn your phone off. Take it with you. Yes, even to the toilet."

Her dinner arrived. While she ate, she put together a list of employees who had access to the entire Rex system. Then she narrowed that list to football people with access. She came up with thirty-two. With luck, among those thirty-two citizens, there would be someone who had gone into business with Frank Leit.

It was easy enough to access their bank accounts via Rex payroll records; and for most of them, she found nothing out of the ordinary. It was incredible, though, how boring their lives were.

One exception to boring…Jeb Connors had an on-line gambling habit. When she checked his HR file, and reading between the lines, it looked like two years ago Connors had been on his way to a top international job. Then Fitzroy had screwed him, but good. Could it be that Connors figured a way to dig into the system and take his revenge?

Even more interesting, the number two man in IT—Raj Banerjee's bank accounts showed more than two thousand large cash deposits over a four-year period. He would certainly have access to everything in the Rex system. And who was giving him that kind of money, and for what? Well then. That was two possible insiders right there to be pushed a little. Just to see what popped out.

But that didn't mean she'd be scratching the Fitzroy twits from her list. Not yet. She would set her New Orleans people on all of them—including the family cousins. With luck, by the time she was back in Minneapolis, she would have some answers.

The next morning, she was up at 5:00. She checked her cell...still with no response from JR. She set the phone aside and finished applying her makeup. Sooner or later she was going to have to fire JR. He was such a damned pain.

Of course he was a pain. That's why he was an assistant. But he was a *loyal* pain, with an unerring sense of survival. And they both knew his survival depended one hundred percent upon hers. Point being, he never left a *need to talk* message unless something was about to fall on her.

So, what was going on? She finished her face and called JR again—nothing. She sent him a text and took off for her interviews.

As far as she was concerned, that meant which old white guy would better serve her interests once she was CEO at Rex? Would it be her 7:30 breakfast—she'd hand-picked him for his marketing ideas. Or David Fitzroy's man, R. Lakeland Conrad. Seriously? She'd be dropping in on his 9:00 o'clock talk over at Rice University.

Just after 11:00, she strolled into the executive lounge at George Bush International Airport and claimed a secluded corner. She asked the lounge attendant for an espresso, took one sip, set it aside and booted her tablet.

As far as her meetings had gone… She'd already vetted both Board candidates, *thank you Specialty Dining.* But a damned good thing she'd had a face-to-face with them. It had taken her more time to drink her coffee than it had to dump her candidate. Let's just say, he might have looked good on paper, but he was pompous, boring and a disappointment. Her story for the executive committee would come in the form of an apology: He had discovered a conflict of interest that prevented him from serving on the Rex Board.

She had an entirely different problem with R. Lakeland Conrad. He'd given a very solid presentation at the Rice University business school. And during his talk on corporate growth in the international market, he'd actually raised a couple of points she hadn't considered. After the seminar, they had a nice chat together. She had to admit, he was personable, affable, he didn't waste time on non-essentials and it seemed to her he was damned smart. Conrad would be a real asset to the board. In fact, she had no objection at all to him except that he was Fitzroy's candidate. What to do, what to do…

She dragged out her phone and checked her in-box—still no word from JR—and she caught herself staring around the room. Given that she was due in an Executive Committee meeting the instant she got back to Minneapolis, now the question was, could she support Fitzroy's man?

A pair of business commuters strolled into the airport lounge. Lawyers, based on their uniforms—the older man just her type. Wearing Giorgio Armani. He immediately laid his exquisite briefcase on a table and grabbed his phone. He'd barely noticed her. Well, that was his loss. The associate—who'd hadn't stopped checking her out—definitely not her type. His shoes were worn at the heel, they should be replaced, or at least polished. And he needed a haircut.

Pity. As she scrolled down the latest list of unopened emails, she picked up the espresso cup, swallowed the last palatable mouthful and spotted an update from her buddies in New Orleans—an amendment to their report on the board candidates.

Well, well… It seemed that R. Lakeland Conrad and his publisher had promoted his 2015 best seller by touting Conrad's fresh take on the world markets. Reviewers had said his theories were pure genius. There was just one problem with that. Dr. Conrad's celebrated theories first appeared in a thesis published three years earlier at the Universidad de Buenos Aires. A thesis written by Jose-Maria Valenzuela.

Naughty, naughty, naughty Dr. Conrad. Nobody likes a plagiarist.

Thorsen emailed her New Orleans investigators, requesting the original thesis—it would have to be an original or one certified by the university's authorities. Fitzroy would be delighted to have her support for Conrad. Down the road, if the good doctor got in her way, she would have what she needed to keep him in line. And, with the board question settled, she finally caught up with JR, who—when he wasn't coughing— sounded like he was whispering from the bottom of a well. His apology for not getting back to her might have lasted five minutes if she hadn't interrupted him.

"You made it sound urgent," she said.

"Oh… I did call. But then I collapsed in the hallway and they took me to ER and I was so woozy and they took away my phone and they had me on so many drugs and the worst part was the doctor in ER was so cute and I looked like crap and—"

"JR, if you're sick, you're sick. But you said in your message it was urgent. What's up?"

"But I thought you'd want to know," he gasped.

"Spit it out."

Coughing for a solid minute. Then a rattling and throat clearing. Finally, "Mr. Fitzroy might change his mind and run for Governor instead of the Senate."

It was all she could do to not pitch her phone against the wall.

David Fitzroy was not allowed to change his mind. He had already made it known he was running for the Senate. Senator Mueller was already involved. It was imperative that David Fitzroy win that senate seat. She would NOT have him sitting less than fifty miles down the road trying to pull the strings of the Board of Directors at Rex. She would not have it. David Fitzroy did not exist in the life she had planned for herself as the next CEO of Rex Sports.

She could hear JR wheezing into the phone. "He's changing his mind?" she said. "Well that is news, isn't it? It really won't impact my projects though. But thank you, JR, for your diligence. You should send yourself some flowers and charge them to my card. Oh, and JR—don't fret about David. Whatever he decides to do, I'm sure we'll all be right behind him."

Chapter 10

Rolf clicked off his billing timer and shut down his computer screen. He raised his voice. "You still working on Etouffee? What's the hold up?"

Hart unfurled himself from his usual computer crouch and shook his head no. "Twelve down, one to go," he said and motioned for the conference room. The Halliday detail didn't make sense.

"Client won't like that," Rolf said and followed the younger man down the passageway and into the little conference room.

"Can't help it." Hart closed the door and took a moment to let the *faster-harder-fierce* message of Rolf's KREATOR T-shirt sink in. "Halliday went off the grid the minute his divorce was final. He has a studio apartment with a roll-over lease but hasn't been there in eight years. The apartment manager's records—that got me to the bank account—confirm Halliday pays his rent by auto-debit. As for the bank account—I can confirm the balance will support a twenty-grand charge but that's about it. The bank accounts are double-washed so even I can't crack the activity reports."

Rolf started reciting his standard list of what to do next and even before he'd made it half-way, Hart rolled his eyes.

"Halliday's mail goes to a law firm downtown. But

according to the Minnesota Bar and the ABA, he's not working there. And that's the real stickler. I can't crack their system."

"What you mean you can't—"

Hart shook his head. "You will agree, nobody's ever stopped me, right?"

Rolf backed his skinny ass up against the door frame and shrugged an *Okay, so?*

"Well whoever set this law firm's system up—if it *is* a law firm—they stopped me. At least so far. I can say Halliday's not working for that law firm, I got that from Minnesota Workers' Comp. Other than that, I can't say anything about the last ten years. Just trust me: Halliday is off the grid except for his retirement account which is still part of the Rex Sports deal and it pays into those bank accounts."

Rolf's eyes tracked around the room and back to Hart's pinched face. "Contacts?"

"Except for the apartment file and that 401K—they list Halliday's ex-wife—his contact data's a black hole. His car shows he's living at that apartment I told you about, but it's never been spotted there. So, bottom line, unless Ms. Etouffee wants us to put boots on the ground, I've struck out." Hart jammed his hands in his jeans' pockets. "How about you?"

"The wog was naturalized two years ago." Rolf scrubbed his nose again. "Not married. I'm guessing he's got illegal family."

"We care because?"

"Because the client wants us to," Rolf said. "Banerjee's hiding something. Drugs, whores—why else more than three hundred cash transfers a year and all under the banks' reporting limit. He owns three houses and three SUV's. Paid cash. He lives in one of the houses but pays utilities and phones for all three of them. International calls all over the place. Those SUV's? Who's driving the other two? I'll get back to the client about whether she wants a staffed follow-up."

Hart rubbed a raw spot at the back of his ear. "Anything about how Etouffee connects to this stuff?" Rolf shrugged.

"Not my business. We sell information. What our clients do with it, not our responsibility."

Chapter 11

Even before Ben left AA, the back of his head was pounding. Twenty minutes later, his hotel room was stifling. Then he was freezing. His left eye wouldn't let him read. He chugged the max dose of his headache meds and emailed the expert that Mike Park had suggested. Then, he didn't so much sleep as he died. Next morning, he hit the computer.

Park's expert emailed saying sorry can't help. Polite, full of apologies, but no. Ben forwarded a copy to Park: *Any other ideas?*

The only other computer guy Ben could think of was Thui, the administrator for his dad's website. He put in a call. According to Thui, there was no spyware on the website's server, no threats or serious complaints. Though a few dozen readers regularly emailed their corrections, opinions, and gripes. The big thing, there were absolutely no complaints from corporations. Which might have pointed at something if there had been.

Well he was not sitting around waiting to hear the cops had seen the light. He booted his dad's computer and started at the top. Reading memo after memo, it was like his dad was sitting beside him. Every page bristling with dates and times, opinions, weird little quotes and phrases, misspellings, best of all, every kind of reference you could hope for. He started a list of the zillion citation numbers that he figured linked to the research files. The trick was going to be how the pieces fit. Eventually though, all he could think of was the last time he'd seen his dad.

Just a month ago, he'd flown down and they'd ended up out on back slope of that damned Scottsdale house, in that spot overlooking the whole Phoenix basin. *Just one month ago.* They'd talked their way through sunset out there. Mostly, about his stint in rehab and what was next for him. His dad kept watching a plane heading into Sky Harbor Airport—it'd looked like a toy hanging in the glow. For the nine-hundredth time that weekend, his dad had pushed for him to move south. And he'd promised to, but later. He'd told his dad the main thing right now was to stay clean and sober. He would figure something constructive to do, he just didn't know what that would be.

They both knew what he had in mind, that he'd head south once he started losing it and couldn't take care of himself. His dad just nodded, then shifted their talk to some story he had going for the website. A blockbuster, his dad kept saying. It would shake the sports businesses to their foundations.

Ben grimaced at his reflection. He'd only half-listened. And now, it felt critical that he remember everything his dad was working on.

He headed down to the hotel's fitness center thinking maybe what his dad had said would come to him if he worked up a sweat. Cardio, free weights, he was doing fine, ignoring the TV and counting reps when the detective on his dad's case showed up on the big screen. The Mayor and some police muckety-muck were claiming they'd caught the home invasion gang—everybody beaming *case closed.*

He pitched one of the hand weights into a wall of chrome. He didn't think about it, just pitched it. Ten pounds. Made a hell of a dent and the sound reverberated like a shot. In nanoseconds, a couple of security guys roared in. "Sorry. I slipped," he said. And once he got things straight with the hotel manager, he headed back to his suite and called Bobby Joe. He'd blown it again. He needed help, just like they'd said in rehab. He promised Bobby Joe that once he got back to Seattle, he'd get with his doctor.

With the fitness center out of bounds, for the next two days, he stuck to the hotel room. His new routine involved reading until his eyes rebelled, eating when he was hungry, doing calisthenics, and sleeping when he couldn't stay awake.

His dad's stuff was crammed with notes on how big money and TV were influencing college sports. That might have jacked up his dad, but it seemed pretty harmless to him. For a second, he thought he'd stumbled on a real threat to his dad, an athletic gear company out of Minneapolis called Rex Sports. It looked like his dad had pulled together a load of dirt on Rex—white-collar crimes like price fixing and something called tie-ins, where Rex was forcing its customers to buy stuff that they didn't want in order to buy stuff they did want. If it was true, that would explain how Rex had gone from a Midwest sports shoe company to the giant it was. But that would only be interesting if you started your day reading the financial pages of the newspaper. Clearly his dad saw it as a huge story and, well, it was. Still, people getting killed over white-collar crimes? That seemed like a no-go.

But there had to be something in his dad's stuff. The killer had torn the place apart to find it. He leaned an elbow on the little desktop and reread what he'd just been through. What he kept sticking on was, his dad knew the killer. His dad trusted the man that killed him enough to let him in the house. So the killer's name was right there in his dad's stuff. It had to be. He wasn't seeing it. Why not?

He called Mike Park. *What am I not seeing?*

"Did you check the download files?" Park said.

Well, that would be a no.

"How about the stuff your dad had stored as photographs?"

The 'photographs' turned out to be newspaper pages in Japanese or Chinese—no way Ben could make them out. But his dad had kept them, written notes all over them.

He ended up walking around the sitting room about nine hundred times. Finally, it hit him. He didn't need a name, not really. He needed the killer to think that fire at his dad's place hadn't worked. That whatever had been in his Dad's garage hadn't burned at all.

The killer had been a blog reader, so why not take over the blog, do a little pump-fake and turn himself into a target. Sooner or later, the killer would come for him.

Just making the decision, his headache vanished. Last thing before he headed back to Seattle, he sent the website administrator his first blog post.

RIP Frank Leit: 1960-2019

Sometimes a great drive stops short of the goal line. Dad's playing in another league now.

Dad's column in the football blog will take a break in honor of his passing. Look for my first post on November 24. My promise to Dad's regular readers, you will get quite a jolt.

Meantime, I know it's mid-season, but I encourage you to spend time with your families.

Ben Leit

Chapter 12

Raj Banerjee stepped into Rex Sports International's IT conference room and closed the door behind him. The Lee twins stopped talking and straightened their chairs around to face the group; Magda pushed a strand of her long black hair behind her right ear and scooted up to the conference table; and Turan, Monsour, Chandra, Deepak, Sam and Nick all parked their newly-silenced smart phones on the table and turned their full attention to Raj.

It was 9:03 a.m., November 20.

"Good morning." Raj pushed his glasses back up on his nose.

"There has been a security breach. I was notified by our outside service two hours ago. Now I am confessing to you that I was thinking a hacker was responsible, which was a very, very foolish idea. I have wasted two hours and found nothing. It is for this reason that I apologize. Now I must ask that you put aside your projects. That you apply your very best effort to resolving this problem."

Rather than address their questions one by one, he described the phenomenon as if it were something alive in the Rex system that could not be seen and that was maintaining access to the system for hours at a time. As he described his own investigation, the energy in the room shifted noticeably. The team members leaned forward. And slowly, methodically, the jottings they made became a plan which they put into place immediately.

The Lee twins would take on the MPF server—which handled all the financial data. Magda would stick with Legal. The other six team members would focus on servers in Minneapolis, Italy, Germany and Indonesia. The whole team would check in every two hours. Their first objective was to learn which servers and what files had been accessed, plus what, if anything, had been damaged or moved or copied. Once they could say with some certainty what had been compromised, then the team would refocus on the breach itself—the trail, any footprints, anything done using a variation in protocols, and on and on. Anything they uncovered would be shared immediately on their comment site. They would work round the clock.

After six hours, the team determined that the Rex servers in Italy, Germany and Indonesia had not been compromised and they refocused on the Minneapolis site. Two and a half hours later, the team re-assembled around the conference table. Monsour and Sam said it best: it was like there was a ghost in the system. A ghost they could not find, that was drawing energy but was leaving nothing tangible that might show how the intruder had entered the system or where he had been.

Raj watched their faces. Everyone on the team looked exhausted and frustrated. And perhaps worst of all, they were shocked at their own failure. If his team couldn't come up with an answer, who could? He told his people to go home. Rest and come back for their normal shift. He would discuss it with Mimi Fitzroy.

The elevator delivered Raj to the administration

building's fifth floor just after 6:00 p.m. Most employees in administration had gone home already. But not Mimi Fitzroy. She stepped out of her office and motioned him over.

Years ago, when he was visiting the family in India, he had tried to explain about Mimi to his mother.

"She is very beautiful," he'd said.

His mother's eyes had clouded with worry.

"My Blessing—" she began in that loving way he knew meant that once again she believed he was making a mistake.

"No, no, Mama. I say this only so you might picture her for yourself. Miss Fitzroy is my employer."

His mother rolled her eyes.

"*Sundara*," he said. "But very small. Petite as you are. Only more so. You might think she is a young girl." It was possible that to allay his mother's anxiety, he might have said, "Her hair is the color of mice and very often fixed together with rubber bands or some such thing. Very much the color of her usual sweater and pants." He had laughed then, hoping his mother would see his description was intended to be humorous.

"Blessing, she is wearing trousers into the office? And she is a corporate officer?"

After a suitable period of despairing at the poor judgment her son was exhibiting, his mother changed the subject. And Raj made a mental note: no more talk of Mimi. Nearly ten years ago and yet he had not mentioned Mimi Fitzroy to his mother since that day.

He hurried down the hallway to where Mimi had stopped outside her office.

She was wearing two sweaters. A white turtleneck and over it, a thick gray one made in a pattern of ropes running from top to bottom. Would she someday wear something that fit her small body?

Raj laid it all out for her, opened a file of printouts he'd made so she could see the system tests his team had performed. He was careful to monitor his voice and hands in order that she understand he was not over-reacting and that the problem his team had encountered was a serious threat.

"We have definitely confirmed a system breach. But we are finding no damage and no evidence of activity in our files—no changes in programming, no markers, no tiles, no flags to indicate someone had trespassed. But the usage numbers, so very many intrusions. I am finding them most troubling."

Mimi's lips parted.

Such an appealing woman. But he should not be having such thoughts. He cleared his throat. "The Lee twins have confirmed BMT's opinion that our financial servers were not breached."

Mimi was looking at him intensely. She continued nodding even after he stopped talking, as if he might say something more.

He returned her nod. But as he did so, Corporate Chief of Operations, Anna Thorsen, stepped out of the elevator and made straight for them—her walk, the long stride of a jungle cat. And her hair now an unnatural red.

What was Ms. Thorsen doing on this side of the building? One look at Mimi and he was certain she had not asked Ms. Thorsen to come around.

In an instant, Raj was a nothing, a shy Indian man, a computer geek, a foolish immigrant who would always defer. He dipped his chin at Thorsen.

"Mr. Banerjee—You aren't lost, are you? Do we have a problem?"

Said as if Ms. Thorsen's responsibilities included IT. But before Raj could answer, Mimi said, "Nothing to concern yourself with, Anna. What's up?"

Ms. Thorsen looked down at the top of Mimi's head as if Mimi were a thing, an unpleasant artifact, as if Ms. Thorsen were regarding the ugly gift that, for reasons of family harmony, could not be consigned to the trash pile. Finally, she said, "It may seem undiplomatic of me, but I have a meeting with Senator Mueller to set things up for your father. Do you know if he's changed his mind about the Senate seat?"

Raj couldn't help thinking why ask Mimi when Ms. Thorsen could easily ask Mr. Fitzroy himself? Clearly Ms. Thorsen was trying to get an answer to a question without asking it.

"I don't have a clue about Dad's plans," Mimi said.

"I'll follow up with David then." Ms. Thorsen glanced from Mimi to Raj. "You're sure I can't help?"

Mimi shook her head no. But still Ms. Thorsen did not leave, and Raj could not help thinking how Ms. Thorsen would look in her true body. Her teeth filed to points, her broad mouth open and snapping, Snapping just as the demons in the movies.

"Is that it?" Mimi smiled at Ms. Thorsen in a manner that Raj very much doubted was sincere.

Ms. Thorsen instantly refocused. Her skin seemed to glitter like a serpent's as she glanced over at Raj. But then—once he turned his Buddha face to her—without comment, she pivoted and disappeared into the elevator.

Mimi waited until the elevator door closed, then

fixed Raj with her dark, dark eyes. "Well," she said. "If your hacker has your team stumped, I doubt I can do any better."

It was not his place to argue. But he did and she listened.

Finally, and much to his relief, she said, "Okey dokey. I'll take it from here."

Chapter 13

Mimi had been running for forty minutes when she stumbled. Stumbled for the third time. She stopped and stared at the surface of the track, the centerpiece of the Rex Sports Pavilion. She bent forward and braced her hands on her knees. The surface looked perfectly clear.

If her brain couldn't manage the simple act of running, how could she ever expect it to come up with the password to the hidden file?

Pushing her body should be a help. Free her up. Let her think. She was a born athlete after all. At thirteen, she'd been number one on the balance beam for the U.S. Women's Junior National Gymnastics team. And number two on the uneven parallel bars. She had steely nerves, she was quick. And just like all the Fitzroys, she was really, really good at her sport.

Sure, she'd quit gymnastics at fourteen, but not for lack of talent. Or commitment. Her coach had pushed her to compete in the bigs and she'd backed away letting him think she was afraid of her competition. Better that than explaining to him that her father wouldn't be satisfied with his daughter merely competing. She'd have to win every meet. The great David Fitzroy would've made such a thing of it, there wouldn't have been any joy left for her.

Her big brother Jamie made quitting easier because he'd been powering his way into the decathlon record books at the time. With Jamie taking the heat from Dad, Mimi had been free to pursue her real passion—mathematics. She'd graduated *summa cum laude* from Stanford and at nineteen was headed to Cal for her PhD in algebraic geometry.

But that same summer eleven years ago, her brother fell to his death. He'd been climbing in Yosemite. At his funeral, her dad had made it clear to her. "Take your advanced degree in something we can use, Mimi, or start work now in Anna Thorsen's group."

Which was why she did her Ph.D. in computer science. It was also why she'd been working at Rex for the past ten years.

Mimi shook off the memories and took another critical look around the inside of the over-sized barn that everyone at Rex called The Pavilion.

Dedicated to indoor sports training, The Jamie Fitzroy Sports Pavilion was more than 140 yards long and 75 yards wide. It stretched up two and a half stories, and from where Mimi stood, the ceiling came together as an elegant spider web of steel beams and glass. The place was stocked with all the equipment an athlete could ask for, plus display cases stuffed with exemplars of uniforms Rex had specially designed for Baird State University—the long-time recipient of Rex Sports' considerable largess.

The regulation track she had been running skirted the Pavilion's interior.

She'd stopped mid-way around the track's north end, directly opposite an exit sign that gleamed back at her. She checked her pulse. The run brought her heart rate up a little, but it'd done nothing to help her refocus. The missing password was the thing. And she was still drawing a blank. She stood one-footed and stretched her quads. Then, more in frustration than thinking what she might do next, she squinched up her face, sat on the track and pulled off her running shoes.

She needed something different, something difficult, something that would force her brain to recalibrate.

She walked over to the floor exercise mat which was part of the gymnastic area set up in the middle of the track. She stretched her back and shoulders, and let her gaze slide over to the equipment. First to the balance beam, her favorite. But it was barely five a.m. She was not about to risk a serious fall when there was no one around to spot for her. So, floor exercise it was. She stripped off her socks.

As a corporate officer, she normally was nowhere near the Rex campus in the middle of the night. But the situation at IT had called for emergency measures.

Once Raj Banerjee had turned the problem over to her, she'd run a system management report looking for anomalies. She'd discounted the results the first time and ran the report again. But there it was: the equivalent of an entire server unit—six terabytes—failed to show up at all. Not as available space, not as data stored, not as locked off. Six terabytes were just MIA.

Now that's a big invisibility cloak, Harry Potter.

The outside security vendor's report of extra system usage made sense if somebody had been using the system without authorization. But what were they doing, exactly? Tagging? Spying? Corrupting files? Stealing data? Raj's team hadn't been able to say. And of course, the deeper question was why. But *Why* would have to wait.

The long and short of it was, she had found a file Raj's people hadn't discovered. Some hacker—she wanted to think it was a hacker—had parked it on a highly secure server. The location of the file proved that whoever created it was an expert and likely knowledgeable about the system at Rex.

Once she discovered which sectors were involved, at a little after 4:00 a.m. she went after the mini-program that controlled the invisible file. But getting *into* the file itself required a password and she couldn't make her brain work.

She could've stretched out on the sofa in her office, caught a few Zs, and then taken on the password challenge. Instead she had decided to hit the gym. The password couldn't wait, not really, but pushing her body might help overcome her mental block.

Which was why she'd spent forty-five minutes running the track in the wee hours—forty-five minutes resulting in a stubbed toe and not one useful idea.

She worked her bare feet against the floor exercise mat and took a long look at the corner where she intended to land. She rocked up on her toes, straightened her spine, aimed her arms straight in front of her and held them parallel to the mat.

She would make a diagonal tumbling pass across the mat corner-to-corner. She would stick her landing. She'd done the pass a thousand times. Really. A thousand. Probably more. She'd always ended the pass with a twist.

She took a deep breath, let it out, then in again, and attempted the first back tumbling pass she'd done in ten years. From the get-go, she got it wrong, missed the twist and landed on her butt. It was that blasted password, the hacker, the whole darned thing. Stupid, stupid. She slapped her hand down on the mat, scrambled to her feet and went at the pass again.

It took five tries—and two more falls—to get it. Not perfect form, but passable. It took her three of those tries before she started enjoying the routine. As she finished attempt five and landed in her stance, the hunt for the password was the farthest thing from her consciousness. For once she actually felt good. She was actually having fun. She had forgotten what that felt like.

Just for the joy of it, she made a simple dance pass along the side of the mat—arabesques, balance moves—she stopped at the corner as if she would make another tumbling pass. She rocked up on her toes again, pressing them into the mat.

Suddenly she could see how the file must have been set up.

Because they couldn't count on the file staying hidden. If it were discovered, the password would need to convince IT that the file was her dad's personal stuff, and most likely part of her dad's senatorial campaign. If somebody wanted the secret file to look like it'd been set up for her dad, it would need to look like something he could remember and use.

She'd already set up a campaign file for him. She'd idiot-proofed it and given him easy-to-read instructions which he promptly forgot. So, for sure, the hidden file was not part of his campaign. Chances were really, really good then that the file she'd uncovered had no reason to be on the system.

Mimi nodded as she stared out across the mat. The

password was right in front of her. She tossed the idea of passwords aside the way she would have a resin bag and made a final tumbling pass, ending it with a vault into a pike double twist.

It didn't matter that she failed to stick the landing. In seconds, she pulled on her shoes and sprinted back to her office. At her stand-up desk, she ran a hand through her hair and rubber-banded it out of her eyes. Then she revisited that mini-program that controlled the invisible sectors.

The whole Rex system was set up to let a user have three tries to enter the right password before the system locked her out. Hopefully the hacker hadn't messed with that.

She'd always hated that her dad insisted on using their first dog's name plus his wedding anniversary as the password on his files. But it sure made her decision a simple one. Was it numbers first or last? She pressed her lips together and typed.

T-U-C-K-E-R-6-1-1.

She hit Enter. Held her breath...nope.

When numbers-first, name-after failed too, she was a little annoyed. But only for a moment. Because a different password proved that the file wasn't really her dad's. What could be better than that?

Who was she kidding? *Better* was sorting out the password. And she only had one try left.

Whoever set up the file was counting on that file looking like a David Fitzroy deal. Which meant, it needed to look political. Third try, God help her, she typed her dad's completely pathetic campaign slogan, THERIGHTFITZ.

And she was in.

The file itself was a wonder. A ton of sub-files, all named as dates. She scrolled to the bottom of the list. Holy mackerel, more than eighteen months of records.

She took a tired breath and copied the hidden file onto her *designing in progress* server. While the copy program ran, she left a *no-call* instruction for her assistant, then showered, and pulled on her regular sweater and wool pants.

Once she had a complete working copy of the file, she gave herself up to reading, following one thread after another. A lot of it was emails, but there was plenty of junk and a ton of research too—on Rex, but also on antitrust and securities law. She was sweating, her fingers kept trembling. If what she was reading was true....

Mimi Fitzroy was not a woman who panicked. That had always been one of her strengths. But at the moment, it sure as heck felt like she was panicking. She was too old for all-nighters but all she could think was what she'd uncovered could ruin everything. And she couldn't have that.

Chapter 14

Thorsen held herself in check as the guy from the Finance Reporting Group laid another page of statistics in front of her. *Do not purse your lips. You will need this man.* What she didn't need was a tutorial on reading financial reports. She simply wanted to know if the IPO rollout would be ready by the time she took over as CEO—and he kept using the word "promising." She couldn't help thinking there would be a *but* somewhere in his next lecture.

A flutter on her hip—phone. She raised her hand to pause the flood of financial projections and glanced at the little screen. It took a supreme effort to remain in her chair, manage a tight smile, and, as if the finance geek had her full attention, peer at more financial projections. She motioned for him to continue.

Compromised, the message had read. COMPROMISED. How in creation could anyone discover her cache of emails? More than that, how could they have made it through the maze she'd set up and cracked the password?

What's-his-name the finance guy was saying, "—a formality of course, but I know you'll want to put your own stamp on it."

Had it ever entered the man's mind that she had other things to do? Thorsen gave him a level look and said, "I'll take it with me."

Seconds later and back in her office, she went through the drill she'd followed so many times to access her ghost file of Frank Leit and his buddies' emails. Virtually on autopilot, she careened through the labyrinth of international servers—in The Hague, Mumbai, Wolfsburg, and back to Rex where she signed on again. But under the name of a Rex employee she'd never met. At the administrator's system screen, she typed **<*SENATE10*. She'd already seen the message to her phone. So, she knew what was coming. And yet, the suddenness of a sulfurous yellow screen with its red border still came as a shock: *SECURITY COMPROMISED 11/21/19 07:08:27-07:17:32 Source: admin.*

Her hand paused mid-air. As it floated down to her desktop, she tossed the pencil she'd decapitated into her wastebasket. Was she safe?

Why was she still asking that question? Of course she was safe. Every time she touched this file, she signed on as a different employee. Time and time again she had changed employee aliases, hundreds of different names. She'd scrubbed every dish, every fingerprint, even laundered Leit's sheets. And her spyware had wiped Leit's computer clean. If pieces of the spyware program existed in Leit's two-year-old emails, so what? The cops would never put that together. Nothing connected her to the pirated file and nothing, but absolutely nothing, connected her to Frank Leit.

Almost on its own, her hand settled back onto the keyboard. She closed out the security message and skimmed the last emails to arrive from the lawyer Kaufman and the other blog writers. The good—or was it bad—news: plenty of emails but nothing had come in from a U.S. Attorney, not to Frank Leit, not to any of them. She ran a check for changes in the file content...apparently nothing, except the new emails. Did it make sense that whoever had accessed her file had merely opened and closed it? Sure it did; and the Seattle Mariners were a shoo-in to win the world series next year.

She leaned back in her desk chair and stared into space. If the data hadn't been messed with—and it hadn't—what had been going on for the nine minutes that somebody had the file open? And, what would they do with what they'd found?

It had to be Mimi.

Thorsen shot away from her desk and paced the room. She could not have Mimi destroying everything. She would not allow it. And when pacing didn't help dissipate her anger, she knew what would. She plunged her hands in the ice bucket JR always set up for her on her credenza. She closed her eyes and waited for her fingers to go numb.

Minutes later and herself again, she returned to her desk and texted Rex's outside security firm. *<Suspicious actions observed by you? Thorsen>* Their almost immediate answer: *<Anomaly observed Reported to IT Dir 11/19>* Thorsen leaned back in the leather chair. Clearly then, it was not some whim that got IT looking for trouble. They'd worked it for two days.

That had to be what Raj Banerjee's pow-wow with Mimi was about.

Mimi would not fail to follow through on the pirated emails. She would never go to her dad though, because he wouldn't pay attention to her. But she would keep the story in-house. Because Daddy had his award coming up and there was the family's reputation to consider and God forbid something should go wrong with Fitzroy's senatorial campaign.

Time for a chat.

Thorsen left her office and marched around the atrium to Ms. Fitzroy's bailiwick where one of Mimi's minions said that the boss was out. Thorsen took in the news and got hold of herself. Christ, she wanted to wipe the simpering smile off that face. Instead, she said, "I just have a couple of things for Mimi. Would you mind letting her know? I'm on my way to the gym."

At her office, Thorsen changed to her workout gear. Time with a punching bag might take the edge off. But punching wasn't a good look with so many people wandering around. She decided on the weight room, loaded another eighty pounds on a machine and wiped down the bench. Once she laid back and pressed the safety catch...once the heft of the bar pressed down...this was what she needed. The slow, even strokes...fifteen reps and a rest, fifteen reps and rest...a stop to load on another ten pounds and fifteen reps...

Sweat bloomed at the back of Thorsen's neck. What if it wasn't Mimi? Was it remotely possible the Phoenix police had made the connection between Frank Leit and Rex Sports' server? Could their forensics team move that fast? Could they have pulled Leit's emails and reconstructed the spyware? Could they be that thorough? That good?

Thorsen abandoned the workout, took the back stairs up to her fifth-floor office and caught a look at herself in the mirror. Tired...she was tired. Tired of the fight, tired of being this close, of not getting what she wanted, tired of employees who panicked when they saw her coming, tired of the ass-covering, of David Fitzroy and his preoccupation with fame, gratitude and adoration. Most of all, she was tired of the sneaking suspicion that whatever she did, Fitzroy wouldn't come through for her.

She locked the door to her office, stripped and headed for her bathroom. She stepped into the shower and waited for the hit of cold. Because cold was the only thing. Because she hated Mimi. She couldn't help but hate Mimi, the stringy hair, the tiny hands, that herbal stink and her dull brown everything. Mimi had wrecked things for her with Jamie and was trying the same thing now with David. She'd hated Mimi the first time she'd laid eyes on her and she still hated her. Even after she was rid of Mimi, however it was Mimi would die, that hate would still be there.

Chapter 15

An hour before lunch, Mimi speed-dialed the General Counsel's office. "Tell Robert Addison I'm on my way over." She didn't wait for excuses and only stopped long enough to run her hands under the hot water tap.

By the time she completed the long walk over to Legal, she was fully geared up. Addison had a reputation for pooh-poohing whatever difficulties people brought to him. Didn't matter. She was definitely ready to take him on.

She would have barged straight into Addison's office except for his receptionist, who had planted herself in front of the General Counsel's door. In hushed tones, the woman said Mr. Addison had been tied up all morning and could Mimi come back another day?

Mimi managed a tired smile. "Sorry. It's crisis time. But I'll handle it." She stepped past the receptionist into Addison's office and quietly closed the door behind her.

One look at the ridiculously huge chairs in front of Addison's desk, and Mimi bypassed them in favor of the more power-neutral conference table at the far end of the room. She glanced at her watch, 11:42 a.m. Twenty-eight hours without sleep.

Head down and staring at his daytimer, Addison

seemed fully engaged in a call, fingers tickling the air. He was a generation older than Mimi. Perfectly sculptured silver hair, tailored three-piece suits, silk ties, manicured hands, way too much for a corporate world built on professional sports teams and athletic equipment, clothing and running shoes.

He'd been hired as General Counsel at Rex the same year Mimi had joined the company. So technically, they'd been colleagues for ten years. They'd never worked together.

Despite the fact she had walked in on him, that she was still waiting for him to finish, that she was listening to his conversation, Addison stuck with his call. Eventually he retrieved a file from a big drawer in his credenza and paged through it.

She knew she was wasting time. She could have summoned the man to her office. After all, she was the corporate officer, not Addison, and she was a major shareholder—again, not Addison. Why had she shown up on his turf? Because she needed to talk with him, in person. And she needed a break from her office. Stupid of her.

Clearly Addison was using the phone call as a power play.

Mimi stood perfectly still behind the conference table and stared out the office window. Just before noon, she spotted a couple of brave souls racing from the design engineering building to the Pavilion. When she looked away from the window and back to Addison, he was still on the phone but he'd swiveled his ergonomic chair to face away from her and tipped back as if he were preparing for a nap. The call sounded nothing like business.

Mimi's arms virtually exploded with the rash she got anytime she had a serious conflict.

She checked her watch again and walked over to where Addison was sitting. She stood beside the arm of his chair. "Sorry to interrupt," she said—sounding, she knew, like *sorry* was far from the truth. She stared down at him, "You need to wrap it up."

Addison looked up at her in apparent disbelief.

"Now. We need to talk," she said quietly, then took a water bottle from the cooler on his credenza, turned and walked back to the conference table. She plonked the bottle down next to her daytimer, took a seat and, when Addison finally ended his call, she started talking.

"I've spent the last five hours reading about Rex Sports. The most important thing being, that for the past seven years Rex has been breaking every antitrust law in existence. Am I the only shareholder who didn't know about this? I thought Legal reviewed these contracts."

Addison stood but continued to fuss with the open files on his desk. "Perhaps you didn't notice, I'm tied up at the moment," he said. "Didn't Nancy tell you to wait?"

Why hadn't he jumped on antitrust?

The idea he was drowning in legal business, she'd heard enough of his phone call to know that was bushwa. "As I told Nancy, this can't wait," she said. "Perhaps you didn't hear me. I've just read quite credible accusations that Rex is engaging in antitrust violations. Exactly what has been going on? And does my father know?"

Addison stared at her. His hand hovered above his desk as if he were inclined to call his secretary. Or

Security.

"Yesterday IT received an alert from our outside security vendor. It's a long story I won't bore you with. The bottom line is, about 6:30 this morning, I uncovered a hidden file parked on Rex's main server. I'm estimating ninety percent of it is personal emails."

Addison's face gave away nothing. But he was clearly pressing his fingertips into his desktop. "Not Rex emails."

"I wish they were." Her eyes bored into him. "Three terabytes of pirated—as in stolen—emails parked on our server."

No response at all from Addison.

"We could handle the theft of Rex emails internally. No, these emails were stolen from outsiders. You may not be aware of it, but three terabytes translate to more documents than Legal has stored on its designated server. I'm thinking that Legal will have to defend a load of lawsuits from the people whose private information was stolen."

At least Addison was listening. Even if he hadn't made it over to the conference table. Her hives continued to spread like acid, running from just below her earlobes to down her neck. With luck, her turtleneck would hide the worst of it 'til she made her escape.

"Here's the thing," she said, "whoever created that file knew so much about our technical protocols, I have to think he's an insider. And if I'm right, then Rex will be on the hook for damages and your people will have to defend those lawsuits."

His hand reached out for the buzzer that would summon his assistant.

"There's more," she said. "And trust me, you'll want to hear me out before anyone joins us."

Addison drew his hand back but stayed by his desk. Did he actually look worried?

"The pirated emails? There's a lawyer in Seattle and three other former football people. But besides them, and what would likely fascinate a jury…the main email victim is Frank Leit."

Now he was listening.

"Frank Leit the football player?" he said.

Despite the fact it still felt like she was crawling with fire ants, she nodded. "You do know Frank Leit was murdered two days ago."

Addison took a moment to dictate an in-corporate press release to his secretary. The gist of it, a lame *we all regret losing a great sports figure* thing. The real point being, nobody at Rex should talk with the press or the cops about Frank Leit, refer them to Legal.

The moment Addison turned off his intercom, Mimi jumped in again.

"Care to join me?" She patted the top of the conference table and kept talking. "I've read enough of that, let's call it a ghost file, to be convinced that for a long time something crooked has been going on. And Frank Leit was onto it."

Addison wearily plucked a water bottle from his credenza and joined her at the small conference table. By the time he sat, his face had returned to its normal tanning bed glow.

"*Assuming arguendo* that this file you say you found is what you say it is," he said and went after everything she'd laid out for him. Beginning with Frank Leit's claims. Which he announced were old news. Rex wasn't breaking the law. And, in his opinion, threatening Leit with a lawsuit hadn't been the answer. "It simply would've given Leit another pulpit and a wider audience." Addison slowly shook his head as if he'd seen it all. "There's always somebody who thinks they know more than the company's lawyers. Leit was just another self-promoter."

"Please do not handle me." Mimi fought her emotions back and faced Addison with as much resolution on her face as she could manage. "Frank Leit was a former U.S. Congressman with real connections. I seriously doubt a jury would buy the idea that Frank Leit was writing about antitrust violations because he was a self-promoter. So please, do me the courtesy of giving me an honest answer. I don't care about why, but if you knew Rex was engaging in criminal deals, say so. Then maybe the company can get out in front of it. So...did you know? You did okay the deals, right? What about my dad and the Board?"

Addison drew himself up. Not merely angry, there was something more going on, but she couldn't pinpoint what it was.

"We discussed Leit's claims at several board meetings—the fact that you choose not to attend those meetings is your problem," he said. "As far as Frank Leit's claims were concerned, after some debate, the Board made a unanimous decision to take no action until such time as Leit specifically named Rex Sports in his allegations. Given that he never referred to Rex or David by name, and given that the man is dead, I have to think his theories died with him."

"I don't. I'm thinking his theories are alive, well, and that the Arizona police will find them mighty interesting," Mimi said.

Addison shot her a tired look. "I hardly think that the police are going to give much credence to Frank Leit's blog."

She couldn't believe it. The man hadn't thought it through at all.

"Frank Leit was murdered," she said. "It won't take the Arizona police more than a day or two to get around to looking at Frank Leit's computer. And when they do, it won't be long before their technicians spot the spyware and the spyware will lead them straight to Rex Sports. So, I'm thinking you had better be prepared to answer some nasty questions." She leaned forward onto the table. "Who came up with the business plans?"

Addison's eyes were the giveaway. Just a flash of panic, but it was there.

"Which business plans?" he said.

"The ones that Frank Leit claims are crooked." She shook her head. "Let's make it simple. Tell me who put together the business plans Frank was talking about. Because it seems to me, if you were involved in them, if you approved them, you have one heck of a conflict of interest."

Addison took a moment to arrange his face into that patrician exterior she was accustomed to seeing in corporate photographs.

"Forgive me for asking, Ms. Fitzroy," he said, "but how long have you been a corporate officer? Is it seven years? Then you know as well as I do how Rex business plans are developed."

She should've known, but she didn't pay attention to crap like that.

"Dad was part of it?" she said and shifted her

shoulders—just to relieve the bloom of hives that had made it down onto her back.

Addison didn't comment on whether her dad was involved. But she would've bet money he knew something about the file or who set it up. Or he'd guessed it.

"Of course, we were keeping an eye on Frank Leit," he said and leaned back in his chair. "Now and then, Legal gets a heads-up from PR. Frank Leit's blog crossed our desks that way. The man was careful not to publish anything actionable. And, as I said, if we had pursued him in court, our image would have been damaged, perhaps irreparably, even if we prevailed in a trial."

She folded her hands on the tabletop and regarded him for a moment. "I understand your advice to the board. But I can't help thinking about the position you're in now. Because if you fail to steer Rex clear of some ugly lawsuits, and maybe even a government investigation, I don't see how you can expect to remain at Rex."

Now that one hit home.

Addison retrieved a legal pad from his desk, then returned to the little conference table where he smacked it down on the glass surface. He removed his suit jacket and made a production out of withdrawing a gold pen from his suit coat's inside pocket. He sat and launched into his own questions about the file: precisely how she'd found it, what she'd done with it, he wanted every detail about it. After twenty minutes or so, he drew back in his chair and tapped a finger against the tabletop. "This file, you say it's been hidden on the server for a year and a half?" He regarded her as if he honestly couldn't recall what she'd told him a few minutes earlier.

The file had been there more than a year, she said, and started theorizing about the person who had set it up.

He interrupted her. "I'm wondering why it took you over a year to discover something as dangerous as you claim. Why all this drama just as your father is about to run for Senate."

It took everything she had to not make any kind of abrupt movement—like run for the ladies' room, strip off her sweater and douse her hives with cold water. "As I said earlier, the file was discovered because of outside Security's notice."

Addison thumped his pen against his tablet and finally made a note. "Get me a copy of it," he said. "And make certain that the metadata is not altered. You can do that, can't you?"

That tone of voice was no different than when her dad had disciplined the dog. She clamped her jaw tight and waited.

"And I'll need the names and email addresses of the sources of the emails," he said and flipped a page of his tablet over.

Absolutely straight-faced, she said, "It would be a mistake to contact them yourself. You lack the expertise to explain what has happened. I can explain."

"That won't be necessary. Legal will be handling all the outside contact here," he said and ticked off a note on his tablet. "Once you've made a copy for me, delete the file. And provide me with a memorandum confirming your discovery, file evaluation, our conference, the file destruction, every step."

Addison stared at her, beads of perspiration showing on his upper lip.

Delete the file. Why hadn't she discovered it earlier? She opened her mouth to respond. But just looking at Addison, she got it. Once people were trying to save themselves, she would most definitely become a target. She closed her mouth, cleared her throat and said, "My department will handle the file according to established professional guidelines." The pompous jerk hadn't even considered she had a year and a half's worth of backups, which presumably contained the same invisible file.

She was so outta there. She marched back across the Rex campus heading for her own office, painfully aware that her face was flaming. Her hives had made it all the way up her neck and were blooming behind her ears. Thank God for the cold. It kept most everyone off the quad and it felt so good.

If she had been calling the shots for the company, and if she had known all this time about Frank Leit...what would she have done? How about investigate his claims? Talk to him. Explore what he wanted. Because...didn't anybody see it? Wasn't the company's lack of action a confirmation that Frank Leit was on to something?

As she hit the doors into the main building, she got it. Addison hadn't said a word about her legal responsibilities and yet he knew she was a corporate officer. Why hadn't he called the lawyer in Seattle while she was there?

She waved off her assistant and closed the door to her private office behind her. Addison wasn't gonna make the call to Seattle. He just wanted to make the problem go away and the easiest way to avoid responsibility himself was to stick her with looking incompetent when everything blew up. And if Addison was already setting her up as the fall guy, what kind of a position did it put her in, exactly?

She needed a plan. And she needed advice. But certainly not from her father. Whether or not her father was involved was a can of worms she wasn't ready to even think about, let alone open. Besides, he wouldn't listen to her. But Uncle Ted would. And he could certainly recommend a good lawyer.

Chapter 16

By late afternoon, November 21, Thorsen was sitting through one of those *sorry-we're-late-with-it-but-here-it-is* meetings with the PR firm David had picked to promote the Triathlon. They covered the table with marketing exemplars. They smiled. They apologized and offered to discount their bill.

Why they'd bothered making the trip to Minneapolis was beyond her.

They were so overmatched.

They were so fired.

Post-meeting, Thorsen returned to her office, locked the door and stretched her long body out on the leather sofa. Her thoughts slipped back to the meeting. David's people had hired those people. They'd been tasked with handling groundwork. Rex's first international triathlon was scheduled three years out for the Pacific Northwest. Frank Leit's blog had a Seattle connection. How handy was that?

She put in a call to Rex Travel and told them to book an open-ended stay, she'd be leaving for Seattle on Monday. David would sulk. But as long as his Man-of-the-Year thing went well, and as long as she'd be back for his senatorial campaign kick-off, he'd settle down. Suddenly, Thorsen sat up so abruptly she felt it in her neck.

Mimi would run to Addison about the hacked file.

Of course she would. And then what? Thorsen could imagine Addison's face—pure panic at the mere suggestion of scandal. Which made sense, given the fact he was part of every hinky deal they'd put together right up to his well-trimmed hairline. For damned sure, any investigation would take a bite out of his bank account and very probably get him disbarred. No way Addison would risk that.

JR rapped on her door, then stuck his head in. "Anna, the General Counsel's office called. Robert Addison needs to see you ASAP."

She bet he did. Well, she was ready for Addison. She retrieved her portfolio, blew through her outer office and headed for Legal. Two minutes later, she managed her face into a benign smile and strode into the Offices of Robert Addison, General Counsel, Rex Sports International. Addison was waiting in a room Legal used for video conferences.

Now why meet there?

Addison's assistant had placed a water carafe and glass in front of the chair Thorsen always sat in for international conferences. At the opposite end of the table, the green beacon from the video system stared back at her.

Recording. Did he think she was so witless?

Apparently. An *I've got you now* expression settled around Addison's eyes as he hovered next to the camera opposite her. He crossed his arms and waited. Well, she could put that right.

She stood behind her chair, raised her eyebrows and peered at Addison. "Robert," she said, "It's a busy day. Suppose you get to the point." She waved her hand at the media equipment. "And you might want to have somebody adjust the sound. The last recording you people made for me, I couldn't hear a damned thing when we played it back."

Obviously, that gave him a bump. But he recovered. He took a seat, maybe a little chastened, and returned to his agenda. He'd called because IT had discovered a security breech, a hidden file. "It's full of pirated emails. IT was doing an audit," he said, eyeing her reaction.

Thorsen made a point of looking concerned. Finally, she sat and pulled her daytimer out of her portfolio, as if she were preparing to make some notes. But instead of addressing his implied question, she fired off a string of her own. Whose emails? What hidden file? Where was it hidden? How long had it been there? Who found the file? And what's being done about it?

Addison's face clouded momentarily. Then he quickly resurrected his head-of-state stare.

Which she ignored. "The hacker or whatever, do they think it's someone from outside, a Rex employee, or what?"

Addison cleared his throat. "IT assures me the file was very likely put together by an insider. But the emails are—Mimi said they were stolen from a sportswriter, a lawyer in Washington and two or three others."

Mimi. Confirmation is always so handy.

Thorsen poured herself some water, sipped at it and nodded for Addison to continue.

He leaned forward. His hands and forearms stretched onto the table, clearly in view of the camera. He explained the legal tangle Rex might face. There'd be hefty damages to pay, but nothing that would take

Rex out of the game. The biggest problem would be a besmirched public image to repair. He would do his best to get the company out ahead of it.

Thorsen licked her lips, slid her glass aside, and leaned an elbow on the arm of her chair.

"You've spoken to the email people. Right? The people whose privacy was violated?"

Staring. No answer.

"You haven't? You *do* know who these people are?"

Addison closed his eyes as if he were fending off a headache.

"Robert," Thorsen said. "Have. You. Spoken. To the people whose emails were stolen? Have you notified the police? Have you done anything at all to protect this company from the consequences of this thing? For that matter, what's being done inside the company? Do you have any idea who put this thing, this file, together?"

She waited nearly twenty seconds. "We're all waiting for an answer, Robert. Whoever this recording is for. And of course, I am as well."

She stared at him. She was good at it, that stare. Her gray eyes bored in. She lifted her chin and waited for him to cave. She counted another seventeen seconds.

Addison continued to return her gaze.

She shook her head as if he were utterly pathetic. "Should I infer from your silence that our IT department is unable to identify the person responsible?"

Addison slowly straightened. "Mimi Fitzroy only found the file today. She's working on it. Personally."

"And that's it?"

This time Addison met her glare with one of his own. "The file has been removed from the system," he said sharply.

Well that wasn't precisely the case now, was it?

"I should hope so," she said. "You've notified David?"

Addison dodged the question.

So he hadn't. Which meant Addison intended to sweep the whole mess under the rug.

"I assume that would be a *No*? You haven't notified the board either I suppose."

When he sighed, she asked if he wanted her to follow up with her people. His face implied he didn't like that idea either. He stood and started for the door.

"Just a couple of other things if you would, Robert," she said and gestured to the camera lens. "While we're making a record, I've been thinking about those rumors the Board has been chewing over. You do recall those discussions, I trust?"

He stopped near the door and waited.

She said, "If what I glean from the Internet is correct, violations of the federal antitrust laws can be tricky. Fines, even imprisonment? And I seem to recall hearing that criminal convictions can make civil lawsuits a cake walk, is that true?"

She leaned forward and put one forearm on the table. "On the record, Robert, talk to me about antitrust law."

His complexion gave him away—he could have happily killed her. He stepped back to the table and stood behind a chair. Obviously, he would have given anything, or nearly, to turn the recording off. And, she had to admire his effort, pulling himself together. He gave her a much more complete answer than she'd expected. Any antitrust claims against Rex would arise primarily from their market share and price control. There was no need to worry, he said and dumbed down his explanation as if she lacked the education to keep up with legal theories she'd covered long ago in business school.

She said, "So you're telling me we have no exposure legally unless it can be proved that someone knew in advance that one or more of the deals Rex made were illegal."

He shot her an impatient look but didn't answer her question.

"I'm asking," she said, "because, as we're both aware, your compensation is predicated on corporate growth. That, plus a flat salary of course. I seem to recall that for the last eight years you've done very well off our corporate growth. Growth based on business decisions *you* have endorsed both on behalf of the Office of General Counsel and personally. You've received over five million dollars so far in compensation, shares and stock options if I remember correctly. Personally, I think pay structures like yours create quite a conflict of interest. I'm sure your predecessor would think so."

It would be a cold day in hell before she brought Ted Halliday back as General Counsel. But Addison didn't dare bank on that. His face flooded with unsightly purple blotches.

"As I recall," he said quietly, "every deal I handled was initially proposed by you and approved by the board."

She stared at him. Then slowly smiled. They both knew he'd okayed at least one hinky deal a year.

"I believe," she said, "if you re-examine the paperwork, you'll see that every deal you signed off on was proposed and approved by David. Not me. As for Board approval, no one on the Board is a member of the bar. We all relied on your advice. As you know. And, as you knew at the time. So, I'll ask again. Are those deals solid? Do I have to hire my own attorney to evaluate the corporation's legal exposure before I take over as CEO?"

She closed her eyes for effect, then regarded him again.

"I'll make it simple. Is Rex vulnerable to an investigation by the Securities and Exchange Commission or the U.S. Attorney?"

Addison cleared his throat and drew himself up. "This office scrutinized every acquisition. We determined each one of them was fully compliant with the law as it existed at the time of the closing," he said. "As for whether you should obtain counsel of your own, there are people who might conclude any answer I gave you might constitute legal advice to you, personally. Regrettably, my position at Rex precludes my providing personal advice. So, I'm unable to comment."

She popped her daytimer into her portfolio and stood. *Unable to comment.* She'd made her point. His ass was grass if they were ever investigated. And he knew she knew it.

As she headed for the door she said, "I don't want people on my team who aren't trustworthy. And, count on it, Robert, I will be following up on this."

Thorsen left the Rex Sports campus at just after 5:10 p.m. "Things to do," she told her assistant. Now that was the truth. She had a computer program to re-set. Dry cleaning to pick up. But first, she needed to pay a visit to Mimi Fitzroy's McMansion.

Chapter 17

Madge Fitzroy Halliday cracked open the massive front door to her Lowry Hill house. "Honey?"

Mimi dragged her fingers through her ragged bangs. "Aunt Madge? Are you okay?"

There had to be something wrong. Something big. Because it was midafternoon and her perfectionist aunt was looking like...Mimi couldn't think, but it wasn't good.

As Madge backed away from the door, her hands fluttered to her bird's nest hair and scuttled across the front of her sweater. She pulled a handkerchief from a pocket, urged the door shut and locked it.

"I'm fine," Madge said. "Fine. Just...over-scheduled...late all day and, uh, Ted's in the guesthouse. And Mimi, whatever you do, do not upset him."

Okey dokey. Mimi headed through the house thinking of all the times her mother had said *fine.* It always felt like the situation was a hair's breadth from outright war. Or else there'd been a war, and peace hadn't exactly broken out yet. Had Madge and Ted had a blow-up? God, she hoped not. Her aunt and uncle were the only people in her life she could count on.

Mimi carefully climbed down the icy back steps and headed for the guesthouse where Ted stood waiting at the door looking both sweaty and strained. And once she stepped inside and stomped the snow off her feet, she got it. It wasn't just that her aunt was in trouble, something had happened to both of them. Because the guesthouse sitting room looked like the inside of a paper factory after the bomb had exploded.

Ted gave her the usual bear-hug welcome, tossed her coat on a pile and steered her toward the only empty chair in the place, right in front of his desk. No chit-chat, no offer of a drink, he planted himself in front of her, leaned his butt against the edge of his desk, and dramatically stuck his hands in his pants pockets.

"So, what's up?" he said.

She was not falling for the Mr. Perky act. "Is Madge all right?"

According to Ted, Madge was fine. That word again.

"We're just catching up around the place. You know how it gets." He shrugged.

Okay, whatever it was, they didn't want to talk about it. And she'd stepped right in the middle. And, she was about to pile more on their plates. *Terrific.* Mimi weighed her alternatives and plunged in.

"I need your advice. I just found a three-terabyte file somebody had hidden on our main server. The whole thing is pirated emails, even the attachments. Bad enough, but there's a ton of stuff about Rex being crooked."

Ted's color drained away. "Emails?"

"Did you know about it?" she said. "You did, didn't you?"

He was shaking. "The board had been… Give me a minute." He turned and fumbled a plastic pill bottle out of his desk. "Don't call Madge." Once he'd washed his meds down and waited a minute, he wanted every detail. The emails, did it look like they were everything somebody might get, junk included, or did the dates on the files look like they'd been cherry-picked?

"There was plenty of junk," she said, "but there wasn't time to check every sub-file." She explained how she thought the spyware worked. "Do you want—"

"Names and email addresses please," he said. "And whatever else you've dug up on 'em. Better yet, just send me your notes on the file, what you've done, what you read, who you talked to... Does your staff know? And this is very important, if there's a way for the hacker to learn you broke into the file. Or, let me put it this way: is there any way for somebody to see that *you* broke into the file? Tell me the truth."

It seemed like he was holding his breath. Was he in pain? Pressing him about it probably wasn't the best thing. If he got worse, she'd call Madge whether he liked it or not.

"You have anything out here that I drink?" she said.

His eyebrows went skyward. "Maker's Mark's in the cupboard above the fridge," he said.

It was pretty early in the day for alcohol. She'd been thinking lemonade or a sports drink. But, "Why not?" she said and collected the bourbon, seltzer and highball glasses. By the time she'd parked it all on his desk, she'd made up her mind. She would not tell him about the mini-program she'd set up to track the hacker. And she wouldn't tell him about the call she'd made from her car telling her assistant to delete her computer history for the day. But the rest, he could have.

An hour later, she was exhausted. But Ted looked

better than he had since she arrived—not better exactly, but his hands weren't as shaky, his chin was much more determined and he seemed a whole lot more focused.

"Have you told anybody else what you found?" he said. "Your staff, I suppose."

"Not my staff. Robert Addison," she said.

"Personally?"

She nodded. "I had to, didn't I? As a corporate officer?"

Ted finished his drink. "If you notified him, what's the problem?"

"I can't help thinking something else is going on. It's like I'm being set up," she said.

His forehead puckered. "Ground keep shifting? Or your job's being re-defined. Or somebody else's mess has been reassigned to you. Any of those sound familiar?"

Close enough. Addison knew nothing about IT, and yet, he'd been perfectly content telling her to delete the file. And more than happy to accuse her of dropping the ball. "Definitely being set up," she said.

Ted opened the Maker's Mark and slowly poured himself a second drink.

"I hate to say it, Mimi, but in Addison's shoes I'd be doing pretty much the same thing. I know it must've felt like you were being handled. Okay, you *were* being handled. But he's the company's lawyer, remember." Ted launched into a long explanation of why Rex's lawyers needed to take control of that email file and be the one to speak with the victims—it was all about protecting the company.

Eventually he stopped talking and tapped his pen against a legal pad.

"Honey, I think being set up is the least of your problems. Don't you see? Uncovering that file put you right in the hacker's crosshairs. For damned sure somebody savvy enough to set up that file, to hide it from you and all your security programs, don't you suppose their programming includes something to alert the hacker if somebody messes with that file?"

She hadn't thought about that. But she hadn't noticed anything either. She let out a breath. "I'll be fine," she said. "I'll document everything I do." She nodded at the look he gave her, as if she were promising to be a good girl. "I won't leave a trail."

Ted drained his glass and sat it down on his desk with a thump. "No point in arguing with you I suppose. But just don't forget what happened to Frank Leit."

"Frank Leit was saying…" She did her best to read her uncle's eyes. "*Is* Rex breaking the law?"

"Has been ever since I left the company," Ted said. "Listen to me. Frank Leit was as straight as they come. You want proof?" He disappeared into a back room and returned carrying a pile of papers. He picked out a memo near the bottom of the stack.

"This is just the tip of the iceberg," he said. "Read this. It's a business plan. Anna Thorsen's idea. Sound to you like what Frank Leit was complaining about? And, by the way, Anna's appointment as Rex's CEO is a done deal. You do know that don't you?"

Mimi kept scanning the documents he'd handed her. Her stomach was doing flip-flops with every new page. Of course she knew Anna Thorsen was taking over from her father. She hated it. But reading those business plans… What had her dad been thinking?

She handed the stack back. "Dad bought into

everything Anna was selling, didn't he? Was any of it Dad's idea, do you know?" One look—her uncle's face was a hundred percent *I told you so.* She should have expected that. After all, that corporate growth scheme in those memos had been the reason for the blow-up Ted had with her dad.

Ted fanned the papers, pointing as he went. "There, and there…and there. It's all Anna Thorsen."

"But Dad was part of it," she said.

Ted sighed. "My point is, the price fixing and tie-ins *originated* with Anna Thorsen."

"But Dad bought it," she said. "And he sold it to the board, the stockholders…to everybody." That quickly, she got it. There was absolutely nothing more she could say.

Fingers trembling, she re-read parts of the papers Ted had passed back to her and, when her stomach refused to stop churning, she poured herself a glass of seltzer and downed it. She couldn't shake the fact her own father had lied to her. He'd made her question her own sense of what was happening. No wonder he kept avoiding her.

Ted started to say something about sorry, but she cut him off. "At Stanford I knew who I was. I had a future in mathematics and plans of my own. I threw it all away because Dad claimed he needed me." She pulled her bag up into the chair with her and started ransacking it for a tissue. "This whole time I've been part of the lie."

Ted took a long time pulling his papers back together. Finally, he cleared his throat. "What is it you want? What kind of a future?"

Cripes, she wasn't about to have that discussion.

"Mimi," he said, "in five years, where do you want to be?"

She couldn't think. She didn't know. But she would not be at Rex. And it would not take five years. She just couldn't talk about it now.

But they did talk, for another hour—about change, about her potential for doing something worthwhile. Somewhere in all the talk, the bourbon disappeared, and Ted made coffee. He brought the pot over, along with a clean mug.

"Honey," he said. "You're not seeing the kind of danger you're in. It doesn't matter in the least whether you're being set up. A year from now nobody's gonna believe you dropped the ball at Rex. Or that you did anything wrong. Nobody will even remember that file. But this thing about Frank Leit—the police will be all over it in no time and whoever killed him will have nothing to lose. You understand? Anybody who knows anything about that email file is at risk. You need to disappear."

"I can't help thinking about Dad," she said. "Isn't he at risk, too?"

Ted gave her a long, serious look. "We're not talking about your dad, Mimi. We're talking about you. Take all the time you need to decide your future. But right now, today, tomorrow, next week, you need to get yourself safe. And you need a good lawyer, one not related to you. I can give you a name."

To make him happy, she said fine. If he set up a meeting with his lawyer, she'd be there. Ted seemed content with that. What she didn't say, what she had to take care of before she did anything about leaving Rex, she had to face down her dad. It was his choice, either

B. Davis Kroon

her or Anna Thorsen.

B. Davis Kroon

her or Anna Thorsen.

126

Chapter 18

Thorsen had intended to spend Friday working at home. She should have had a quiet day reading the Securities and Exchange Commission reports Legal had sent over. Instead, at 8:30, she slammed the final draft of the 10-K she'd been evaluating into her portfolio, snatched up her phone and speed-dialed her assistant. "Get Tim what's-his-name who'd drafted that 10-K in my office. I want him there in thirty minutes."

"But I thought you were—" JR began.

"Thirty minutes!" She jammed the phone off, tossed it in her portfolio and flew out the door, which she managed to slam so hard it rattled the windows of her condo.

Tim what's-his-name was pacing her outer office when she strode in.

She stripped off her coat, her fur hat, and motioned for him to follow, saying she had a couple of questions. She did not say precisely what they were. Instead she made a beeline for her desk and locked her laptop into its network docking station. Tim had stopped a good ten feet back from her desk, clearing his throat and shifting from one foot to the other.

As if it were an absent-minded gesture, Thorsen waved him over to a small round table. She laid her copy of the 10-K down between them, then shoved JR's coffee/tea set-up aside and insinuated herself into a chair.

They read through the document together. They read aloud. As they came to the little sections she had tagged, she checked his expression but didn't raise her objections to the long and complicated report. She would save that for later. To begin with, they discussed nearly every paragraph as if they were writing it jointly, cooperatively, supportively even. She leaned forward and listened, especially to the tone of his voice. She nodded at his explanations, now and then she made a note.

Eventually she acknowledged how difficult it was to artfully present Rex's growth issues to a regulatory agency "without drawing too much attention to the company's...let's call it success in negotiations," she said, then stood and walked away from the conference table. She paused to fiddle with something on her credenza to give him time to think. And with her back to him, she said, "Let me explain why I wanted to speak with you personally." She gave it a moment and turned to face him. "As this document stands—and I appreciate how thorough and careful you've been here—but your draft raises four or five serious questions about the company."

Tim stiffened. *Questions* must've shot through his system as if she'd jabbed him with a hot poker.

"I'm sure when you think about it, you will agree that any unexplained reference might cause the S.E.C. to consider whether Rex might be hiding something. The last thing we want is to imply, however innocently, is that Rex should be investigated. You see that, don't you?" She leaned forward as if she were trying to see whether he agreed.

She didn't miss his surreptitious effort to wipe a hand on his pinstripe pantleg. Instead, she let the moment stretch into an awkward pause before she returned to the table. "I don't mean to put you on the spot," she said and gave him her most sympathetic face. But Christ, if the twerp couldn't hold it together when she'd barely rapped his knuckles, what would he do if somebody really made him sweat? She picked up a bottle of water—did he want one?

"I'm sure you see," she said, "if the S.E.C. were to flag our 10-K, it could make a pretzel of our next five-year plan. That's best case. Worst case, if they were to find something—not that they would, but if—the feds could restrict public trading of our stock."

Watching her words hit home was as satisfying as a vodka martini. And restricted trading had been an especially nice bomb to drop. Finally she said, "So let's see what we can do." She scooted closer to the table and commenced revisiting the entries she'd flagged one by one. She left that pesky Indonesian comment for last and worked her face into a kind-but-confused puzzlement as her finger hovered over the footnote. Why was he raising the company's history in Indonesia at all? Was there something she didn't know? No, she knew precisely what had gone down in Indonesia.

On the other hand, what Tim didn't know was a lot.

She'd been the face of Rex Sports for all five negotiations. She'd visited every subcontractor factory Rex bought and personally toured the one that burned to the ground. Of course there'd been a stink about the fire at the time. But she'd taken care of that.

She was not revisiting that part of her life again.

Especially not with the S.E.C.

"No, no, no," Tim said. "It's just that the political climate there is…well, you know. Their leaders have made some very unfriendly comments about the West so I thought, better to be upfront. That way it's clear that our corporate stability—"

Thorsen nodded and used a red Sharpie to delete the footnote.

"We don't need to mention it at all then," she said. "We wouldn't want to worry the S.E.C. with what might happen a half-world away, would we?" The poor sap couldn't get out of her office fast enough.

She downed a protein drink and, out of habit, made a quick check of Frank Leit's blog. Ridiculous given the blog was dead… Only, apparently, Frank Leit's son had a different idea. It was a short post. *R.I.P. Frank Leit…*

Sweat sheeted her back. Ben Leit was NOT part of her plan. And he certainly was NOT taking over his father's blog. Not while she had breath left in her body.

Chapter 19

A few feet away from Ben's seat in first class, the cabin attendant was opening champagne. Even from where he sat, he could taste it and his palms went slick just thinking about a drink. *Just water thanks just water thanks just water.*

The woman next to him, in her fifties he would have guessed, leaned over to him.

"I'm thinking you know my friend, Bill W. Am I right?"

She wasn't looking at him at all. She was focused on the wine flutes coming their way. And he got it. He started to nod, to say yes. But even before he could answer, she motioned to the cabin attendant. "Would you mind? When you get a chance, I'd prefer an orange juice," she said and shifted back into her seat.

"Good idea," Ben said to the attendant. "Me too."

Once the attendant left, he turned to his seatmate. "Ben. Two-hundred twenty days."

"Ameera," she said "Eight years, four months, seventeen days. You can always get juice."

****

The first night back in his Seattle condo, he hit bottom—or it felt like it. He didn't have a clue how to go forward. To distract himself, he took a crack at writing his next blog entry. He got as far as the first sentence, which was crap, tried it again a couple hundred times, considered whether staying sober was worth it, rejected calling Bobby Joe, and finally hit the sack.

The next morning, the phone woke him up. For one second, he had that sick feeling it was happening all over again. Instead, Mike Park had come up with an expert. Ben glanced at the clock—6:00 a.m.—and swung his legs around to get the details. Park said, "Zach Berman. When it comes to email conversions, word is, Berman's been there and got the T-shirt. And he's working right where you are. He's head of IT at some place called the Kaufman Group."

Paul Kaufman? Ben's pen lifted off the notepad. "You're sure?" he said. There were plenty of big law firms on the West Coast, maybe seven in Seattle. And Park comes up with an expert who works for his own lawyer? Why hadn't he thought to call Paul in the first place?

The news felt so good, no way he could go back to sleep. He hauled on his sweats and headed down to the parking lot.

The whole hill was enveloped in that inside-the-cloud misty rain that happens before a front rolls in. Between the dripping tree canopy, the sun not being up and the mist, he could barely see down the side street. He didn't care. It felt terrific just to be home, to run, to be alive. At the bottom of the condo stairs, he paused beside the covered parking just long enough to pull up his hood and got a lungful of that loamy smell you get in Seattle in November.

He took the downhill section of the road slow, side-stepping the ruts of fallen leaves. Once he crossed Aurora, he started seeing people on their way to work, then more joggers. And by the time he made it on down to South Lake Union, it was getting light out and there were even a few boaters out working their gear.

Berman… Even the thought of getting at his dad's emails gave him a kick. He checked his watch. Two hours 'til the law office would be open. His usual run would take an hour. He took off around the lake figuring to head back once he got to the University Bridge. What was truly great about hiring his IT guy from Paul's office, he could work on his dad's stuff right there. They had three floors of the Smithson Tower, which meant there was plenty of space for special projects. He could rent some of it for a couple of months.

The more he thought about working inside Kaufman's firm, the more it made sense. His dad had been a long-time client. *He* was a long-time client. He already knew his way around there—at least the floor Paul worked on. If he needed extra help or equipment, Paul could get what he needed.

By the time he got to his turnaround spot at the bridge, a couple of rowing teams were on the water. If it was humanly possible, he felt even better than he had when he'd started the run. He stood watching as the sculls passed until the cold hit him, then, finally, he turned for home.

An hour and a half later, Ben walked into The Kaufman Group's law office. Berman was waiting by the elevator—olive skin, dark hair and eyes, not more than five-foot-nine or ten, younger than Ben—leave it to Paul to hire an ex-jock. Probably the guy was a former running back, or maybe a wrestler, because he hadn't lost the thick-shouldered, power-build those guys have.

Berman led the way back through the north hall to a corner office. He had two walls full of awards and degrees from Stanford and Cal, the other two walls were glass, with a heck of a view of the Belltown District. Once Ben got past the scenery though, he couldn't help thinking it was just an upscale version of Mike Park's shop, but without the big dog.

Berman unloaded a guest chair. Ben sat and explained what he needed.

For a second, Berman looked blank. "What about the police investigation?"

Ben shifted his focus to the view. What could he say about the investigation? He didn't know what the cops were doing. Not really. He ended up talking about Mike Park and the emails, saying that he needed that email access to keep the blog going. For his dad's estate. "You know, the blog."

Okay, it was a lie. But you do what you have to.

Berman took about twenty minutes explaining what Mike Park had already explained. But Berman did it in way more detail. As far as Ben could tell, the "don't touch the emails" thing all came down to the idea that emails have two parts. One part was what ordinary people see and another part only the experts see. The part the experts see is in code. The code identifies the true source of the email. He got it, the code would be key to identifying the sender. *Conversion* is what exposes the hidden code and freezes it so it's part of the individual email. That way, the emails can be part of a database.

"I can set up your email conversion, no problem." Berman picked up his phone and got the vendor going.

At most, it took the guy five minutes.

As Berman hung up, Ben couldn't help thinking, finally, he had a real, doable Plan B, with emails he could look at. *Touchdown!*

That was when Berman started in with the bad news. First, the conversion process would take a few days—there was nothing Berman could do to speed it up. Second, the Kaufman firm didn't have any extra space it could rent to Ben. And third, assuming that Ben was thinking about a database of the converted emails, plus his dad's memos and so on, Berman didn't have time to teach Ben about setting the database up or working with it.

"And you will definitely need somebody, somebody really good, to help you. At least when you're starting out," Berman said.

Ben licked his lower lip. "Isn't there something you can do to get me going?"

Berman checked his Outlook calendar and sighed. "Maybe the firm's human resources people could find somebody to help. I'll do what I can and get back to you, okay?"

Ben left Berman on the phone to HR and, at the elevator, decided to try an end-run. Maybe a little leverage from the firm's founding partner would make a difference. He took the elevator up two floors, where he learned that Paul, who never did trials anymore, was tied up testifying as an expert in Chicago. Wasn't that just terrific. If he'd been talking football, he'd have said it was fourth down with eight yards to go—definitely time to punt, at least as far as the law firm went. He thanked Paul's assistant and headed back to the elevator.

The giant windows in the building's two-story lobby had a clear view of stalled traffic. The weather had gone from rain to monsoon; even people with umbrellas were standing in doorways.

He debated hanging around the lobby, maybe catching a break in the weather. But who knew when it would let up? Besides, he always felt better when he was in action. He headed across the street to the garage, the whole way trying to convince himself that getting any kind of help with his dad's emails was better than no help at all. So he had to wait three days. Who knew what could happen in three days?

At his car, he tossed his dripping raincoat on the passenger seat, climbed in, and sat there with the heater going. Any sane man would've backed off and let the cops run their investigation. He might've done that too if the cops had been willing to look at what happened to his dad with an open mind. But home invasion, that was just an excuse for closing the case.

He dialed down the car heater and it hit him: maybe his name wasn't as big as his dad's anymore. But what if he kept the spotlight going on his dad's murder? What if he went on a whole publicity campaign—print media, internet, TV, radio, anything that the killer might see or hear? The killer would have to come after him.

Well then...even without his expert or the emails, there was a heck of a lot more he could do. And he had three days to do it.

He started with Henry on the Sports desk at the Seattle Times. Henry had been after him for a story ever since he'd left the Giants. He put in a call, bought Henry lunch and gave out the first newspaper interview he'd given since leaving New York. Front to back, he talked up his dad's story: school, football, what kind of man his Dad had been, public service, what he'd been working on at the end. By the time Ben wrapped things up, he figured he could count on Henry to get something hot into print that the AP would pick up.

Then he called the local ABC affiliate. It took a couple of minutes, but once he talked with the right producer, he cut a deal with KOMO-TV. KOMO would give him the main segment on a special they were putting together on sports figures with a Seattle connection. They did say Ben's piece might be shortened for the main broadcast, but they'd put the whole interview up on their web site.

Three hours later, the KOMO crew showed up at Ben's condo—cameraman, sound guy, producer, a light setup, the works. Ben made sure they got plenty of stuff on the condo's location, shots of the building entry, views of South Lake Union from the balcony—anything he figured might help his dad's killer get to him. He punched up the interview as much as he could, going on about his dad's blog, the charity it supported, and he ended with a great sound bite. He set it up like an afterthought and even threw in one of his dad's grins.

"Dad had a big project going." He said it straight into the camera. "I'm building on it as fast as I can. In two or three weeks, I'll have a story for you that'll stand the sports world on its head."

Chapter 20

Less than two minutes after opening the link to Frank Leit's blog, Thorsen closed it and pushed away from her office desk. "R.I.P. my ass," she muttered. And, to shake loose of her fury, she paced. Would she never be rid of Frank Leit and his hangers-on? She tried staring out at the weather—no good. Ben Leit making it his business... Not happening. She flexed her latissimus dorsi. That was no help either. She had a 11:00 a.m. meeting she couldn't duck. And meetings after that one, straight through 'til mid-afternoon. There wasn't time to investigate Ben Leit, let alone do something. Not personally, not if she were going to get the detail she'd need. Not if she wanted to shut him down before he got going.

She dialed her New Orleans investigators. A man answered. "Specialty Dining."

What was that hard-to-place accent, Austrian? Dutch?

"I'd like to place an order for delivery," she said. "Is it too late for this evening?" Translation: she wanted something ASAP.

"We are only too pleased to be of service, madam. A complete dinner or—"

"Just appetizers this time. For forty people," she said. Meaning, *investigate and spare the legalities but no break-in, and I want the report ASAP.*

She hated the predictable phone dance. But she appreciated the purpose—to avoid those nasty and embarrassing wiretap records that might prove she was asking for information or assistance that the law frowned upon.

It would be an honor to serve her, the man said, and the line went dead. Just as it always did. And her phone rang again after three minutes. Just as it always did.

This time, a woman. "We apologize for losing your call, madam."

Thorsen figured she'd changed continents. Had to be the woman was calling from Europe or Southeast Asia. The slight sound delay gave it away.

The woman confirmed the appetizers would be delivered promptly. She then provided a one-time message address which Thorsen noted in the palm of her hand. "For Madam's use should she wish to provide specific instructions regarding the service," the woman said and ended the call. Thorsen dialed the new number, entered a password, then relayed her very, very complete instructions about Ben Leit to a digital recorder located on a site that would exist for minutes at most—only long enough to receive and re-deliver Thorsen's message to someone working God knew where.

In spite of the protocol, it was always a pleasure to be dealing with professionals.

For the next five hours, Thorsen was in and out of meetings at Rex, listening to facts she already knew and crap she didn't give a damn about and wouldn't go forward with once she was in as CEO.

Finally, just as she rolled into her office at 3:00

p.m., JR of the single ear stud earring, who made it his business to know everything about everybody and would be thrilled to find out more... Her ever-ready assistant, JR, stopped in her doorway. As usual, he was positively quivering.

"Just so you know: our main server is down." Said as if he believed the news might mean there was something worse going on than a server being down.

Thorsen eyed the laptop sitting on her desk, still in its network docking station.

"They say it should be up in an hour or so," he said watching her, "but you should work from your hard drive, okay?"

She couldn't believe it. If IT had the server down, they were fucking with her file. Because, no matter what Addison had said, Mimi Fitzroy would never delete that file without making a copy. And Mimi would never store it in the cloud or leave whatever she'd stored it on in some desk drawer at Rex. Mimi would squirrel it away at her house and obsess over it.

Thorsen blinked once, twice, and JR repeated himself.

"I heard you." She snatched up her coat and hat. "I'm late."

Forty minutes later she slowed her Maserati and cruised by Mimi Fitzroy's Victorian—one of those elegant old, three-story family homes with a couple of turrets. One year earlier, Mimi bought it—complete with its decorative shingles and four-color paint job. The story was, the house had been on the city's demolition list. Then a crazy blonde with a TV rehab show had restored it. When Thorsen learned Mimi's house had been part of the show, she'd watched the reruns. You never could tell when knowing the lay of the land might come in handy. First though, she needed a sense of the neighborhood.

A quiet street, no parked cars, no sign Mimi's front walk had been used since the snow. But the public sidewalks had been cleared and the snow piled by the curb. The entire way along the block, no lights on, no sign of kids. She drove past Mimi's house to the corner, turned right, up the grade and turned right again into the alley. She passed a long line of garages—again, no sign of life. In spite of the cold, she rolled down the car window and listened for dogs...nothing. She cruised west along the alley and paused just past where Mimi's garage opened onto the alley...standard automatic garage door, no side door.

Thorsen cruised down the alley for another block. Turning right, she put herself three blocks from Mimi's. She parked, walked back and stood out of sight of the side street. She pulled a little black gizmo from her pocket—God she loved electronics. It took less than two minutes to find the right frequency for the garage door. Once inside the garage, she located the control switch, closed the automatic door and pulled out her little toolbox. Seconds later, she was inside the house.

Chapter 21

Rolf leaned a hand on Hart's desk. "Done yet?"

Without looking up, Hart finished inputting a phrase, saved his work and brushed back a long strand of hair. "Like I said before, the deal doesn't feel right."

Rolf picked at a fingernail. "Like I've said before, we sell information."

Hart turned back toward his computer. "Right, information. So how do we know Etouffee isn't blackmailing—"

"Forget about Tea-for-Two, that was before Uta took over. Etouffee just wants to put her hands on the guy. My guess, it's a business deal in the making and she wants to see the man behind it. You're done with the Halliday report?"

Hart poked his glasses back up on his nose and glanced at the work order in Rolf's hands: a rush project, a full book request on Ben Leit, the NFL football player. Hart's thin lips disappeared entirely.

"Ben Leit? Man, I gotta tell you, there's something wrong here. Information's one thing, but this guy's a public figure, you know? I mean you do know who Ben Leit is, right? Big-time football player... American football? And what's this woman doing anyway? This must be like the fourteenth search she's ordered."

Rolf bent his scarecrow frame, leaned a little closer to Hart and lowered his voice. "Twentieth, as if that would matter. Look, Etouffee pays up front, there's always a bonus, and, it's not blackmail. Uta looked into the client; she says Etouffee is front for a mega-corporation. So we're covered. There's a bonus here. You want the work or not?"

Hart stared at his lap. "Anything else I could work on instead?"

Rolf eyed Hart. Finally he said, "This is a straight location. From 2000 to October 10, this year, Leit lived in Manhattan, a condo at 169 Spring St. He moved on October 10. No forwarding address. Check my notes at ETF24-21."

Hart eyed the Rule of Twenty protocol chart on the far wall: bank charges, deposit sources, account history, credit check, business account charges, volume of cash transactions and digital records, court history. It was a long list of sources to be checked and Hart's eyes followed it through to the end. He turned back to Rolf. "You run the whole list?"

"Most of it. We're up against the clock," Rolf said.

"Then why don't you finish it? And forget that Rule of Twenty. It'll only slow you down. Best source is the realtor that sold the New York condo. That and The Giants' offices. Get the detail on the condo sale. And there must be a payoff on his contract. That'll give you the bank account, and his location," Hart turned back to his computer screen.

"I don't have your touch." Rolf pressed a Post-It on the work order. "No risk to you. If Uta says the client's good, you can bank on it. Trust me. And—" He tapped the paper. "Monday at the latest, okay?"

Chapter 22

The whole way home from the meeting with her uncle's lawyer, Mimi kept thinking about Frank Leit. Uncle Ted had maintained Frank Leit was right, that Rex (or at least somebody connected to Rex) was corrupt. Somebody? Who else but her father? It made her sick.

And then there was everything Uncle Ted's lawyer had said.

She pulled into her garage, dumped her coat and keys in the mudroom, and set off through the house. She needed to think. A workout would help. She headed up to her bedroom, yanked on her workout gear, and started on up to her third-floor gym. Her body froze on the fourth stair tread. A shiver shot down her neck and the tiny hairs on her arms stood erect. Her chest pounded. She checked her pulse and couldn't help listening for something more—the creak of a floorboard, a knock, something.

After the news about Frank Leit and finding that file, and that pompous ass Addison…maybe she was just jumpy.

She swiped her hand into her hair, pushing it back. She could call Security, that's what she was paying for. But the last time she'd called Security, back when she'd first bought the house, she completely over-reacted. She hadn't felt safe. Because, who knew how many people would recognize the house after it had been on "Rehab America" for weeks and weeks during the remodel? Maybe more honestly, she didn't feel safe because, for the first time, she was living alone in a big empty house. Plus, the guys who'd moved her in knew she was a Fitzroy. And they knew she had a lot of cash because she'd stupidly flashed it when she tipped them. She knew what could happen. That's why she'd installed a security system in the first place.

Back then, she'd called in a panic and Security came roaring in like a squadron of Navy Seals on a rescue mission. Naturally it was all her imagination. Imagination or not, the next day she'd bought a Glock 19 and taken lessons. She kept it in a safe in her bedroom.

She let go of her breath, turned, and took three steps down to the landing outside her bedroom. In seconds, she punched in the code for her gun safe and retrieved her Glock. She threw the safety off, snugged the Glock between her backbone and the waistband of her shorts, and, on second thought, grabbed her Mace. As she started back up the stairs to where she'd stopped on her way up to work out, there it was again like a cold shower, that feeling of somebody...

Her face and neck stung like she'd been swarmed by bees.

After taking a deep, centering breath, she switched the mace to her left hand, retrieved the Glock, and forced herself up to the third-floor landing. The only sound, the mechanical whump-whump of the fan. She played her fingers against the pistol grip and edged herself against the door. If the guy was up there, she'd flatten him.

The third floor was one big room with a treadmill, elliptical trainer, weight bench—the whole megillah with only one way out and no place to hide. Ready for she didn't know what, she stepped back and kicked the door wide open. Nobody. She could breathe. So then why was she still so creeped out? And why would somebody break in and not go straight for her safe?

Half-way down to the second floor she saw what had spooked her. The guest room door was closed. She always left it open. So did her cleaning lady.

Think: How many people had Addison talked to in the past five hours? And who were they?

Six steps to the landing. She hit the alarm.

Security answered on the first ring. "How can we help?"

"I've had a break-in."

"Is the intruder still there?"

"Not sure."

It looked like, whoever it was, they'd tried to crack her computer and failed. While she waited for Security, she set a computer program going that would quarantine anything she hadn't authorized to be on the hard drive. Done, she grabbed her Glock, plus the Mace, and headed down to wait by the front door.

By the time Security arrived, it had started to snow. Again.

Security turned out to be Burt and two younger guys carrying night sticks and walkie-talkies. The young guys took off immediately to check outdoors, the basement, all the places she hadn't been and hadn't thought about. Burt ran through his preliminary spiel about what they'd be doing, disappeared to confer with his men, and she headed back up to her office.

She looked hard at her desk, at what was there, what was moved or missing—blotter, pens, mouse pad, a photo from Stanford days, UCB plug-ins. Everything was just like always. No, not the plug-ins. The red and orange ones were out of order and her extra keys were on the floor. She couldn't help thinking about the "home invasions" she'd had while she was at Stanford. There'd been at least four of them, and they always the same kind of hint that it wasn't a thief, that she had a stalker.

"You're all clear." It was Burt, standing in her office doorway. "But come with me."

He pointed across the hallway to the guestroom. He stopped just inside the doorway, turned off the overhead light and aimed his flashlight across the plush carpet.

With the different angle of the light, she could see footprints on the Oriental rug. One set tracked right next to the room's perimeter and stopped in front of the closet, where obviously the person had turned more or less in place, and left the room the way they'd come in.

"Those are me." Burt trained his light on the second set of prints. "These aren't."

The prints went straight from the bedroom door, to the bathroom, back out around the end of the bed and disappeared on the far side of the room. They returned to the bedroom door on the same route. How had she missed them?

"You have company?" Burt shot her a sideways glance.

"Not for months."

"Boyfriends?"

She gave him a limp smile.

"A cleaning service?"

"Magda comes in on Wednesdays. She cleans the whole house and she's very careful to leave everything the way I want."

Burt motioned her to follow him. At the end of the bed nearest the windows he squatted "Take a good look."

Two clear prints, way more than a foot long and maybe twice the width of her hand—crushed into the deep pile of the rug. They were angled like whoever made them had looked out the window.

Burt hovered his own hand over one footprint. "A man, maybe a big boy."

"In trainers," she said.

"That would explain the width."

"A man," she said, "or a really big woman."

Burt looked back at her, a little surprised. "She'd have to be pretty big." He stood and started for the door. "There's more."

Downstairs he showed her the scratches on the key plate of the door into the house from the garage, very faint, but the marks were there. He suggested they sit at the breakfast counter. He had questions, opinions and advice for her. But she wasn't paying attention. Not really. Because the break-in wasn't some ordinary burglar, she could see that.

Burt shoved a work order in front of her. She signed and headed back upstairs to secure her computer. She stared at the screen. Either Frank Leit's hacker must know she'd found the file and figured she'd taken it home with her, or… No. It was too much like California.

She should have thought of Anna Thorsen right

from the start. Thorsen had plenty of nerve. And *really* big feet. She'd focused on Addison before because of how he'd blown her off. Because he'd made her mad. And he would have to okay any deals the company made, wouldn't he? Maybe he didn't see them as crooked. Or maybe Thorsen had forced him to go along with her. It would be like Thorsen to drag some man into her plan and keep him in the dark.

Oddly enough, that was the good news. Thorsen might be a bitch and a back-stabber, and for sure wasn't above screwing with people. And winding somebody up would be just like Thorsen, she had that cunning. But Thorsen was no threat to Mimi. Thorsen had too much to lose professionally. Like everybody was saying, Thorsen was set to be the next CEO.

Mimi rubbed the bridge of her nose.

She was right. She could feel it. Thorsen and Addison were both involved. That didn't explain how they managed to pirate the emails, or set up the ghost file. Did they hire somebody? Was a third person involved? Was it somebody at Rex? Because, for almost certain, neither Thorsen nor Addison had the technical chops to set up that pirated email file themselves.

She patted her hands against her computer keyboard as if she were saying goodbye and stood up from her chair. One thing for darned sure, she was not sleeping where somebody might break in without setting off the alarm. And, with her dad's Man of the Year dinner less than twenty-four hours away, she definitely needed her sleep.

The thing that kept eating at her—she'd ended up in tears about it at the lawyer's office—was whether her dad was really involved. Ted hadn't actually accused her dad of coming up with the antitrust thing, just with going along. But how could she be sure her dad hadn't been part of it right from the beginning? He always had to win. And winning by a tiny margin was never good enough, he had to win by a mile. Maybe that's how it started. Thinking he deserved better than everybody else, that he was above the law.

She called the Radisson, booked a suite and packed. She could live there while Security did whatever they needed to do at her place. And by the time she settled in her hotel room, she had the makings of a plan.

She would be at Rex when ABC interviewed her father tomorrow morning. She would confront him about Frank Leit's antitrust thing. Was he or wasn't he part of an antitrust conspiracy? She'd say she wanted the truth. It wasn't just Frank Leit saying the company was dishonest; Ted was saying it too. She would say *Dad, I don't need an immediate answer from you. Just the truth.* If she put it to him face-to-face, she'd know if he was lying.

She would go to his dinner, whatever he said. She would do it because she loved him and because she had promised him, she'd go. As for whatever happened after the dinner, she'd sort that out later.

Chapter 23

Saturday morning Mimi rolled into Rex executive parking in plenty of time to watch her father's pre-award interview with ABC television.

She'd never been thrilled about attending the Man of the Year thing. She didn't enjoy meet-and-greets, she wasn't a Baird State alum and she didn't want to give her father the impression he could use her as a prop for his Senatorial campaign. He had way too many skeletons in his closet—for starters, there were the bankrupt competitors, and then there was the way he'd flim-flammed control of the company away from the rest of the family. There had to be people at Baird State who were furious at the way he'd taken over the school. Maybe that's the way politics worked. But she wanted no part of it.

The closer they got to The Big Day, the more it seemed to her that the Man of the Year dinner had all the earmarks of a disaster in the making. There'd been too much publicity, too much counting on it launching his image, loading in stuff about her now-sainted dead brother. It was too much everything.

But she'd promised to be there. And in a weak moment, she'd ordered a fabulous dress. She'd even hired a stylist. She would show up, look good, and keep her fingers crossed that things didn't get too sticky.

Meantime, there was her dad's TV interview; it

ended up taking more than an hour.

Mimi stood in the back of the media room. It was like she was watching a stranger spin out a newly-minted version of himself: politically savvy, sincerely casual, earnest, kindly, disciplined.

What troubled her wasn't her father's persona, or how people described him. For years she'd seen him go into his song and dance. It had always left her feeling sad and lost. But this time it was worse. Because watching him now, she wished it was true that her father was that phony blow-hard, instead of being the man behind the crimes Frank Leit had been ready to expose.

Fitzroy-the-candidate dodged the interviewer's final question with a silver fox grin. "I'm just lucky."

She loved her father. But *just lucky* definitely wasn't the phrase she'd have used to characterize him.

Once the TV host wrapped things up, Mimi made her way over to where her father stood chatting.

Her dad was beaming. "Let's duck in here," he said and pointed to a small kitchen that served the media room. She had her opening salvo ready but—

"Whadya think? Did I strike the right note?"

All she could think was go with the flow if it helped relax him. "You couldn't have been better," she said. "You really—"

"That's the ticket. I needed to hit that mark. I'm just a regular guy. But a businessman. Now, come on in here." He stepped into the kitchen and backed around to face her.

As he backed up, he bumped into a counter and she realized, the kitchen was barely big enough to hold a rolling cart for drinks trays and hors d'oeuvres. The only way for him to leave before she'd had her say was to push past her, out into the media room. So she had him.

He had that indulgent face going, but his eyes were searching her face and she could feel her don't-be-mad-at-me-daddy smile slide into place like she was still nine years old and hadn't properly put her wet boots away. "So," he said, "what's this about not picking you up tonight?"

"Well," she said, "with the weather and my dress, it just made more sense for me to stay at the hotel."

"Not willing to go to the show on the old man's arm, huh?"

"Come on, Dad." *Ugh...wheedling.* She took hold of his hand. "Listen, I just need to talk with you. Before the dinner. Just for a minute. It won't take long."

He gave her the same look he'd been using on the TV people. "Fire away."

"It's about a thing I just read."

He pulled back, his eyebrows skyrocketing in mock surprise. Someone else might have thought he was joking, but she knew him. She was being warned to keep it light.

He said, "You're not gonna make this a downer for me, are you?"

"Dad, I'm serious. The more I think about it, the more I worry. I worry for you. For your campaign, the company. Look, I'm sorry, but Frank Leit's website—"

He jerked away from her. "Jesus, Mimi. I'm not wasting my time rehashing Frank Leit and his bullshit."

He pushed past her and snatched the door open so fast she actually had to jump out of the way. And by the time she could see where he'd gone, he was surrounded

153

with people. Naturally, Anna Thorsen had planted herself right at the center of the impromptu audience. With her new haircut and color, Anna bristled like a fire-engine-red porcupine. Maybe that was the thing for would-be CEOs. Less sports model and more edgy network news anchor.

For one moment, Thorsen's gaze locked on Mimi, then it skidded around the room and returned to settle on Fitzroy. Thorsen leaned toward him, said something, and he glanced at his watch. In the second before Thorsen disappeared her dad out the door, he did look back at Mimi. He'd been smiling for the TV crew. But the look back to her implied that they would be talking later. And it would not be good.

Chapter 24

Raj Banerjee slid a sports drink over to Mimi. The fingers of her right hand had not stopped drumming the top of his worktable since she'd sat down. And that was nearly fifteen minutes ago. He was feeling such concern for her. She was ghostly pale…though he had not mentioned this to her.

"You are working too much perhaps."

She ducked her head. "No. No more than usual."

"You did not work through the night on the hacker?"

Her lips tightened. "We've resolved that."

At least nine times her body had startled at noises in the hall. She was not meeting him eye to eye. "Resolved," he said. "Good." He leaned into the table and looked at her more carefully. Her breathing was so very shallow and her good face pierced with tension.

"Your father has his big celebration this evening," he said. "This is an honor from his university, yes?" He smiled at his friend with an open heart, with his whole face hopeful, as if he were imagining the Man of the Year dinner. Though in truth, he was thinking she was so very unhappy and that he must do something to help.

She pressed her lips into a tight, fishy smile. "He had a television interview this morning. Maybe you know that. He seemed happy with how it went." Her smile evaporated and she looked away.

Raj let the flat of his hand drop to the tabletop. "Mimi, I am telling you this is not right. You say it all is resolved this business with the hacker as if you would have me believe everything in your life is happiness. It is not happiness. And we are not children. We are friends, Mimi. I see your fingers, how you drum them. You do this when you cannot decide or when you worry. You do it now." He could see she was angry with him. But he could not stop. "My friend, no matter what you are telling me, I know that all is not well for you. Tell me, please, what may I do to help you? If this is about the breech of our security—"

"It's handled," she snapped. "You've seen the directives to personnel. Outside Security has imposed new routines—"

"Stop. Mimi, please stop. Did we not agree to keep one another informed of all incidents, all troubles, all repairs? Am I not correct?" He shocked even himself. The words had flown from his mouth before he had considered how they might sound. Now he could not look at her. She was lying. So disrespectful. But he had said too much. He apologized.

She seemed to listen, but then she glanced once more at the door. When, at last she met his eyes with her own, she sighed, squared her body to the table and told him what had happened after she'd taken on the work for his group. She explained about the ghost file, how she had found it, what it contained, the risks it created, about the murder of a man in Arizona.

"A murder? Your father knows of this?"

"I told the General Counsel," she said. "Addison's theory is I should copy the file, give him the copy and delete the original." She had not deleted it, she said.

Instead she had copied it to her private server, she'd left the original ghost file in place, and written a small program that would alert her if someone opened it.

He cast a quick glance at his hands so she would not notice his thoughts...what a fool the man Addison was to think that deleting a file would make this business of the hacker disappear. "Do we know who it was set up the file? He must be exposed—"

She fixed him with her lovely brown eyes. They were wide as a cat's.

"No. Addison will do what he's doing. Which I think will be nothing at all." She scooted closer. "I didn't say that... But listen, IT must do nothing about the file, including you. This is the story, and you must stick to it: the only thing you know is that you received a message from Outside Security. Your team did their work. We later learned the notice was an error. It was their mistake. You and our department, you didn't find anything because there was nothing to find. Okay? And we have not discussed this."

When he asked, she said she had not told her father. *What to say? What to say?* "This man Addison, you are trusting him?"

The worry in her eyes told him she did not. *What could he do to help her?* Clearly, she was more afraid than he had first thought. He stretched over to his desk, dug a flip phone and charger out of a bottom drawer and handed it to her. "It belonged to my mother. It is old but it still is working. It needs only to be charged. It is programmed to call me wherever I am. Only me. I will find a way to help you. This is my promise."

She took the phone from him, slipped it into her sports bag, then scooted the strap up high on her shoulder.

"And Mimi," he said. "You must be very careful with yourself."

"You too," she said and was gone.

Chapter 25

An hour before kickoff of the Man of the Year Dinner, Anna Thorsen climbed into David Fitzroy's limo and smoothed herself into her seat.

"Glad you could join me," Fitzroy said watching her. "Nice dress."

The compliment wasn't like him. And it sounded perfunctory. But she flashed him a smile. "I thought Mimi was—"

"Already at the hotel." Fitzroy turned away and made a point of gazing out the window.

The limo took off and she glanced down at her lap. So, it was going to be like that: tight mouth, twitchy fingers, fiddling with the bow tie. All because Mimi had not joined him for the limo ride. Fine. She settled back. Eventually she got a long look at Fitzroy.

She'd need to straighten his tie before they landed at the hotel. But the midnight blue tux suited him, made his salt and pepper hair seem more polished—part George Clooney, part Ted Turner. Distinguished and hot was a tough assignment to pull off. But, she reminded herself, good looks might help close the deal on his senatorial campaign. On the other hand, giving people the silent treatment wouldn't make for a very successful evening.

She ticked down the rest of her to-do list: seeing to Senator Mueller, the Rex board, planting another takeover rumor, setting Mimi up for the society columnist… She'd pulled out all the stops to assemble a room full of political help. So the Man of the Year had damned well better get over his case of sulks.

She slapped on a concerned expression and peered over. "Senatorial candidate nervous?"

Fitzroy finally looked at her. "Man of the Year, nervous," he said and made a half-hearted attempt at a grin.

"You'll be great," she said. "Just keep your chin up and your good side to the cameras."

She leaned back into the leather seat and inspected her manicure in the avenue's on-again, off-again ambient light. Senator Mueller was armed and ready for Fitzroy and the rumor mill was already pumping full blast. No big deal if Fitzroy was preoccupied—as long as he held up his end of the deal.

For the next four hours, his job was to hit the political ball out of the park. If he did, he'd go into the senatorial campaign as the front runner in an open-seat contest. She needed him to win. Being the front runner and having the Senator's backing would be the key to doing it. As for Mimi, whether Mimi rode with them to the dinner, what Mimi knew or didn't know, what kind of trouble little Ms. Fitzroy would try to stir up—none of that really mattered. Because by mid-December, Mimi Fitzroy would be out of the picture.

Ironically, if the evening was a tipping point for Fitzroy's political success, she couldn't help feeling that it was also potentially life-altering for her. It was crucial that Minnesota's power elite, and particularly all those Rex shareholders, bought into her image and message. If she wasn't exactly a descendant of Grandpa

Fitzroy, she was the only person capable of leading the company. She had the nerve, the savvy and connections to take Rex to the next level and the one after that.

She slowly drew in a breath and equally slowly released it along with the knot of impatience she'd been pushing down. A quick glance at Fitzroy and she couldn't help imagining how it would play out that evening...provided he stepped up to his assignment. Before her last Houston trip, she'd recruited a pair of handlers to see that the senility set stayed clean and sober. And, more importantly, she'd enlisted a few Baird State alums to keep Mimi away from her daddy. She'd been specific with every one of the Mimi Wranglers. *Ms. Fitzroy is tiny, a mousy-type but very smart, buckets of money; get yourself in lots of photos, show her around, keep her busy, booze is fine but nothing that might involve the police.* She did not tell them she was relying on at least one of them getting it right. But she was. Her money was on the engineer.

Fitzroy shifted in his seat and stretched his neck.

Almost as an echo, she flexed her shoulders. The metallic embroidery and beading on her jacket itched where the collar brushed against her neck. Typical—the thing cost a fortune and it was still miserable to wear.

Still fixed on the passing lights, he said, "She read some of Frank Leit's lies. She's decided he's right,"

Thorsen reached over and touched his arm. "And you said?"

"I told her I didn't want to discuss it." He went back to staring into the night.

"I'm sure she didn't mean to upset you," she said.

Originally, she'd seen the dinner as an opportunity to once and for all convince Fitzroy that Mimi couldn't be his successor. But clearly, now that Mimi had bought Frank Leit's story, it was time for Mimi to self-destruct entirely. Not at the dinner of course. Though even that would be fine as long as Fitzroy was nowhere near the blast zone.

"I'm not upset," he snapped. "I'm fed up hearing about Frank Leit. He's dead. Did you know that? Somebody killed him? And now my own daughter's pushing that bullshit. Jesus. Those deals he's been harping on—I had them vetted six ways from Christmas. Bob Addison cleared them, you cleared them, the whole damned legal department cleared them. I'm done talking about it."

Two blocks and he was still fuming.

Thorsen sighed. It was a regretful sigh, loud enough he'd hear her. "I am sorry, David. I'll talk with her. I'll think of something to say to reassure her about the deals." She glanced over to him...nothing. She'd always thought the stumbling block would be family, especially the Fitzroy kids. But with Jamie out of the way, and the cousins disqualifying themselves right and left, she had not foreseen that David himself would turn into an obstacle.

She stretched her legs and glanced over at Fitzroy. Eliminating Mimi, that was the key, and the last hurdle. If Fitzroy made his campaign official in mid-December, then Mimi would have her accident.

Thorsen suppressed a smile. She'd pick a down news day for the sad event. Before Christmas, so PR could make the most of it. With the right images, the TV news could play Fitzroy's grief against the usual video clips of Santa and the inevitable needy families. He'd be okay.

As they stepped from the limo onto the red carpet, she gave Fitzroy's arm a squeeze. "Give President Wainwright fifteen minutes," she said. "You know the drill."

He shot her a genuine smile. "Right. Schmooze the line at the door with the old man. Make him look good, he'll make me look good."

TV and print press had their people strategically set up throughout the space. Most prominently at the main entry to the hall. Thorsen was more than ready for them. She'd spent her mid-teens providing Vogue and Elle with the kind of glamour shots the press wanted. For this event, that meant her red hair sculpted into a micro bob. The whole look, striking but elegant, a power broker if one had ever been born.

She stood tall, her shoulders and neck relaxed, a hint of cleavage, and her movie-star smile on high-beam aimed straight at the camera. Behind her, already surrounded by admirers, the debonair David Fitzroy was finally in his element.

Eleven minutes, three investment chats and a half-dozen aged-out junior leaguers later, she bent her knees ever so slightly and smiled at a sharp-eyed little old man. "Senator Mueller," she said and clasped the hand of the eighty-year-old senior statesman. He looked her up and down as if he were purchasing a racehorse, then made a thing of admiring her glorious jacket, and whispered that the word was definitely out. David was running.

If the evening was going to pay off for her, it had to seem effortless. She let the old man lead her the long way around the room. The twinkle in his eye was still in place when she deposited him next to Fitzroy. On to step two. *Where was Mimi?*

Skin tingling and careful not to rush it, she strolled past the entrance and the event bar where she noted one or two interesting tuxedoes—no sign of Mimi yet. Summing up, there was way more gray hair in the room than she would have hoped, plus, enough hairspray, aftershave and perfume to camouflage a zoo. She floated through the throng, smiling, taking a hand. The questions ran the gamut, from "What do you think of that new Italian movie with the girl?" to "What are those damned fools in Washington going to ruin next?" A half-dozen times, she was stopped by a gaggle of would-be mothers-of-the-groom. All with the same question: *Where was Ms. Fitzroy? Surely she was coming?* Thorsen assured them Mimi would be there. It was like promising chocolate to the secretaries.

Of course, keeping Mimi away from her father for the night was critical because they couldn't permit Mimi to take on her dad about Frank Leit's theories and have Fitzroy go off like an ICBM. But she sure as hell didn't want to end up explaining why Fitzroy's own daughter didn't care to attend.

Mercifully, Miz Fitzroy finally made her entrance. And what an entrance it was, down the grand staircase.

Clearly somebody had hired a stylist, a whole team. And they must've worked overtime, starting with the dress, a bias-cut navy silk gown—a *gown* for God's sake, complete with a slit up the side of the skirt, a slit worthy of an A-lister at the Oscars. They'd done her makeup. And, as the *piéce de résistance,* they'd cut and colored her hair a deep chocolate brown. Mimi Fitzroy was a dead ringer for Audrey Hepburn. Doe eyes and all.

Ten to one, Fitzroy wouldn't realize the beauty on the stairs was his daughter.

If Thorsen was staring, Mimi was staring right back—a look that said *I know what you did*. It was the same poisonous look Mimi had shot over the dinner table the first time they met.

As Thorsen made her way to the bottom of the staircase and Mimi began her descent, a photographer appeared from nowhere and aimed his camera at both women. Thorsen made a quarter turn—it was automatic, her 400-watt smile. Besides, whatever Mimi suspected, the little bitch couldn't prove anything. No fingerprints, no hairs, there was no *proof* that she'd been at Ms. Fitzroy's house off Dean Parkway. No proof that she had any connection to Frank Leit or the email file.

Mimi stepped past her and might have disappeared into the crowd except one of the would-be escorts stepped up—then the other guys, one by one—big smiles all around. And the media people climbed all over one another to make Ms. Fitzroy the unifying presence in their stories, especially the StarTrib's society photographer. All that attention resulted in endless group shots of Mimi and Bachelor One, Mimi and three socialites, Mimi and Bachelors Two and Three, Mimi and her Aunt Madge, Mimi and every eligible man in the place as well as with several aging professors—enough photos for an eight-page spread if the papers had wanted one.

At nearly 7:30 p.m. Thorsen excused herself from a gaggle of Business School people to correct a few seating assignments at the head table. In particular, she needed to ensure that *she* was sitting next to Fitzroy;

then, on her left, Baird State's Director of Athletics, and beyond him, the left-handed Mimi. Once the others were seated, if Ms. Fitzroy objected to her place at the table, it would be too late to do anything about it. And, thanks to the photojournalists, Mimi—a rather a sore-footed, frazzled rendition of Mimi—was last to arrive on the dais.

During salad, the Athletic Director confessed to Thorsen that he'd thought *she* was Fitzroy's daughter. No, she said and smiled as if his error were flattering. But she felt a little thrill play along her neck. For years her goal had been to be the true Fitzroy daughter, for Fitzroy to see that Mimi would never cut it as a corporate head, that Mimi had no brain for business, that blood wasn't enough. But that she, Anna Lise Thorsen, was everything he desired in a daughter *and* business heir. All he had to do was hand her the keys and walk away.

Thorsen lifted her wine glass, surveyed the packed ballroom, and glanced to her right at Fitzroy. Clearly; he'd left his disappointment about Mimi in the limo. Meaning, once they got past the dinner, the more Mimi talked about Frank Leit and his theories, the more it would alienate her dad or anyone else that might stand in Thorsen's way.

Thorsen tasted her wine and replaced the glass on the linen tablecloth. Her forefinger lingered against the stem. Who would've guessed that Frank Leit would be a help?

Weeks earlier, Thorsen had imagined the best ending for the evening would be for Mimi to slip away without speaking to her dad—no congratulations, no *Wonderful, Daddy,* none of the tripe Fitzroy expected from his admirers—but she hadn't been so naive as to count on that happening.

As the evening rolled on, Baird State's President monopolized Fitzroy, Thorsen chatted with the Athletic Director, and Mimi continued to sit at the far end of the head table, staring out at the room, picking at her dinner. During his award speech, President Wainwright provided the perfect excuse for Mimi to jump ship—a tear-jerking eulogy for Jamie Fitzroy in which Wainwright droned on and on about Jamie's death in Yosemite.

Regrettably, Wainwright's speech, even with all the melodrama about Jamie's death, wasn't enough to propel Mimi out the door. Nonetheless, Thorsen couldn't suppress a tingle at the thought of little Miss Fitzroy's reaction if only...if only... She turned her face toward the spotlight and squeezed out a tear. It slid down her cheek. The second one must have glistened. She made a thing of getting into her purse and producing a white hanky. She blotted her eyes, turned into and away from the light. *Too much?*

Mimi froze as if she were suffering from some internal electric storm. She sat forward on her chair. Her little chin trembled. She gripped the edge of the table in a stranglehold and slowly, almost mechanically, she picked up her evening bag. For a moment, it seemed like this might be it. But no, through the remainder of Wainwright's presentation, Mimi remained riveted to the edge of her chair, even through her father's thank you remarks.

Fitzroy did a flawless job on his blessedly brief speech. As he finished, the audience scrambled to its feet and roared their approval. Mimi made a dash for her father. She was beaming, calling to him, clearly proud, clearly determined.

Thorsen jammed her own chair back before Mimi could get to her father.

Mimi stopped, her eyes teary, still focused on Fitzroy. "Dad," she called. Her voice sounded desperate. Her face shifted from blotchy to ashen. She shook as if she might explode. Her lower lip trembled. Her eyes watered. And the typhoon came ashore.

"For Chrissake, Anna. Can you please, just back off?"

Ms. Fitzroy's question would make the first paragraph of the StarTrib's front-page story on the dinner because no one had thought to turn off the microphone.

Chapter 26

It was out of her mouth before she knew it.

On any other occasion, the celebrants' conversations would have continued, dwindled away and the crowd would have happily dispersed. Instead, it was one of those moments when a crowd is suddenly, if only momentarily, silent. So, with the audio system running full blast, her fury carried perfectly through the dining room, out into the reception hall, and into the memories of every man and woman who was present.

Heads turned, necks craned. Almost everyone in the room froze. But not her father. Judging by his face, nothing, absolutely nothing was the matter. He glanced at Baird State's President and glibly diagnosed the situation.

"It's been twelve years since we lost Jamie," he said. "An emotional time for all of us. But especially for Mimi…" He sighed.

But she was not taken in. It didn't matter what her father said. Or how calm he appeared to be in the moment. Because he had latched onto her arm. She couldn't help but wince at his fingernails digging into her elbow. She would definitely not get away from him 'til he'd had his say.

He steered her off the dais, through a side door, and into a hallway. "I will speak to you in the limo," he said.

She quietly reminded him she was staying at the hotel.

He ducked his head a moment, then resumed his military pose. "The hotel then. Fine." Grim-faced, he ushered her back into the nearly empty ballroom.

The band was busily breaking down their music setup and a half-dozen hotel workers were already re-organizing the space for whatever was scheduled for the next morning. Only Anna Thorsen, her Aunt Madge, and a pair of her dad's would-be political handlers remained behind.

As her dad stopped beside Thorsen, her aunt snatched her dad's free arm. At first glance, her aunt looked calm...pleasant...happy even. But the hand she extended was trembling.

"David," her aunt Madge said, "don't do this."

Her dad turned to Anna Thorsen. "You take the limo." Then he pivoted to face his sister. "Stay out of this, Madge."

He shot a dismissing glare at his sister then turned. "Mimi... Move it. Where's your room?"

"I can see myself up," she said.

"Not a chance," he said and propelled her into an elevator.

They rode up to her floor in complete silence. Once they reached her room, he put his hand out, silently demanding her keycard. When he made the same gesture for the third time, she pulled it from her evening bag and, looking him straight in the eye, handed it over.

He pushed her inside, stepped in behind her, and closed the door.

He didn't speak at all, not right away. Instead he headed straight over to the windows. For several minutes he stared out at the cityscape. Finally, as if he'd decided how he would handle the situation, he turned his back to the city view and regarded her.

"What is the matter with you?"

She knew he wasn't expecting an answer. This was always his opening gambit—always followed by something like he'd expected more of her, she was educated, she'd had every opportunity, she could have made something of herself.

He cursed the day he'd hoped she might become something. Then turned away from her, paced, and turned back to stare at her in disbelief. "What were you thinking?" he shouted.

She could have explained herself. A week ago, she probably would have reminded him she'd given up a brilliant career because he'd asked her to help him at Rex. She'd have pointed out that she'd kept the company growing by developing increasingly sophisticated design software. God, maybe she'd have begged for some recognition.

"You're jealous," he said. "You're sick with it. You stink of it. You have absolutely no reason to be jealous of Anna Thorsen. She's no threat to your position."

He said he'd never expected her to have the business sense that Anna had. All he asked of his daughter was her support. Why couldn't she at least deliver on that? He raved on and on about Anna, Anna's years at Rex, Anna's business acumen, Anna's ability with people, how Anna had filled the void.

The void was Jamie. But he didn't say that. He didn't need to.

She knew she should say *something*. Was she

jealous? As a kid, probably. But not for years. She was fed up with Thorsen, that was all. The woman's behavior at the dinner was infuriating. Truth was, Thorsen had played her and foolishly she'd taken the bait.

But Thorsen wasn't the issue. Not really. The issue was Frank Leit—his ideas, his blog. And antitrust. And fraud. That's what was behind her dad's anger. She'd felt it all evening. He'd avoided her, barely looked at her. The real question was, how deeply was he involved in the crooked deals.

He slapped a hand down on the back of an overstuffed chair as he passed it. "No reason at all to be jealous," he repeated. "I don't understand it. For the life of me, I don't."

It was cold in the room. A shiver ran through her and she felt herself moving. Slowly, almost automatically, she backed her way to the open doorway between the suite's sitting room and bedroom.

The moment she stepped back, her father rounded the other side of a writing desk and closed the distance between them. As he paused there, his hands gripped the back of a decorative desk chair. He hunched forward, shaking. His face was gray with anger.

She opened her mouth. "I'm so sorry, Dad. Really, I—"

He smashed his fist down on the desk. "Not me. Apologize to Anna. What's the matter with you? And if you can't work with her, I need you to say so."

When her mother was alive, her mother had been the only one he loved. When her mother died, it was Jamie, only Jamie. Now, so obviously, it was Thorsen.

She drew in a breath, counted slowly to ten and left

it all in that room: apologies, promises, all of it. Clearly, it didn't matter to him what she said.

He was talking when she took a step back into the bedroom. He was talking even when she closed the door. She could still hear him of course, but she was no longer going to listen.

Chapter 27

As usual, Thorsen woke before dawn. No way was she letting Mimi get away with that tantrum. For years Fitzroy had been complaining that Mimi was unstable. Time that instability was terminal.

After tossing every conceivable piece of crap she might need into a duffel bag, Thorsen headed for the Radisson and parked on the street. According to the dashboard on her Maserati, the temperature was a balmy nineteen degrees.

No action until 9:30 when Mimi's Lexus finally rolled out of the hotel garage and headed straight to Miss Fitzroy's McMansion. It was definitely an option to stage a suicide there. But there were way too many witnesses out clearing sidewalks for Thorsen to seriously consider that move.

At the McMansion, more waiting. In the alley in back of the house. For more than an hour.

When the Lexus finally took off, it was still below freezing. Mimi drove to the Rex campus, spent five minutes in the executive building, then took off again, making quick stops at two drug stores before heading down to the financial district to Fifty South Sixth Street. The Lexus disappeared into the office building's underground garage.

Thorsen parked down the block and checked the building's tenant names on her smart phone.

Commercial real estate, law, accounting. Who has business meetings on a Sunday?

Another long wait. She'd blown nearly six hours, had to move her car twice and still no action. If something didn't pop soon, she'd bag it.

At 2:30 p.m., Mimi's Lexus rolled onto the street.

Tailing a luxury minivan made it simple. Thorsen dropped back into the thin traffic thinking all she had to do now was track the Lexus until Mimi landed somewhere private. On the off chance that the perfect setting for Mimi's demise still might present itself, Thorsen hung with her original strategy of following three or four blocks behind the Lexus. But wouldn't you know, mile after mile Mimi seemed to be driving aimlessly around. Then, at just after 3:30 p.m. the Lexus headed out of town and turned off the highway at Minnehaha Falls Park.

Thorsen was not about to roll into the parking lot right behind the Lexus. Instead, she cruised on down the main road and took a later turnoff, putting her closer to the trailheads and more than a hundred yards from where the empty Lexus sat.

She checked her side mirrors, reclined her seat and waited.

The overnight snow had stalled, likely from the cold. And the sky had backed off to a forbidding gray. In a playground across from the rest stations, three women huddled to one side while their kids squabbled.

Thorsen dragged her duffel onto the passenger seat. She was wrestling on her hiking boots when she spotted Mimi heading straight for the main trailhead wearing a long black parka.

Thorsen glanced at the dashboard—twenty-nine

degrees out. The overnight temperatures were predicted to be in the teens again, so… If a hiker fell, if she passed out or hit her head, chances were good she wouldn't make it through the night. If she went into the river, well you could hang it up.

Thorsen had been around the Fitzroy clan long enough to know everything worth knowing about Mimi and a lot that wasn't. For example, she knew Mimi's closets were organized white to light, gray to black, that there was no color anywhere. She also knew that Mimi folded her dirty laundry before it got sent out.

She knew Mimi took Ritalin when she was little. She knew when the Ritalin stopped. She knew when Mimi'd gone on Prozac and when she quit. When she went into therapy, and when she quit that.

There were no men in Mimi's life, not since graduate school, no women either.

Two or three times during Mimi's stint at Stanford, David Fitzroy had sent Thorsen to California. Ostensibly the trips were for Rex. But Fitzroy had made it clear, "You girls are going to be sisters-in-law; you should be friends." Afterward, Thorsen always filled Fitzroy in about the fun she'd had with Mimi—the dinners, local theater in Palo Alto, yada, yada. Of course, her reports didn't include the best part. On every visit she'd arranged a little something for Mimi to discover long afterward, so it had no connection to her visit. Most of the time it was something like a beer stain or an oily paper napkin, something wrong with the twerp's desk. The last straw was stolen panties.

Why didn't she get rid of Mimi then, when the twerp was in Palo Alto? There'd been a reason, it just took her a moment to think…Jamie… She would've lost Jamie if his sister had died, if he'd guessed...

Thorsen watched Mimi disappear past the trailhead sign, then pulled on a thick jacket, tied the flap up over the bottom half of her face, and climbed out of her car. With a knit cap pulled down tight over her hair, she zipped up her keys, grabbed a camera and slammed the car door. Easy enough to track a black parka from a parallel trail. Especially a black parka with a big white stripe up the back.

Across the parking lot, the three women on the playground turned to stare and Thorsen's ramrod posture melted. Her head drooped, and her torso settled into an insolent slouch as she took a few steps away from the cars. *Fine, ladies. Get a good look.*

One of the women called, "Young man, the park's closing pretty soon."

Young man. Now that was sweet.

Thorsen ignored the woman and lumbered away— head forward, shoulders hunched, letting her boot heels leave long drag marks in the snow.

The straight trunks of trees stood out like matchsticks against the white slope and the low light bent them into long shadows on the ground. Tracking Mimi, the one sticking point would be camouflage. But for any would-be witness, she was just a gangly kid with a camera. Besides, there was almost nobody left in the park. It was too damned cold to be out.

As soon as she was out of the women's sight though, Thorsen shifted to high gear. And a damned good thing she was fast, because by the time she finally caught sight of the black parka, Mimi was almost a hundred-fifty yards ahead. No problem, just like the other times she'd stalked Mimi. The trick would be to keep the quarry in sight.

She could feel the old jets revving, the familiar hum rising along the back of her throat and spreading down, out across her chest. That feeling always took her where she needed to go.

Mist from the river had sealed everything with ice. Even the snow was crust-over-powder, burying a couple of thickets of what must have been blackberry vines. Where it was bare, the understory lay studded with ice and frozen snow. Beautiful if winter scenes appealed to you.

She could just make out the distinctive rustle of ski pants. That had to be Mimi hustling along the Overlook path—the Overlook, nicely isolated as she remembered. It was all good. And the temperature plummeting couldn't hurt either. She sprinted to the crest of a rise in the path and stopped—black parka. A wide smile spread across her face.

Mimi Fitzroy had been an angry kid right from the first. An eleven-year old who sulked her way to and from the dinner table. It was remarkable how good it felt to finally be finishing this thing.

She closed more of the gap on Mimi and stopped maybe twenty yards away.

The only sound in the deeper woods was the river off to the left. The temperature must've dropped again. Which made sense, given that, even with the snow to reflect it, the light was playing out.

At the top of another little rise, she spotted a way through the brush to the trail Mimi was following. Stepping out in the center of her own trail, Thorsen stretched her back, and spun out a test kick. Not exactly great form, but she was a little tight from the cold and her effort to walk noiselessly—plus, the boots were all wrong.

She was thinking about the cold, that she'd be fine in spite of it, when out of nowhere, a huge black dog exploded down the path toward her, whirling in the snow. From fifteen yards, this one looked innocuous enough, loping, clowning. But then, it skidded to a stop. The hair along its back stood thick and angry. It lowered its body and crept forward giving her a low rumble—its yellow eyes fixed on her. It laid its ears back, bared its teeth and began to circle her warily.

Why did there have to be a dog? Dogs always hated her. And she did not have time to screw around with this one.

She was nanoseconds from taking the thing out with a kick, but then she heard voices...a man and woman. They stopped maybe twenty yards away, whistling, clapping their hands and calling for the dog to come.

Time for Shy Boy. Thorsen backed off the path and kept backing toward a copse of trees. The man ran the last few yards up the path, lunged, and caught the dog by a harness. As he snicked the lead into place, he glanced nervously at Thorsen. "Nero's never done that before."

Well, she wasn't buying it. Instead, she kept going with Shy Boy: flailing, stumbling around in the snow as if she was freaking out and didn't know what to do... *As if.* Her breath had that familiar hot, jumpy edge to it and the tension traced her arms and legs like electric threads.

She held herself in check and clung to the nearest tree like a terrified kid. She counted twelve breaths, then dropped her hands down in front of her crotch and turned so the guy would guess that the kid had wet himself. The man abruptly muscled the woman to her feet, they got the dog under way, and hurried toward the parking lot.

Thorsen watched until they disappeared down the trail. Finally, satisfied they were gone, she let go a shudder—a trick she'd used before to get rid of extra energy.

Those fools had made her lose sight of her target. Damned lucky she had the self-control she had. Part of her still wanted to see the terror bloom on their faces when she took out their damned dog, then crushed their skulls and left all three bodies in the snow. But that would have been stupid. And she was anything but stupid.

She sprinted up the path to check on Mimi and pulled up short where the path made a bend. The black parka was maybe seventy yards ahead of her, seated on a bench facing the river at the edge of a precipice.

It took a while for her to work her way from the path she'd come in on to a spot behind Mimi. Thanks to the roar from the river, Mimi would never hear what hit her. Just ten feet more…

Thorsen paused to savor the moment. The one remaining threat to her take-over sat hunched forward against a little breeze coming off the river. The striped hood pulled tight. It seemed like Mimi was looking at something.

Two more steps and Thorsen stopped—the perfect distance.

Maybe the hood turned just as Thorsen spun out her kick. Maybe it was the boot or the difference in their height. Whatever it was, the kick felt like it hadn't quite connected. At least not the way it had with Frank Leit. Of course, Mimi never played for the NFL.

Didn't matter. Mimi Fitzroy lay slumped face-down in the trampled snow.

Thorsen took a quick look around—no one. She knelt, rolled Mimi over and unzipped the long black parka. It was like undressing a doll. She pulled the coat free, wadded it up, and sailed it out toward the river. Then she picked up the body and boosted it up onto her shoulder. What did the twerp weigh? Not even a hundred pounds.

She stepped over the safety railing and walked to the edge of the cliff. For a moment, she stood looking down at the river. It wasn't quite a straight drop to water, but close enough, at least twenty feet down. Maybe more. And, as she'd predicted, the river was high and running a torrent. She tossed the limp body out into the air and seconds later she could just make out a muddy shape in the surging water.

She watched the river for a while. Nothing more to see, really, but she'd thought getting rid of Mimi would mean something to her. She'd been building up to it for years. It felt like nothing, even less than Jamie. Who would've guessed?

Neither one of the Fitzroy brats was as exhilarating as Frank Leit had been.

Chapter 28

Mimi came to in the near dark. She was freezing. The air smelled dank and moldy. For sure she'd fallen. She'd hung up in some kind of brambles and landed halfway into a somersault with her head and shoulders below the rest of her body. And the river—her heart lurched against her ribs—the river surged right below her. The muddy water was so close she could feel it, could taste it in the air. And there was nothing but brambles between her and being swept away. God, where was her parka? How would they ever find her? She was panicking, and she mustn't, she knew. Panic led to mistakes and even one mistake could kill her. She took one deep breath, then another. *What are you going to do to get out of this?*

Her right arm had been trapped under her by the fall. But her left hand was free. She ran her fingers over her head and face. The damp had already crusted her hair and eyelashes with ice. She was stinging in a hundred places and it killed her to breathe. She squirmed against the thicket she'd landed in. If she could just get her torso turned without dumping herself into the river.

But it felt like her legs, her feet…even her undershirt was caught in a thousand places. And it didn't help that she was upside-down, or almost, staring up at the sky. On top of everything, it was getting dark.

Then, for a moment, the clouds parted, and the river came alive with moonlight.

And she got it. There was a massive brush pile right at the river's edge just upriver from the Overlook. She remembered staring at the color of it in the afternoon light. She must've landed on it. If she could untangle herself and climb over it, she could get closer to the bank itself. And from there she could maybe get back up to park land. But the bank looked like a mud and a rock cliff face...and being that high and with an angle that steep, how the heck was she going to make it up?

South of her though, she could make out scrub trees, clusters of them reaching all the way up to the park. If she could maneuver over to the trees, she could climb up from there.

She worked the sleeve of her undershirt down over her left hand as protection and got a grip on the blackberry canes. Then she levered herself off her right shoulder and arm, and slowly managed to body surf the lurching thicket. And oh, sweet Jesus, what she hadn't seen before—a tree that had fallen top-down into the river. It was covered with mud and debris near the water, but the trunk ran nearly half-way up the bank. And the trunk was more than a foot thick. Blessed Mother... If she could make it over there, she had a ready-made bridge to get her away from the river.

After what felt like hours of tangling and untangling herself, she latched onto the big tree's side branches and wrapped herself around the icy trunk. Just for a moment, she laid against it, caught her breath, then began to climb.

The fallen tree rested against the stand of trees it

once must've been part of. Hand over hand, from sapling to sapling, she worked her way over to an old aspen with a split crotch, one part rising nearly straight up, and thick enough to support her weight. Wedging herself into the tree's crotch, she forced herself up and up.

Though the work of the climb kept her focused and going, her hands and feet were already nearly numb. More than a few times she tucked her hands into her armpits to warm them and tried to guess how long she'd been there. But every time she stopped climbing, it hit her how much pain she was in, how the cuts in her hands burned, how much trouble she was in, how time was running out. But what option did she have but to keep going. Every foothold, she was closer to her car.

Eventually she came to a place where the trees spread out and the only way she could progress was to hang by a knee and swing—like a pendulum—using her momentum to stretch and make the grab to a new tree. Twice she missed her target. Once she fell when a branch gave way and she barely managed to save herself. In the end, though, the technique worked, and it didn't matter so much that her ankles, fingers, the backs of her knees all burned where she'd worn her skin raw. Much worse was that the only light left was coming from the reflection of the moon off the snow. What would happen if that went too?

She found a place where she could stand on a heavy limb that, she was convinced, stretched out toward the park itself. She tried to walk the limb like a balance beam and nearly ruined herself when her foot slipped sideways. Tackling it again, she sat and scooted, climbed over side branches, scooted and climbed...until the floor below her opened up blue-white. Even in the half-light, she was almost certain. It was almost too good to be true. But it had to be shadows on snow.

Park land. She could drop to the ground.

Hugging the limb, locking her hands together, she swung over to one side and let her legs dangle...nothing but air. She couldn't risk breaking a leg. Even a twisted ankle might keep her from getting back to her car. But clearly, spending the night in the open was unthinkable. And she hoped her instincts were still good enough she would land without killing herself. She took a deep, agonizing breath, held it, offered a little prayer, and let go.

She landed on her side in a snow drift.

She sat up, tried standing, and quickly braced her hands on her thighs to keep from falling over. She hurt everywhere that still had feeling. And it hit her, what on earth happened to send her over that cliff in the first place? Had she been pushed or hit or... They always talk about random victims, was that what she was? Just a woman alone that somebody tried to take out?

Get back to the car. She found a patch of moonlight, wiped her hands on her pants and, as best she could, checked out what she could see of her legs and chest. Her body clear down to her thighs was covered with the muck she'd been crawling over. Her hands and forearms were bleeding. Something was wrong with her neck. And her fingers and feet had virtually no feeling left. As for her ribs, she didn't know if she'd broken something, but for sure, taking a deep breath nearly wiped her out.

None of it mattered. She was alive. The pain

shooting up the back of her head was proof of that. She just had to make the walk back to her car.

Four steps and she fell over a tree root, a real face plant into the ice-crust. *Stupid, stupid.* She got to her knees and swiped a hand across her nose and mouth. And started to bawl.

Not. Having. That.

Back to her feet. She wrapped her arms across her chest, tucked her freezing fingers into her arm pits, and walked. Nausea and dizziness be damned. She walked though she couldn't feel her feet. She fell twice more because, somehow, she lost the trail.

By the time she got to the trailhead, she was staring at the ground directly ahead of her. Looking for the next place to put a foot and making her foot go there. Left. Right. Left. Right. As she reached the parking lot, she was repeating *Car. Car.* Over and over.

The Lexus sat exactly where she'd left it.

She fished the top pocket of her jeans for the car key—nothing. Then she remembered: she'd zipped it into her parka. *Okay Mimi. All that have-a-backup-plan stuff that people razz you about? Here's where it pays off.* She sat in the snow next to her tire and pulled off a boot. She used the boot heel to break loose the hide-your-key box from under the ice of her left-front wheel well.

Naturally, once she worked the little gizmo open, her fingers shook so badly she dropped the key. Then she couldn't get the thing to work in the door.

In desperation, she stuck her fingers in her mouth long enough to get some warmth going and that, somehow, helped to get the key in the car door. She climbed in and got the blessed, blessed heater going.

Once she began to get warm, once her hands, and feet and face began to burn, everything she'd tried not to think about on the walk washed over her: her head, her neck, her ribs, the scrapes, the nausea, how near she'd come to...

She pressed the Blue Tooth button on the steering wheel and said *Uncle Ted.*

Ted Halliday answered his cell phone on the second ring.

****

According to the doctor at ER, she had a concussion and cracked ribs. After the tests, a tetanus shot and stitches, the doctor said they would be keeping her overnight.

The moment the orderly wheeled her into her room, Madge and Ted peeked in.

"Oh honey, what happened?" her aunt said and commandeered the chair by the bed.

After a long drink of water, she said, "I needed to think. I drove out—"

Uncle Ted shushed her. Then found a cotton blanket, tucked it over her and stepped away from the bed. "What day is it, honey? What day of the week?"

The doctor had asked her that too. "Sunday. Unless it's after midnight." Her head was killing her.

"Good." Ted shot a look at Madge. "What were you working on last week, you remember?"

Nodding made the room spin but yes, she remembered. "The A432 project, and then, you know, that file—"

"Right." Ted dragged his phone out and held it against his thigh. "Now tell me everything you remember from the time you left our house Friday."

Once she opened her mouth, she couldn't stop herself—first the break-in at her house, her dad's interview, then what had happened at the dinner.

Ted's eyebrows slowly worked their way up to his nonexistent hairline. "That's enough for now," he said. "We'll take care of getting your car and organize the things you might need. It's time all three of us got the hell out of Minneapolis."

Chapter 29

Home, Thorsen finally had time to consider Specialty Dining's reports. But first she needed a long shower, and a power nap. At eight o'clock that evening, she pulled on sweats and planted herself in front of her computer.

There wasn't much in Specialty Dining's report on Ted Halliday that she didn't already know. The fact he'd been off the grid the past ten years...her guess was, he'd climbed into a bottle and never climbed out. Interesting that Raj Banerjee owned three houses and his bank accounts didn't show income from them. So, who was living there exactly, family? And did she think they were legal?

Scrolling down the PDF, Connors might be a fool, but he looked clean.

The Fitzroy cousins—three of them had stuffed their Rex shares into trusts. Why wasn't that reflected in Legal's registry? There were no large deposits anywhere, no emails between the cousins and the Rex system except Fitzroy's assistant, and, except for some cash from Grandpa's estate, no transactions worth pursuing. They might be lazy brats, but it looked like they were clean.

The more she read, the more that old feeling crawled on her skin. She was missing something. She could feel it. Probably she was just obsessing about

Mimi. But little Ms. Fitzroy was now officially out of the game.

Food. She pushed away from her desk and padded into the kitchen. The housekeeper had left a lasagna, a salad and a garlic bread setup. Oven, salad bowl, timer, back to her desk.

If it wasn't Halliday, or Conners, or the Fitzroy cousins, then who?

Banerjee, she needed to follow up on him. And get into those houses.

Who else had access to the system? Not Legal. Wrong. Technically, Addison did have access to everything. She hadn't really considered Addison because any attention from the feds would put him front and center for a criminal charge. He'd had a fit when she'd pushed him last Friday. Was it possible the feds had offered him a deal? He might jump at one if it meant he'd get away from her *and* avoid prison. But no. Addison wasn't that nervy, or that bright, and he certainly couldn't have cracked her hidden file. She'd always had to lead him wherever she wanted him to go—and he'd gone. So no, he was just pissed she'd pushed him into a corner. More to the point, if Frank Leit had been scouting for an insider, he sure as hell wouldn't settle for the likes of Addison.

The oven timer dinged. She filled her plate and returned to the den. What was bugging her was Addison had pushed back. True, she'd smacked him down, but he'd pushed.

She ate and stared at the computer screen, reading and rereading, gaining nothing more than a certain pleasure from the clipped prose of Specialty Dining's reports. Those people ought to be offering her a discount for the work she'd given them.

Her better self said take it slow, stay the course, keep track of Addison, offer Fitzroy the sympathy he was going to need because of losing his daughter. But get him out the door and into that Senate seat. And, let the place settle down.

She'd give a bundle to know whether the feds had a working file on Frank Leit's claims. She was also more than a little curious about whether Addison had jumped ship. Not knowing was like an itch she couldn't scratch.

Chapter 30

David Fitzroy hadn't slept since his daughter went off the rails. He couldn't understand how she could have behaved that way. Ever since the dinner, he hadn't been able work on his campaign. He hadn't been able to focus on a damned thing.

He was still obsessing when the Board of Directors' secretary joined him Monday morning for his regular Executive Committee meeting. He'd intended to apologize to Anna Thorsen before everyone arrived. But Anna, who was never late, was late.

And his mood was not improved when two of the other committee members failed to show and somebody finally thought to tell him that his sister—the missing Madge Halliday—was out of the country.

Meeting cancelled, Fitzroy left the committee secretary to handle the fall-out and suggested that Thorsen meet him back at his office.

Eventually she strode in and dropped into a low conference chair. She made a thing of crossing her legs and flexing the muscles of her calves. Did the woman think that she'd been groomed to fill in for him because of her legs?

Without asking what he'd wanted to discuss, Thorsen launched into some scheme she had. No surprise, since she always had a scheme going. True, it was how she'd made it to Number Two in spite of the fact she was a loose cannon. But that didn't mean... He'd accepted that about her long ago. In fact, he'd been okay with it as long as she was knocking out the competition for Rex. And just so long as she was *his* loose cannon.

Thorsen didn't seem to notice as he began to pace his office. Typical...instead of asking how he was, she went over the changes she had in mind for the company "once you're in Washington."

He suppressed the need to sigh or stretch or walk away. Facing facts, the woman didn't wear well. In large part because he always had to be on the lookout that she didn't con him into something. On the other hand, he'd seen Thorsen wrap up negotiations nobody else could've handled.

In Indonesia, she'd led the charge, and closed deals to purchase four sweatshop companies that had been working for Rex's competitors. The only holdout against Rex's buy-out offers went out of business after a big factory fire. No connection with Rex's offer, but the result was, that for over a year, Rex's competition struggled to fill orders for shoes.

Thorsen was still talking when Fitzroy stopped in front of his credenza and fiddled with a model the Design Department was working on.

More than once he'd considered getting rid of Thorsen. But she was good for business, and that was key while he was tied up with the campaign. In the long run, she was not the best man for the CEO spot. Not that she was too young, though she was. And not that she was self-absorbed or a narcissist, plenty of corporate players were. There simply wasn't a loyal bone in her body.

He stopped in front of a window overlooking the quadrangle. The early snow was swirling at every building, burying a cluster of evergreens—Thorsen's voice was like that, sweeping past him and doubling back.

Finally, she stopped talking. He turned. She was looking at him expectantly. Meaning he was supposed to say *Yes. Great idea.*

"So… What do you think?" she repeated.

What did he think? That sometimes honesty is the best policy.

"I'm sorry, Anna," he said. "To be honest, I was thinking about Saturday evening." He walked over to one of the club chairs across from her. He apologized for what had gone down at the dinner. He probably went on too long saying he didn't understand why Mimi had behaved as she had.

"I want you to know, I'm sick about it," he said.

For once, Thorsen let him finish, then shook her head. "Nothing to apologize for," she said. "My fault. I pushed Mimi too hard trying to make her the star. You were a smash hit with the political crowd, and I assumed she would enjoy a little attention. She looked so lovely. Incidentally, I hope you told her that."

Did she actually believe he hadn't noticed how Mimi had looked at the dinner? It was a typical Thorsen end run that finished with the spotlight back on her insight and generosity.

He'd apologized. That was the point of asking for Thorsen to drop by his office. Now it was time for her to shove off. Was it Houston or Seattle, this trip? He'd lost track. But he'd be glad for a break from the woman.

Fitzroy's assistant tapped lightly on his door and, as she walked over to his desk, she shot him a *you-need-to-see-this-right-now* look. She laid an oversized envelope on the blotter and took off.

"Of course Mimi was upset," Thorsen rattled on. "But, really, David, no harm, no foul. Besides, you and I both know I'll have tougher critics than Mimi gunning for me the minute I'm official. If I can't handle a little drama now and then—" She smiled at Fitzroy and raised her eyebrows. "Okay?"

Without comment, Fitzroy walked back to his desk and scanned the package. *HAND DELIVERED—PERSONAL AND CONFIDENTIAL.* He turned the envelope over, fingering a flap that presumably had been firmly sealed shut when it hit his assistant's desk.

He checked the label. Offhand, he couldn't place the name of the sender, but hand delivered. Didn't people email documents now?

Thorsen stood and stepped up to Fitzroy's desk. It wasn't lost on him she was doing her best to see who the package was from.

A patch of skin at the back of his neck began to burn. "Schull, West and Masterson," he said. "Any reason I should get something hand delivered from them?"

She shrugged and motioned for him to open it.

Fitzroy retrieved an opener from his desk drawer, fiddled with the envelope, then stopped and looked to Thorsen. He raised his eyebrows and waited until, finally, she started for the door.

Anyone else might have thought her hesitation was genuine. But Fitzroy recognized the move. He'd seen her do it right before she knocked the whole board on their butts with her pitch to become Number Two.

"Something more?" he said.

"Just a thought before I take off for Seattle," she said and let a pause hang in the air.

Fitzroy laid the envelope on his desk.

"Why not make a change in Mimi's responsibilities?" she said. "A new title for one thing. Give her more independence. Not that it has anything to do with systems, but Mimi is so bright. I didn't mention it earlier, but I'd like to take your idea of sports education to a new level. Why not create a foundation? Put Mimi in charge. She could work independently of me and answer directly to the board."

Fitzroy glanced down, as if he were preoccupied with the envelope. Did the woman really think she was entitled to tell him how to handle Mimi? That he'd strip Mimi's corporate title? Or was it that she imagined she could take Jamie's place. He might have thought of Anna as part of the family when she was engaged to Jamie. Let her think that for now.

He rubbed the back of his neck where it was bothering him.

The next year would tell him a lot. If his senatorial campaign was a bust, he would come back as CEO. He had enough clout to be certain of that. If he made it to the Senate, fine. Thorsen would hold the fort while the board found the right replacement for the long term.

"A foundation," he said as if he would shove Mimi out of the family business or consider funding something so completely independent of his control.

The moment he paused, Thorsen cut him off. "Think about it. You take the credit. Our little secret," she said and took off.

Fitzroy turned back to his desk, pulled out the envelope contents and started reading. The cover letter was formal, polite and to the point. Addressed to him but with a copy to Rex's General Counsel. Why was that?

Mimi was resigning effective immediately. Any communication should be addressed to Ms. Fitzroy care of Stuart Masterson, her lawyer. The other enclosure was a signed Power of Attorney giving the lawyer authority, among other things, to cast Mimi's proxy votes in the shares she held.

Fitzroy laid the thing on his desk, sat, read and re-read the letter. He knew that law firm name, at the moment he just couldn't think from where. His own daughter had resigned just like she'd shut that damned door. A bolt of acid hit his gut.

He could not have Mimi sign away her votes to someone else. Without her votes, he couldn't predict what might happen if things came to a showdown. Wait just a damned minute. Could Mimi assign her lawyer the right to vote her shares? Legal questions, he hated legal questions.

She'd resigned to punish him. She'd misconstrued what he'd said about Anna Thorsen. That was the thing. Mimi was his only child. He merely wanted her to see that she was a necessary part of the team. That he needed her to get along, to not create problems for him. He hadn't meant to push her away. He'd been upset was all. And she knew the kind of temper he had.

She could not resign. Mimi was being influenced by somebody. When he thought about it, that had to be what was going on. He'd bet on it. She would never have resigned without somebody suggesting it.

Whatever they'd told her, he could turn it around. He just had to get hold of her, talk with her, that was all. He couldn't let her think he didn't care about her.

He'd go see her. He'd tell her how sorry he was. He'd make it right. She could have whatever she wanted. For the present, Anna Thorsen would have to run the company. But he'd offer Mimi anything else.

He turned the letter face-down on his desk and speed-dialed Mimi's office. They said she hadn't come in.

"When she does, ask her to call me," he said and dialed Mimi at home. He couldn't believe it. The number was no longer in service. His heart rate ramped up uncomfortably. Her cell—the message referred him to some other number where he got a recording that said to leave a number, and someone would call him back.

This was not happening.

He was sweating. His chest was pounding and, though it didn't seem possible, his gut was worse than ever.

He called the three key people in Mimi's IT group. All they knew was Mimi had emailed the group that she would not be available. They were sorry.

He pushed away from his desk and paced the office. At his credenza he stopped and made himself a drink. One sip—it felt like he'd swallowed poison. He set the glass aside and stared around the room. There must be something he could do.

He speed-dialed Legal, asked for Robert Addison, but hung up before Addison answered. Talking with Rex's General Counsel would mean talking about Saturday night, precisely what he did not want.

His sister might know where Mimi was. For all he knew, Mimi might be sulking at Madge's kitchen table. It wouldn't be the first time. But Madge would never have encouraged Mimi to resign. Madge's home and cell numbers went to the same recording—*The party you have called will be away for an undetermined period*. He was going to have a heart attack.

It wasn't that his daughter had hired a lawyer. It wasn't even that she'd decided to strike out on her own. It was her timing. And the way she'd gone around slamming hotel doors, hiring lawyers...

Christ, how could he have forgotten?

Stuart Masterson was one of the lawyers that had represented his former brother-in-law all through the mess of Ted Halliday's departure from Rex. Masterson had raised such a stink behind the scenes that the board caved, and Halliday ended up with a platinum parachute.

Fitzroy bolted out of his chair, snatched up the letter, and hauled on his overcoat. He slowed just long enough in front of his assistant's desk to say "Neva, cancel my meeting and call this guy." He tossed the papers on her desk. "Stuart Masterson. His number's right there. Tell him I'm on my way over."

The fifteen-minute meeting with Stuart Masterson left Fitzroy in an even worse mood. As soon as he returned to Rex, he burst into the General Counsel's private office and kicked the door shut.

His ulcer was now officially a hot knife through his gut. But he had no intention of giving in to the pain.

"I need an investigator," he said. "We have to find Mimi."

Addison speed-dialed his assistant. "Get that

investigator on the line. The one Tom's been using."
Addison lowered himself back into his desk chair and
blinked. "You need to know, Mimi came over here
Friday—"

Fitzroy shook his head. He wasn't going to listen to
some patronizing crap when they were in a crisis. He
glared at Addison. "Her lawyer tried to feed me a line
about client confidentiality. Like I had no idea what that
meant."

"Let's see what we can do." Addison punched an
amber light on his phone and introduced the
investigator.

Fitzroy laid out the basics for the investigator.
"Bottom line, I need my daughter back here and
involved in the company." He left his General Counsel
to wrap up the details and went back to pacing.

He'd handled the meeting with Stuart Masterson all
wrong. But he couldn't get over the fact he was forced
to deal with his daughter's lawyer. He knew he'd been
a textbook example of what not to do in an adversarial
meeting—it certainly wasn't the first time he'd been in
one. He'd been too loud. He'd been belligerent. He'd
snarled at the help and made an ass of himself. He
couldn't help it.

Addison ended the call and said something.

Fitzroy didn't hear what it was but somehow knew
he'd been spoken to. He stopped pacing and mopped
his face. "I'm fine. Fine," he said. "Friday you said—
why'd you talk with Mimi?"

Addison appeared to steel himself. "Someone has
compromised the server for the executive offices," he
said and launched into a report of his meeting with
Mimi and what Legal was doing to protect the company

and mitigate any damage.

Fitzroy stared at Addison. He could have wept at the bone-numbing stupidity of the man. Didn't Mimi's department handle computer problems? Mother of God, had she or had she not told Addison she was going to resign? That was the issue, wasn't it?

"Why didn't she just walk into my office, kick the door shut and tell me she wanted to leave?"

For a moment Addison's face reverted to his usual mask. "I'd probably feel the same way if my daughter were—"

He could have decked Addison right there. "We're not talking about your daughter!"

Addison stiffened, pursed his lips and, for a moment, pressed an upraised forefinger against them. "You're absolutely right, David. I'm sorry. I was attempting—albeit inadequately—I was attempting to say that I can understand how you might feel."

"Well you can't possibly understand," Fitzroy said and went back to pacing. His hands trembled so much he jammed them into his pockets to get them under control. Mimi had chosen the worst possible time to jump ship. With his campaign heating up and all the media attention, he needed his daughter front and center. He'd been counting on her to vote her shares the way he told her to. Especially in the event Thorsen got out of line.

He was sweating. He dragged out a handkerchief and wiped his hands.

Finally, Addison cleared his throat. "You're right, I can't understand what you're feeling. But I don't understand her leaving either. When I talked with her at your dinner, she didn't mention leaving. Or resigning. I thought she was happy for you."

Fitzroy abruptly stopped his pacing and stared at the carpet. "That lawyer's helping her to disappear."

He should have seen it. Mimi was under somebody's influence, and who does she hire to represent her? Ted Halliday was behind it all. *Ted Halliday* who had tried his damnedest to steal Rex right from under him. If Ted Halliday had his hooks into Mimi...

Addison rose and gracefully stepped around his desk. He didn't confront Fitzroy, but somehow became an obstacle in the midst of all the pacing.

Fitzroy pulled up short and glared. "She's too easily swayed," he croaked. "Too emotional."

Addison blinked. "If you ask me, she has remarkable self-control and I'm convinced she knows her own mind."

Fitzroy let out a bellow, a mix of rage and pain. "I want you to hire an outside counsel," he said. "Get the best in the country. You've seen the papers. Mimi's signed a proxy. I want that proxy invalidated."

Addison choked. "I've already looked at it, David."

Fitzroy glared at Addison and caught his breath. He knew he was out of control again, but he was not going to debate the point. "Do whatever it takes," he said. "I do not want Mimi's shares voted by anyone but Mimi. You understand?"

"David... I'm not sure we can."

"Manage it!" Fitzroy barked, then turned and slammed out the door.

Chapter 31

One last thing before taking off for Seattle—Thorsen opened Specialty Dining's rush report on Raj Banerjee thinking she had time for a quick read. By page two, clearly, she needed an extra three hours for some reconnaissance. She grabbed her purse, headed for her car and, as the elevator doors opened on parking level one, she shivered. She was not cold, and she couldn't spot anything wrong. But there had to be something.

At her car, she stopped, listened and there it was again. She turned and carefully surveyed the garage. And caught her breath—so uncharacteristic of her—not thirty feet away, a Lexus like Mimi's. How was that possible? It hadn't been there five hours earlier.

She scanned the garage to confirm she was alone, walked over to the Lexus—no mistaking that license plate—and pressed her palm down on the hood of the car. Dead cold. As things stood, she barely had time to take care of the Banerjee question, and now this goddamned car? She pulled out a tissue and wiped her handprint away. She couldn't help the feeling something had lightly brushed the back of her neck.

She climbed into her Maserati, dug out her phone and called the inside number for the company jet. Could they delay her flight to Seattle and let JR know? Ridiculous to worry. *She* had not been seen at the park.

If anybody checked, the women at the park and the fools with the dog would all say they saw a boy.

Suddenly, one of the garage elevators opened and JR rushed toward her, sweating, hyperventilating. Thorsen rolled down the car window. "They give you my flight time?"

"Seven tonight," he said and popped his own phone in a pocket. "But what's more important, because you need this, I promise, it's so hot. Have you heard? Mimi Fitzroy resigned. Some law firm had a letter hand delivered to Mr. Fitzroy."

Obviously, JR was dying to regale her with the rest of the fallout from Mimi's resignation. But she was not about to go there.

"Thanks for letting me know," she said and started her car. "Message me if you hear more. But I need to handle a few things before my flight."

JR's mouth snapped shut. He spun out a neat pirouette and took off.

Thorsen waited until the elevator doors closed, then turned off her car, snatched up her phone and called IT. "Mimi in?"

IT gave her the story they were undoubtedly dishing out to every caller—Ms. Fitzroy had emailed she wouldn't be in. That was all they knew. How about the time on the email? They didn't know. A lie. Somebody had opened the damned email, there'd been a date and time sent. She was tempted to ask if they could check for her but pushing them on it would make her sound desperate.

Whoever she was talking with apologized and launched into a string of useless suggestions on how she might locate Mimi. She cut the idiot off mid-sentence and immediately put in a call to Robert Addison, who confirmed Mimi had resigned but didn't elaborate. When Thorsen pressed him, he confirmed about the letter, but that was it.

"I see," she said. Had *he* recommended a lawyer for Mimi? Had he known she was looking for one? No and no. Addison didn't know squat. And he was worried—not that he said so, but it was there in his voice.

No point in giving Addison anything more to work with. She tossed her phone on the passenger seat, then bowed her head and pressed a place on the trapezius connectors at the back of her neck. Just when had Mimi hired a lawyer? When had she had time? *Think.* Mimi'd spent over an hour at South Sixth Street on Sunday. Plenty of lawyers there. But Mimi could not have worked out every detail of a resignation and signed it all in one hour. No high-end lawyer worked that fast.

Thorsen leaned back against the leather seat, her left foot lightly tapping the floor panel. *Executive Garage Security.* She scanned the corporate directory on her smart phone. It took four rings before someone answered.

"I'm trying to reach Ms. Fitzroy," she said. "When did her Lexus arrive?

"Miz Fitzroy… According to the log, 10:47 a.m."

"Did you see who was driving?"

"Security brought it over from the main parking lot."

"What was it doing over there?" She counted out ten seconds. "Well?"

"Dunno. Parking's log sheet shows last night Ms. Fitzroy dropped the key in the lock box with a note for

Parking to bring it over to us."

That didn't make sense. "Miz Fitzroy brought it in?"

"I assume so. Okay, *whoever* it was brought the car in then."

Christ.

"Do you know when the drop box was last checked?"

"That sort of depends."

Another citizen working beyond his abilities. She ended the call and leaned back, tensing and stretching her legs to shake the impulse to punch something. Definitely time for an inventory.

First of all, Mimi—was dead, ridiculous to think otherwise. Mimi's body would turn up like a popsicle. If a body didn't turn up, well, that was a problem for later.

The car—the park service tow company must have picked it up and brought it back. They'd have spotted that the car was registered to Rex. That made more sense than it did to think Mimi had survived and driven back to a Rex parking lot she didn't use and left the key in Security's lock box.

As for the resignation letter—the whole resignation must have been put together weeks earlier to take place after the dinner, probably long before Frank Leit met his end. As for the pirated emails… With Mimi out of the picture, who gave a rip about them now? Addison? Possibly. But she could handle Addison.

Chapter 32

Raj Banerjee took the call in his office at Rex Sports. It was 2:52 p.m. It was his cousin. She would never telephone him at work and now, what is this?

"You must come," she whispered. "Now. A woman. From your company."

For a moment, he couldn't find the words. "This woman, she is very small?"

"No-no. Big, very big. With lion hair, red like flaming."

Raj bolted for his car. Ms. Thorsen being at his home when she would know that he would be at his office working? And his cousin weeping that she is discovered, that her family will be deported. He could hope Ms. Thorsen merely was looking for Mimi Fitzroy, which was bad enough. But he could not help thinking whatever Ms. Thorsen was doing was much worse.

Twelve minutes later, he stepped through his back door. His cousin peeked at him from the pantry, one hand holding the louvered door against her chest. Eyes wide, she motioned at the sound of talk coming from the living room.

Raj crept across the kitchen, stopped at the swinging door into the dining room and listened. His mother was speaking in that effusive voice—her imitation of an overly-eager, not-so-well-educated-

Indian. "Ah yes, he is so much enjoying the game of football." His mother rattled on with one story after another of his boyhood. Raj could not help but roll his eyes. He had played football when he was a boy of nine. Football had not been his passion for many years though his mother made it sound as if he were still part of an amateur club.

"Football?"

It was Anna Thorsen's voice. He could imagine her leaning forward in her chair. Her long legs thrust out into the room, her sharp eyes glittering at his mother. He pushed the door open into the dining room, calling his mother, feigning surprise at the sight of Ms. Thorsen.

A brass tray with tea and sliced cake was sitting on the ottoman.

He knew his mother's trick. Preparing and serving tea was giving her time to assess a visitor. The whole time of boiling the water, measuring the tea, heating the pot, cutting and arranging the cake, the long minutes of fussing—his mother had filled the time. Undoubtedly, she had prattled away to Ms. Thorsen as if her mind could not hold an idea. She would have started with Ms. Thorsen's appearance, then jumped to how it was to visit America, American children, supermarkets, then back to Ms. Thorsen's position at Rex Sports, then his mother would undoubtedly compare her daughter's life in Manchester to her son's lifestyle in Minneapolis— his mother reveled in that word, lifestyle—then she might drop a morsel about the family's life in India and how she was missing her son.

It would take a master, or a child who had endured years of such inquisitions, to spot the attitudes and expressions his mother used. Let alone to expose, for what they were, the excuses Thorsen had made for visiting his home.

Banerjee stopped halfway between the sofa and a very clearly surprised Ms. Thorsen.

As he stepped into the conversation, his mother rose and placed her hand on his arm. "Blessed, would you join us?"

He kissed her cheek, sat and leaned closer. "Ms. Thorsen is a very busy woman, Mama. If she took the time to come here, I believe she is needing my help." His mother rose and made a production out of leaving and closing the hallway door.

Raj caught the flash of rage as it passed through Ms. Thorsen and he reminded himself to be calm. He had nothing to hide.

Ms. Thorsen apologized for dropping in. "I hope I didn't upset your mother. But David is very worried about Mimi," she said. "And on my way to the airport, I thought of you. Any idea what she's planning to do? You must know her father is trying to reach her."

Raj held tight to his Buddha face and nodded.

This woman was showing up at his home in the middle of the afternoon, speaking as if he would be not at his work when certainly he would be at his office and she could have checked and spoken to him there.

Thorsen inched forward in the guest chair. Her eyes shifted gray to black. "Let's be honest, Raj. Half of Minnesota knows what happened at David's dinner. Entirely my fault. I tried to apologize to her then, but," she shrugged, "I thought maybe you..." Her voice trailed off.

Anyone else might have seen that face as soft,

regretful, an earnest appeal that he should help her.

He reminded himself to *assume the virtue of tea* and cupped his hands in his lap. "I would not wish to dispute you," he said. "But if you are asking, am I knowing where Ms. Fitzroy has gone, I am not. I did not know even of her leaving. It is true we are colleagues. We are working together very closely. But I know nothing of her personal life."

Thorsen shifted to reminiscing about Mimi, arriving finally at the day she had come upon him in the hallway, talking with Mimi on—was it just last Wednesday? Mimi had seemed preoccupied, she said. And he had looked very tired, very stressed. "Was there really nothing wrong?" Thorsen said. "Because at the time, it seemed to me that there was."

He could feel her stare crawling over him, probing for an opening. He did not know where Mimi was, he said.

Thorsen shifted her gaze to the carpet, to the tea, to the draperies over the front window. The whole time slowly shaking her head. She pressed her forefinger against her lips—was it all drama for his sake? What was it she wanted from him?

"With all the talk about my next position at Rex—" She was watching him, looking for an opening. "Everyone seems to forget I'm still working as the Chief Operations Officer, sometimes the responsibilities…"

He nodded.

"I rely on you and your team," she said. "Are you certain there is no problem with the system security? Mimi didn't mention anything that—Look, we all have reporting responsibilities. Including me. So help me out here, Raj. You say you don't know about Mimi's disappearance, but you must know what was going on over at IT."

He knew better than to look away. His answer must be candid. He must not be remembering a rehearsed story. "I understand," he said. "I regret I am unable to tell you where Ms. Fitzroy has... I, too, am very concerned that she has disappeared...with no word to me and so suddenly. It is true, I last spoke with her Saturday morning. Yes, there had been a security alert. It came on Wednesday. We worked on it all day. A false alert, as I learned later. After so much work. I was told later there was no problem."

Ms. Thorsen seemed to accept his answer.

But even *he* heard something in the kitchen. He forced a smile. "My mother begins our dinner." Ridiculous, of course. His mother had never prepared food herself.

Ms. Thorsen leaned forward, licked her lips with her beetle tongue. And uninvited, she reached to refill her teacup. "Your mother is a very interesting woman."

Ms. Thorsen could hardly know how interesting his mother was. His mother had read history at Lady Margaret Hall, Oxford. Then returned to India and practiced law until she became a judge. Among her children were two physicians, an Episcopal priest, and three software engineers. She spoke perfect English. And now she helped immigrants navigate the labyrinth of American behavior and immigration law.

He smiled, nodded. "I am thinking the child does not see what is interesting in the parent. But yes, my mother is interesting. She lives in India. Perhaps she said this."

"You must miss her. But you have family here. Besides your mother." Thorsen's eyes flicked to the swinging door into the kitchen. She was looking for him to explain the noises there. Expecting him to delay his answer, to mention his mother again, or perhaps to pick up a piece of the yellow cake, to stuff it in his mouth to give himself time to formulate an answer. To say more of Mimi. To speculate. And truly, the thought of working without Mimi twisted in his heart. But he would not give in to it.

He forced a smile. "Perhaps you do not know, Ms. Thorsen. I am unmarried." He took a moment to pour himself a tea. "I have my mother, who visits me here as you see but as I am saying, she lives in India. Some of my cousins also are in India," He gave her a wistful look. "My brothers and sisters are—what is best to say? In England. Also, in Australia and Canada, and two cousins temporarily in South Africa."

He was taking tea with a tiger. No, with something much worse.

"Your mother tells me you are a football fan." Her eyebrows up at the end of her question. As if she were genuinely interested. As if they were chatting at a company party, as if they were sitting in *her* living room, as if she were not looking for a way to trap him, to make him betray the families in his other houses, the families he was committed to help.

"But you are seeing my mother is joking. At school, I am playing goalie on what you would call a soccer team."

For a millisecond, her eyes narrowed. Then she fished her way through the current swamp of international star soccer players. When he did not respond, she switched to cricket.

"Very popular in India," he said. "But I find cricket very slow and boring.

"NBA?" she said.

Even where he was sitting, he could feel the tension in her as if she were about to pounce, to sink her long teeth into his neck and shake the life from him.

He forced himself to laugh. "I am the odd man at Rex," he said. "Truly I am not so interested in sports as when I was a boy. I read technical journals, I play a little tennis. But cannot name ten professional players in any sport. I apologize."

Thorsen sat forward, the flames shooting off the crown of her head. Abruptly she glanced at her watch, stood and pulled together her things. At the front door she paused. He had expected perhaps one attempt at cordiality as she departed, but no. There was only a last look. As if he were not worth eating, merely a greasy thumbprint on an otherwise unappealing dinner plate.

Chapter 33

Thorsen pushed her way into the private flights' passenger lounge, handed off her bags to the attendant, and set up shop in a corner just in time for the place to empty out completely. Her eyes were killing her. She pulled out a wad of medicated tissues, kicked back and let the towelette do its job.

It was that damned car of Mimi's that had thrown her off pace.

No. There'd been something wrong even before the car. For one thing, there'd been no fun in getting rid of Mimi. Stripping her down, the feel of her, the scent of her parka, sailing her out into the dim light. Disposing of Mimi should have given her a high that lasted a week. Instead...she'd had more kick getting rid of a sack of garbage. She'd walked back to her car with not so much as a tingle. Why was that?

Jamie'd been spur of the moment. Maybe that was it. Jamie had tried to dump her for chrissake. No wonder it'd felt so sweet as he turned loose and skidded down Half Dome. His howl had cut through her like an orgasm.

It'd been way better planting that kick in Frank Leit's ear. Like booting the moon. Like doing poppers in the old days. No, like a hit of pure oxygen. It should've been better with Mimi...after waiting so long to get rid of the little bitch.

Well it wasn't better. So, get over it. Mimi was dead. Get back to business and ID Frank Leit's insider. Could be Banerjee. But he hadn't recognized Frank Leit's name. Or the names of Leit's other blog writers. More importantly, he didn't appear to give a rat's ass. He was terrified of her, of course. But whether she could trust his story about the false report of a security problem… He wasn't so foolish as to feed her a story she could easily check. As for her ghost file, with her little report program going, she could relax on that front. At least for the time being.

She shifted over to the lounge sofa and stretched out her legs.

Dropping in at Banerjee's had definitely not been a waste of time though. That vein at his temple had spasmed every time she'd mentioned family or looked at that swinging door. Either he was housing illegals, or, was it beyond the realm of possibility that he was laundering money for somebody? Green card or not, a conviction would get him deported. It would be easy to use that to turn him around when the time came.

She ditched the medicated tissues and fished her phone from her bag. Two hours to flight time, she speed-dialed Fitzroy's private number and left a message: Any word about Mimi? Did he want her to postpone the Seattle trip? If so, she needed to know by seven tonight. Otherwise she was landing sometime after midnight. But let her know how she could help.

She jammed the phone back in her bag and walked over to the windows. It killed her that her thoughts kept circling back to Mimi's Lexus. How the hell did it get from Minnehaha Park to the main Rex parking lot?

The lounge attendant popped up beside her.

"Something I can help you with, Ms. Thorsen?"

"No." Said with way too much force. "Sorry. Thank you."

It was ridiculous to let the damned car get to her. She'd been there. She'd tossed that little body in the river. Mimi Fitzroy was dead, simple as that; she'd either drowned or died of exposure.

Time—she had more than an hour until take-off. It felt like she had an entire army of ants crawling over her and she trusted that feeling. She'd missed something… She forced herself to take one, two, three, four deep disciplined breaths. She closed her eyes. If, IF Mimi survived, it made sense that after Minnehaha, she would try to disappear.

So let's just take care of that.

Thorsen pulled up the Specialty Dining phone number, then paused, thinking she was not about to waste her time while Specialty Dining came up with an answer that she was perfectly capable of engineering herself. It took twenty minutes to hack her way into the airport passenger lists and scroll through the bookings for late Sunday the twenty-third and Monday, November twenty-fourth. No Mimi Fitzroy, no Miriam Fitzroy, not even an M Fitzroy among the bookings. Eight minutes later, nothing on Amtrak.

Rex's pilot strolled by and gave her a high sign. If she wanted, they were cleared to depart early.

"Twenty minutes," Thorsen said and went back to staring at her phone. Absolutely no record of Mimi after Sunday morning, November 23rd, when the Radisson had charged Mimi's bank card for a suite she'd stayed in on the twenty-first and twenty-second.

Forget about the getaway. IF Mimi had survived

the fall at Minnehaha, where would she go? Not home. Not to Daddy. How about back to the Radisson to re-group?

After some careful questions, a few lies and groveling, the Radisson confirmed Ms. Fitzroy was no longer a registered guest and had not stayed with them since Saturday night. Bonus—they coughed up the out-of-state phone number that Mimi had called the night before that Man of the Year Dinner. Reverse-searching the number, Thorsen came up with a home phone listing in Guerneville, California, for Charles and Connie Allen.

Connie answered the call.

"I'm calling from Ms. Fitzroy's office?" Thorsen spoke in a voice with so much air in it, she might have lifted off like a helium balloon. "Um-m-m. Everyone's very worried. You know?"

The thrill of hearing Connie Allen catch her breath rippled over Thorsen.

"We really needed to locate her? Um,... you know? Is Ms. Fitzroy there?" Then in a whisper, she said, "My boss is getting kind of desperate."

"She's not here yet," Connie said, "but we are expecting her. If you want, I can take a message."

Chapter 34

Ben let out a whoop. He could hardly believe his luck. Ninety-three boxes if he'd counted right, just like in Arizona—a second set of his dad's papers. Who would've guessed they'd been sitting in his folks' house on Lake Washington? He popped open the top box in a stack and pawed through it, then opened another one—the same kind of stuff but a little different. He'd hit the motherlode. Heart pounding, he stripped off his coat and went to work. Starting back at the first box, but this time he read the details, one memo after another. But man, there was so much to get straight and it was taking forever. He ordered in food, slept on the sofa and worked as quickly as he could.

By midday Monday he decided he had to face reality: he'd been diving down one rabbit hole after another and all he'd managed to do was get lost. He'd wasted three days. When was he gonna hear back about expert help?

He caught his first real break Monday afternoon when FedEx showed up with his dad's cellphone. He spent the rest of Monday making dozens of calls to the numbers in his dad's phone and most of the time he ended up talking to somebody's voicemail. Finally, at 10:37 Monday evening, a Ted Halliday checked in.

"I worked with your dad for over a year and a half."

Worked with? The guy sounded like a TV sports announcer on steroids but who cared...just so Halliday was the real deal.

"You worked with Dad? How?"

"I'm thinking we need a sit-down. How's tomorrow sound?"

Tuesday morning, Ben headed over to the place Halliday had said he was staying, on Magnolia Boulevard. Ye Gods. And he'd been expecting a condo. It looked like a full-size English manor house, probably built in the '20s, set way back from the street with a panoramic view of the Sound.

Ben climbed out of his car thinking Halliday had referred to the place as their *pied-a-terre.*

Halliday opened the outsized door. "Mr. Leit..."

Not what Ben had expected at all. The guy was as big as an NFL lineman. With a square head with a half-acre bald spot shining on top. In fact, Halliday looked like the kind of guy who could hold his own pretty well except maybe for the sports jacket and slacks.

Halliday's eyes darted at Ben's face then immediately scanned the street.

Something had the guy spooked. So what was going on?

"Damned sorry about your dad. Come on in." Halliday waved Ben into a foyer that matched the Olde English exterior of the mansion—polished wood, marble floor, all the bells and whistles, right down to the echo. He directed Ben on into a library that overlooked the Sound. "Anybody follow you here, did you notice?"

At first, it seemed like a stupid question. But truth was, he hadn't considered it—though he probably should have, considering the interviews he'd just given the press—he didn't have a clue if he'd been followed. He hadn't noticed anybody. But if Halliday was his dad's insider…he was sweating, so maybe that made sense.

The big man pumped up his eyebrows. "I caught that TV interview you did. Looks to me like you're picking up where your dad left off. Are you sure you want to do that?" Halliday nodded at a pair of wing-back chairs angled in front of a whale-size desk and suggested Ben take a load off. Instead of joining Ben, though, Halliday headed over to the double front windows and started messing with the drapes.

"Damned risky if you asked me. I get it, you want to do something about your dad, of course you do. But just so you know, we think whoever murdered your dad also tried to kill my niece. You need to drop this whole thing you're doing now."

Ben cranked his body around to get a better look at Halliday. "Somebody tried to kill your niece? And you think it's connected to Dad… Who are you?"

"I used to be on the Rex Sports Board of Directors. I also spent ten years there as Rex General Counsel."

"And what about your niece?"

"We found her collapsed in Minnehaha State Park. Somebody had knocked her out, left her for dead. We were thinking—"

"And who is we?"

"My wife, my niece and me. Let me back up. Until a week ago, my niece was Vice President of IT and Patent Development at Rex Sports. My wife's on the Rex Board." Halliday scrubbed his hand across his bald spot. "After we saw your interview last night, we were thinking you should take a lower profile." He peered at Ben over the top of his glasses. "In fact, why not shut down the blog for a while and disappear."

"Disappear...because of what happened to Dad, and your niece." Ben shot Halliday a look. "You're gonna have to convince me on that one."

Halliday strolled back behind the desk and sat. "After I heard what happened to your dad, I figured my wife and I had to be next. Instead, it was my niece. She nearly died. And that tied it. I set things up so we could disappear and yesterday, all three of us—my wife, my niece and I—went off the grid."

From the look of his eyes, Halliday was trying to push back a load of panic. And he wasn't having much success—he was sweating like a linebacker after a full workout and the fingers his left hand trembled every time they lifted off the desktop.

"So," Ben said. "Have you talked with the Scottsdale PD?"

Halliday's mouth tightened. "No. Why should I? I only had one phone call with Frank. We never emailed or Facebooked or any of that crap, and I never wrote him. Scottsdale doesn't know about me."

"I got your number from dad's phone."

Halliday's eyes darted away, then back to Ben. "Right. They would've had his phone, right. No, they haven't called."

Ben licked his lower lip. "The thing is, Mr. Halliday—"

"Ted."

"Okay, Ted," Ben said. "Anyway, the reason I called... I'm hoping you can fill in a few blanks for me about Dad's blog, especially how he was getting his information." He waited thinking Halliday might jump in, but the man seemed to be stuck thinking. "Let me put it this way... If you were connected to Rex, I get how Dad would have wanted to talk with you. But how'd he find you?"

Halliday's face relaxed. He leaned forward onto the desk and smiled. "Actually, I found him. I spotted your dad's blog on that football website. This was two years ago. He kept posting about the boatloads of money Rex was pouring into college sports—he wasn't naming Rex of course, but I knew. His point was, money like that was destroying college football. I mentioned seeing Frank's blog to a pal of mine, a law school buddy, and it turned out, my pal knew your dad's lawyer. I called the lawyer and told him I knew enough about Rex Sports that Frank Leit might want to have a little chat with me."

"So then you got together with Dad and—"

"No. I only met your dad once. I spoke to him one other time by phone, but that was recently."

"But Dad was such a hands-on guy. He was always meeting people to talk. He'd even fly into New York for a sit-down with me, just—"

Halliday shook that one off. "It was too risky. Half the people at Rex were trying to figure who your dad's insider was. If they'd spotted Frank in town, they'd have put a tail on him. No, we worked out a system to feed him stuff through an intermediary. I downloaded Rex documents onto thumb drives, sent them to the lawyer, and his office handled the shipments to Frank."

Halliday shot Ben an indulgent smile. "You know what a cut-out is?"

Apparently it was okay if a dumb football player

doesn't have all the answers. The guy was sure in his element. "Tell me," Ben said.

"A cut-out is a middleman who keeps the people who are actually doing the deal protected. First and only time we met. I told your dad I'd need a cut-out—just in case he ever had to explain how he got the documents. Better if he got them from his lawyer and not me. And he agreed. It was safer that way for both of us. A lawyer can't talk, see?"

That'd be like his dad to make sure everybody else was taken care of.

"But I never—" Halliday turned away.

The door opened and a kid poked her head in. "Lunch in half an hour," she said but ended up coming on over to where they were talking.

Halliday pushed back from the desk and stood. "My niece, Mimi."

Once Ben got a good look, the niece wasn't a kid. She was a grown woman, just the size of a twelve-year-old. And, she was a stunner—not some young babe, more like…she was beautiful like a wild deer.

"Honey, we're kind of tied up right now," Halliday said.

Ben stood and stepped free of his chair. "I'm Ben Leit," he said and offered her a hand.

Mimi headed for Ben and shook his hand. "I'm so sorry about your father," she said and took the wing chair next to him. "I think I should hear this."

"Okay by me." Ben sat and turned back to Halliday. "You were saying."

Halliday blotted his forehead and refocused on Ben. "Your dad and I met in Minneapolis. That was nearly two years ago. Before I started…uh…I told him then that Rex was not merely circumventing the NCAA rules, it was up to its shoe tops in white collar crimes." He shot a glance at his niece and planted a paw on the desk. "You remember, honey, I showed you part of what I had when you were in my office last week."

A shiver ran down Ben's back. "Just a second. If you had proof two years ago that Rex Sports was breaking the law, why didn't you—"

Halliday flicked the question away with a hand. "You need to understand. Ten years ago, Rex reorganized, changed the way it did business. I was forced out of the company. And Mimi, I know what you're thinking."

From where Ben sat, whatever Mimi was thinking, it wasn't good.

Halliday tapped the desk. "Honey, listen to me. Back when I first spotted what was going on, if I had used my contacts then to expose Rex, it would've looked like revenge, pure and simple. Even two years ago, things were so unstable, bringing the feds in might've brought the whole company down. And I sure didn't want to destroy things for all of us. You know that."

Ben shifted in his chair. No way was he gonna buy that *saving the company* crap. He could recognize a loose cannon when he saw one. And when he checked for Mimi's reaction, she looked frozen and her hands had a stranglehold going on the chair arms.

Still the man in charge, Halliday cleared his throat and turned back to Ben. "It's just occurred to me, that's another reason for you to back off. It's not just you're putting us all at risk, did you know your dad was talking to the feds? That's why he called me, to give me a head's up. He told me he'd heard from the feds. I told him, go for it."

Mimi blurted, "You what?"

Obviously, she didn't like it, him taking control, he got that. But right then, he didn't care. He leaned over to her. "Let me do this, okay?"

He turned back to Halliday. "Dad was talking with the feds? Which feds? Was it a U.S. Attorney? Was it somebody he knew from politics? Who?"

"They'll want to keep control of their investigation. You know that," Halliday said. "They're not going to appreciate your efforts, however well-intentioned they are. You need to just sit tight."

"Dad didn't say who he was talking with?"

Halliday shook his head no. "He didn't."

"Did anybody else know? Did Dad say?"

"How the hell should I know?" Halliday was puffing like a lizard, sweating profusely. "And I sure wasn't about to mention it to anybody."

Suddenly Halliday started fishing in his jacket pockets. He finally managed to pop something in his mouth. But the distraction gave Ben a chance to slip into that zone where everything disappears except his downfield target. And there it was: his dad talking to the feds had to be what had kicked the killer into gear. And whoever his dad had been talking to, that number had to be on his dad's phone.

A resounding whack on the desk brought Ben back.

Mimi was standing with the flat of her hand planted on desktop. Her eyes were wide, her chin quivering. "I should have seen it last week. It wasn't Aunt Madge you were protecting. This is all about revenge on Dad. It's why you quit, why you forced

Aunt Madge to divorce you. If it hadn't been Frank Leit, you'd have found somebody else. But it was you feeding Rex documents to Frank Leit. You've been lying to all of us."

Halliday was shaking his head. "Mimi, this is neither the time and nor the place."

"You set Frank Leit up," Tears were rolling down her cheeks. "Now you're doing it again. With his son, setting him up. You want to get him killed too?"

"I told Ben to shut down the blog. You heard me. I met Frank Leit two years ago, Mimi. Don't you remember what was going on? We were after the truth, Frank and I. Once the U.S. Attorney gets involved, there'll be the usual bad publicity, a plea agreement and a whopping fine. But things will get better."

"Getting at all that truth, you made sure you were protected though, didn't you?"

She stepped into the foyer, grabbed the door and slammed it behind her.

Chapter 35

Rolf pushed himself back from the comatose stand-alone computer. He could not believe he'd been defeated by a pack of lawyers. He could not believe he had just watched a message melt down the screen as if his monitor was having heatstroke. On his third try, they had not only shut him out, but his system suddenly locked solid and refused to boot up—the only good news, he had used the safety stand alone and not Specialty Dining's main network.

He could not believe he had failed. He would not accept it.

When the Madge Fitzroy Halliday assignment had landed on his desk, Rolf tracked her from the date her divorce was final (ten years ago) right up to Sunday, November 24. He knew when Madge turned her home security alarm on and off, what TV shows she watched, what brands of toothpaste she bought, when and where she went clothes shopping, the cruises she'd considered and the ones she'd taken. He had her right down to the color of her lipstick and when she changed hairdressers. He knew about her appendectomy and that she'd had foot surgery for bunions. He had the names of her physician, her priest, her old lawyer, her new lawyer, and a couple-dozen volunteers she worked with on her do-good projects. He was inches from wrapping up his report and getting out from under this miserable project.

All that remained was to crack the system of this new law firm she'd hired.

He'd used all his skill, and he had plenty, to break into their system. His back was already killing him. And now this.

He unplugged the stand-alone. If anybody could figure a work-around it was Hart—even if Hart had refused to do more work on the Etouffee project.

Slowly, and careful of his rebellious sacrum, Rolf made his way over to the cubicle where Hart was staring at the two screens he had going. Hart's fingers raced over the keyboard; and the images and text on the screens shuffled as if they were riding a tiny whirlwind. Rolf waited until finally the action slowed, Hart's hands slid to his desktop, and both screens went dark.

Without looking up, Hart sighed. "Don't ask me to work on her stuff, okay?"

"I just need you to tell me where I screwed up," Rolf said.

"Right."

A disembodied voice shot over the cavernous project room. *Do you guys mind?*

Rolf turned, snatched the notes from his desk and both men left for the conference room where Rolf booted the main display system and logged into Specialty Dining's proprietary software. "Either it's picked up a bug or... It's that Halliday thing I took back from you."

Hart grabbed a papaya juice and sat. "Ted Halliday dropped off the planet after the divorce. What else is there?"

"I'm not working on Ted. It's the ex-wife."

"Look." Hart sighed, "I'm sorry you got stuck with

this thing, but I'm done enabling whoever is after these people."

"I'm not asking for your help on the assignment, if you'd pay attention for a second. I'm talking about a problem with our system. Our programs didn't protect me. That's why I pulled you in. I have Madge Halliday right up until Sunday the twenty-fourth. A local hospital. The daughter took a fall on a hike."

"Wrong," Hart said. "The Halliday's don't have kids. They do have a niece. Named Miriam Fitzroy, goes by Mimi."

Rolf dismissed the anomaly as an Admissions error.

"Nothing else with the hospital though?" Hart said. "Hospital not your problem?"

Rolf smiled. "Standard HIPAA drill: I threw our Cumin program at them, watched their security unravel then I followed up with the usual Cardamom bomb."

Hart made a note on his palm. "I like that. Sequence instead of simultaneous setup, right? How long before they got their system back?"

Rolf grinned and nodded. "Six minutes, seven seconds."

He said right after the hospital, Madge Halliday disappeared. He'd done the usual 'count down,' reviewing Madge's actions the previous two weeks. Until Sunday night, there were only two things out of the ordinary. A dinner honoring her brother, David Fitzroy, the CEO at Rex Sports. There'd been a load of news coverage including about a family blow-up with the daughter. But nothing wacko for Madge. The other thing: five or six calls to a law office between the twentieth and the twenty-fourth—not her regular lawyers—all the calls were made on one of the alternate Halliday cell phones.

Hart checked his calendar. "She called some lawyer on a Sunday?"

"On a Sunday. They talked eight minutes. She had an appointment with the guy for Monday the twenty-fifth at 7:30 a.m."

"You know this how?"

"Her Outlook," Rolf said.

Hart nodded. "So she sees the lawyer Monday."

Rolf shook his head no. "Can't prove it by me. Nothing since Sunday night."

"So check the lawyer."

"Well—"

Hart rolled his eyes. "I get it. Last year you hack the National Security Council's office and with the bonus you got, you went to Jamaica for a month. On *my* chops. And now—"

"Yeah, well that was last year," Rolf said. "It's a new game over there now."

Hart snorted. "Bottom line: you can't get past a bunch of lawyers in Minneapolis and you want my help so you can claim another bonus?"

Rolf fiddled with the computer keyboard, then pushed it over. "What did I miss?"

Hart peered at the screen, then input a sequence that ramped up Specialty Dining's Rotterdam system and, with a few more keystrokes, the program should have given them entry to the law firm. Instead, a simple black and white message filled the mega-screen: UNAUTHORIZED USER / ENTRY DENIED.

Hart leaned back from the conference table. "Mannnnnnnnnnnnnnnn."

"Try it three times, you'll fry our whole system," Rolf said. "They've already knocked out one of our stand-alones."

Hart shoved the keyboard away. "So who are these guys?

"That's where it gets interesting. Madge Halliday isn't the first person who's disappeared after she hooked up with these guys," Rolf said. "I'm thinking they have a deal going with the Department of Justice. At least it looked like it when I took a peek at their public history. I'm thinking they help people who need new identities. So maybe your instincts about Etouffee were right."

Chapter 36

Fitzroy joined his campaign team at his conference table. Bill, Isaac and Nate—one way or another, all good for five-hundred grand each, minimum. And the others—solid faces, lots of brains and connections. All that money and power. It'd been precisely the right time to make a run for the Senate. He'd pulled together the unbeatable team.

He made it quick. He would not be mounting a senatorial campaign this year.

There were the usual protests and two seriously disappointed faces. Whether they were glum for him or for the way he had dashed their hopes for fame and fortune—it didn't matter. They all wanted to know why.

He offered a wry smile. "I wish I could tell you more. But you know how it is with a man's business and personal life—sometimes you have to hold things close to the vest, and this is one of those times."

He thanked the group and made his way around the table—a personal word for each of the backroom boys. Within five minutes, he was alone.

Robert Addison showed up at 2:00 p.m. precisely—unshaven, unwashed and rumpled, as if he had spent the past twenty-four hours working nonstop. He was carrying two black three-ring binders, each one thick as a man's hand is wide. Both packed full and bristling with colored tabs, post-its and paper clips. He flopped them down on the conference table and stood behind a chair.

Fitzroy had fully prepared himself with medication, water, and several hours spent reviewing his personal notes on the contracts he'd signed for the company. He pulled one of Addison's binders over in front of him, sat and began flipping through the documents.

Clearly nervous, Addison pulled a written resignation from his jacket and laid it on the table.

Fitzroy shoved it to the side without reading it. "Make no mistake, I don't see you having a bright future with Rex. And I will have to discuss this whole matter with the Board. But for now, Robert, I want you front and center to help make sense of this mess. Understand?"

Addison fished out a handkerchief and wiped his hands.

Fitzroy got it: the way Addison kept trying to find an exit, clearly he was looking at a man with his tail in a crack. In Fitzroy's experience, that meant there must be something more.

"The worst of it," Addison said and cleared his throat, "before we talk about the deals. I need to tell you. When I first looked at the records on our system it seemed like Anna Thorsen didn't play a material part in any of the deals."

"Now just a damned minute," Fitzroy said.

"*At first glance,*" Addison said. Then he walked Fitzroy through the review process. "If you didn't do more than look at Rex e-files and the contract books, you'd think Anna had nothing significant to do with the deals. Even the Indonesian ones. Anna's only role there *appeared* to be limited to attending a few meetings."

"But that's not how it was," Fitzroy said.

Addison held up his hand. "My first pass through these files, I didn't look too closely at the Ace/Walkup negotiations. But by the time I was looking at the second project—and I remember that project very well—I knew something was wrong with the file's documentation. All kinds of memos were missing or altered. That's what led me to check my old work file. I ended up cross-checking my work file on every one of the deals."

Addison reached over to Fitzroy's binder and flipped to a section toward the back. "I hate to tell you, David, but the corporation's contract files have been sanitized. Bound books have been un-bound, altered and re-bound. Charts and drawings are changed or missing—in some cases, memos and emails have been modified, or outright deleted. Even my associates' work files are missing. If I hadn't stored mine off-site…"

Fitzroy held his breath. It was a fucking nightmare, a revolver aimed straight at him. He couldn't help imagining the snick of the safety, the trigger pulling back and back.

Addison suggested that he hire an outside expert to perform a complete audit of every deal's documentation. The audit should include everything from Fitzroy's and Addison's files, even IT's backup files. And if Fitzroy agreed, they should contact the lawyers for the other parties to the deals.

Fitzroy sat stunned. He'd be ruined. Unless he had excellent luck with the courts, he'd end up in prison. He couldn't help thinking about the fight he'd had with Ted Halliday over who would become CEO. If only he'd lost the battle, none of this would've happened. Ted never liked Anna. Ted would've spotted her maneuvers in no time.

But Ted didn't win the fight. And as things stood, everyone would still be expecting him to retire and Anna to take over. If he didn't retire, it was entirely possible that Anna would force him out. All she had to do was leak the sanitized files to the shareholders.

It killed him to think that the girl he'd had such hopes for, the lovely girl he'd mentored and encouraged, had turned on him. But there it was. Slowly he drew in a deep breath. "Do it," he said. "Hire your expert. It'll have to be bulletproof. You know that."

Addison thumbed to another section of the notebook. He said his charts focused on the five deals that had the most influence on Rex's position. In each case, the increase in corporate profits made it clear, the acquisitions were made as part of a scheme to dominate the market.

The biggest impact had been Rex's buy-up of the five companies that actually cut, sewed and glued Rex brand apparel, especially its sports shoes.

"Because we tied all the subcontractors to Rex, I remember," Fitzroy said. "Our two biggest competitors went out of business." He bent over the chart, tracing the numbers with a finger. He should have stayed on top of things. Certainly, he shouldn't have let Anna handle that side of the business without more oversight. But everything she came up with had seemed to work so well.

Addison drew himself up. "We sold shoes at a price that was seventeen cents a pair below the total cost of design, testing, manufacture, shipment and sale. In and of itself, that might not be against the law. But price cutting to force our competition out of that market—definitely a problem for us. What makes matters worse is that we came back the next year with essentially the same shoe and sold it at five times the price."

Fitzroy looked up from the papers. "I don't understand how you could let this happen." He cleared his throat. "I trusted you. I never spotted you for a crook."

The word "crook" seemed to shock Addison. He reared back, set his jaw then pushed his chair away from the table and started for the door. "Do what you need to. I understand. Fire me, whatever. But I'm done with the cover-up."

"Sit down," Fitzroy barked.

Whether it was the tone of Fitzroy's voice or the implicit threat, Addison returned to the table and sat.

"Now," Fitzroy lowered his tone back to normal. "Walk me through how the specific deals went down."

Addison wetted his lips. "I didn't see that first one with Ace/Walkup as over the line," he said. "It was a bold strategy, but not problematic. Not exactly. So, I signed off on it. When the next deal came along, I questioned it, but Anna said you'd okayed it, that you were hot to wrap it up. I should've stopped it right there. I should have run it by you personally. But I didn't. And you remember, the bonuses that year—we all cleaned up on it. Over a million for me when you add up the bonus, the stock and options. Oh, I knew we had a monopoly in the European market. But once I'd let those two deals slide through, there was nothing I could do to stop her. I tried once. And she made it clear: cooperate or she'd report me to the State Bar, and God knows who else."

They talked briefly about going to the authorities right then, but decided, it was a no-go.

Fitzroy scrubbed his hand across the back of his head. "From where we are right now, if we go up against her… We need to be damned careful, Robert. And we'd better be prepared for what she might do next."

Chapter 37

Thorsen hit Seattle like a tidal wave. She set up her temporary office, wrote a point-by-point memo laying out the details for her temp assistant, caught up on the latest Mimi news via her assistant JR's email, then slept for three hours, showered, dressed and drove to a hairdressers' to change her red hair to honey-brown. She made it back at her hotel suite just in time to give her temp Maya the skinny on how they would be working. Once Maya swore she understood, Thorsen disappeared into a sit-down with a new ad firm, a boutique company she had personally vetted—clearly an improvement over the goons she had terminated five days earlier.

Meeting over, she shot Specialty Dining a *what's up* email and ten minutes later, their Ben Leit memo rolled in with one miserable tidbit she could use—a column in the Seattle Times claiming that Ben Leit was back in town. What was wrong with her New Orleans people? They couldn't find one billing address for him? Seriously? Her head hurt. No doubt because Maya the temp had interrupted her three times already with questions JR could have answered for himself.

She opened the sliding door to the balcony and stepped out. The sprawl of green park across the street spread all the way to a cluster of restaurants cantilevered out over the ramp to a boat moorage.

Beyond the sailboats, a bay or lake or maybe it was part of the sound—she would check the map.

Everything was so green. And it was threatening rain again. This was the shift she needed: the wide lawns, the sound of the seagulls and the occasional float plane taking off. The chill helped clear her head and she ended up staying out on the balcony long after she should have buckled down to work.

But she could feel it. She was wrong, looking for the wrong thing. Was she wrong about Seattle? No. She was using the wrong name, that was all. It was Frank Leit's address, that was the key.

She headed back in, unlocked her computer, and five minutes later, there he was, Frank Leit, still on the King County property tax rolls. And, thanks to Google, she was able to check out an aerial view of the target house on a wedge-shaped lot abutting Lake Washington. According to the map, an area called Webster Point, right at the tip of the peninsula. A little thrum ran up her fingers and thrilled her palms. She zoomed the detail up as high as it would go. Enlarging the image distorted it, but she could make out most of what she needed to know. The main floor of the house had a white deck facing the lake. The deck ran the entire width of the house. Beyond it, the yard terraced a couple of times down to a walkway out to a floating dock.

She'd put money there were three floors to the place. Just the way the shadows slanted. Underneath that big deck, she thought she could make out a daylight basement with doors opening onto a cement or stone…she couldn't make it out. Was it a patio? Whatever it was, going in under that cover…excellent.

Given that Specialty Dining couldn't spot the Ben Leit name on anything, it made sense he was living in the place. If he wasn't, then she'd be waiting for the New York City Post Office to respond to her *forwarding address requested* mailer. For damned sure, she had no intention of waiting around for that when she had other options.

While she was nailing things down, it occurred to her there was no harm in checking out the status of the Frank Leit investigation in Scottsdale. According to the Arizona Republic, the cops were still giving out the story that Frank Leit died during a home invasion. No mention of Ben Leit except that he was Frank Leit's kid. *Thank you, gentlemen.*

She itched to get going. But if she had one weakness, it was her propensity to shoot first. If she wanted to avoid that misstep…time for a little homework. She pulled on the apparently-regulation street uniform for Seattle—trainers, running sweats and a light, rain-repellent jacket, nothing matching—she told Maya she'd be out for a while, and headed down to her rental car. Thirty minutes later, she drove into Laurelhurst. She parked three blocks away from the target house and set out on foot.

The neighborhood felt slow the way neighborhoods with locking gates, tennis courts and security guards feel—Stepford Slow. A stranger would stand out like a giraffe. More to the point, a stranger who hung around would be taken for a would-be burglar.

She could risk one look at the house on foot. Then she'd have to beat it.

She parked in University Village, walked into the neighborhood and strolled past the target house. Then, she headed back west past the place, concentrating on her posture and bio mechanics as if she were finishing a cardio walk. The whole exercise left her in an utterly terrific mood. So good in fact, she had to remind herself to now and then pretend to chat on her smart phone. Every house on the street, including Leit's place, had security out the wazzoo. Which meant that likely she was already on camera. No way would she be accessing the place from street-side.

The big surprise, for a couple of million dollars, the target house wasn't exactly the mansion she'd expected. From the sidewalk, it looked pleasantly large but like a lot of two-story bungalows she'd seen in Seattle: three dormers facing the street, two-car garage. From the window layout, she guessed there was some kind of foyer and central stairs to the upper story. Interesting that the lake-side ground floor she'd seen in the Google photos was completely hidden from where she stood street-side.

So what else couldn't she see?

She had that thrum going again, a reassuring message from her body, she was right on target. True, there was no car in the driveway, and she couldn't see any lights on or make out any movement in the target house, but that proved nothing about Ben Leit's whereabouts. Ben Leit was there, she knew it. She kept walking.

Just past the house, she pretended to use her phone and stood for a while stretching her quads and 'talking.' Slowly she turned in a circle, aimlessly staring. She gave the house a last glance, strolled back toward her car and sat for a moment taking stock. She needed a good look inside. That was doable. With all those recreational boaters and kayakers on Lake Washington, if she approached Leit's place from the water, she'd be part of a crowd.

So, she'd be going in from the lake. And definitely she'd be going in after dark.

She called her temp and discovered all was well. "Then see you tomorrow," she said and spent an hour checking out water transport. A rowboat was no option, too heavy and too slow. A kayak—good flexibility on the water, but it wasn't her style. She settled on a racing scull—less maneuverable than a kayak, but it would be way faster. She'd rowed in college and there were plenty of sculls on the water.

She made a few calls to dealers. A couple of retailers were happy to take her order, but it would be weeks before delivery. She moved on to *Sculls for Sale* on Craigslist and left word for a call back. Evergreen Rowing offered to order her a new scull or they could hook her up with a guy who seriously wanted to sell his Hudson single. She called the guy with the Hudson and made a deal over the phone. For an extra $500, he was happy to deliver wherever she wanted. *What address?* She'd call him back in thirty minutes.

She drove west along the ship canal, looking for the Seattle Rowing Center, where she rented storage space for the scull. That settled, she called the guy with the Hudson back and met him an hour later. Just that quick, her plan was underway. Definitely time for a test drive.

Chapter 38

Thorsen laid her scull at the edge of the ship canal, then squatted and rigged a waterproof pack behind the footboard—a pack with plenty of room for the gear she'd bring on her next trip. For her test run though, she'd only have her binoculars.

She stood and checked out the traffic. Enough boaters she wouldn't be noticed. The sky was clearing to the east; not much chop to the water. Chop might slow her down, but this wasn't a competition, after all, she just wanted an up-close look at Frank Leit's house. The issue was silence, speed and invisibility—the scull offered her that.

She waited to launch until a string of kayakers puttered by, then curled herself onto her craft. It'd been twelve years since she'd competed. But her motor memory was long and keen. Out of habit, she tested the scull's glide seat. It worked fine on the stroke but seemed to stick on the return. She oiled the runners, reseated her feet in the footboard blocks and adjusted the straps across her canvas trainers. A little more tinkering and...perfect.

She leaned into her crouch, her heart drumming against her thighs. She could taste the energy of the boat and smiled at the pleasure of it. Finally, she checked the fit of the straps for her feet. Critical to get them right because once she finished at Leit's place, she might need to be off in a hurry. She'd want full power on the stroke and a damned quick return—that meant a perfect fit and no messing around.

Speed. Power. And style. She'd be the whole package.

One more check of the canal for traffic—she locked her feet on the footboard, crouched forward and eased out onto the water.

It was over a mile to Lake Washington. Rowing that stretch gave her time to attune herself to the weather and the surface. On and off, shafts of sun glinted off the water. She caught an oar twice. At first, she thought, because she was gawking at ducks. But her left wrist was tight—the price of lifting weights. She refocused on body position, her style and rhythm, and quickly settled into a solid, efficient stroke and return.

As she crossed Lake Union, a smile lit her face. She still had damned good form. She'd more than pass muster with any gawkers hanging around the passage between Lake Union and Lake Washington—the Montlake Cut someone had called it.

Through the Cut, it was a straight shot to Frank Leit's house, a half-mile at most. And minutes later, the scull settled a hundred yards offshore. The house sat nearly fifty yards back from the lake. And, theory confirmed, the house definitely had a daylight basement with French doors out to a terrace. The two upper stories both had decks overhanging the yard.

If only the Planning Commission had had architectural drawings. Three floors meant more space to search, more places to hide, more options for security but she'd manage it when the time came. A few more strokes east, she eased up and swung the scull around to face north. The light had shifted—and she got it, a big cloud bank was rolling in from the west. So there'd be more chop going back, definitely more than when she'd started out. The chop would affect speed. But the wind might die down. If it didn't, no problem. She'd competed in way tougher conditions in Poughkeepsie. She re-angled the scull and dug out her binoculars. In case she'd been noticed, she made a point of checking out the football stadium and the Montlake houses south of the university before refocusing on the Frank Leit house.

There were lights on across the main floor of the house, but no one in sight. So presumably Ben Leit, was there all right. The place had enough doors—the deck, the patio and a door on the west side of the house—she could take her pick when the time came. As for the yard, the over-height fences and bushes to the east and west would make the access a breeze. And the long slope of the yard—a vertical drop, maybe fifty feet from the terrace down to the water—that might come in handy if she needed to split on the run. As for the flower beds, she could hurdle them easily.

She counted six flood lights in the yard. She'd have to think whether it was worth it to take them out. The good news, there was an old dock. Weathered and likely slick but she could tie up there after dark. There or at the boathouse. Curious about that boathouse though...no sign of a boat. The crap hung on the side must've been somebody's idea of decor.

The boat house would give her better cover than the dock. The question was whether or not it was viable. She'd need to tie off and make her way into the yard without bringing the damned thing crashing down.

She'd check it out on her way in.

The downpour took her by surprise. She stowed her binoculars, brought the scull about and squinted into the wind. Definitely wind, not just rain, and it was a full-on storm. The chop rocked the scull ominously and she hit out across the open water.

Speed would be key now. But bring it on! She hit out for the Cut, Lake Union, then up the Ship's Canal. Her deep-throated laugh pealed out across the lake and lost itself in the wind. A tough fight was what she loved most. Nothing could ever beat her. For damned sure, not some piddling rainstorm.

Chapter 39

Ben got back to his car just as the rain started. He glanced out over the Sound. On a good day, the view toward Bainbridge Island knocked him flat. But this was not good a day. The weather had shifted from light rain to a deluge that drummed against the roof of the car. He leaned back in his seat, closed his eyes for a second, then dug the papers Halliday had given him out of his jacket pocket.

Truth was, he couldn't concentrate for thinking his dad had died because of Halliday's drive to get even with a bunch of in-laws at Rex Sports. What kind of a man sets his family up to be ruined and humiliated? Because that's what a federal investigation would bring.

It was obvious why Halliday had picked his dad to bring down Rex Sports, though. People would listen to his dad. Because his dad wasn't just a former congressman, he was still a really big deal. Christ, one look at his dad's blog and Halliday must've figured he'd found the perfect pawn.

Lightning—just a few blocks to the north—and the temperature inside Ben's car plummeted. He pulled out onto the street. He'd gone maybe four blocks when... *Was that Halliday's niece?* The rain was sheeting so hard, it was impossible to be sure. He parked in the bus zone and rolled down the passenger side window.

She was huddled in the far corner of the bus shelter

with an enormous backpack sitting next to her and, by her feet, a suitcase big enough she could've crawled inside it, with the backpack, and still had room. He'd be an idiot to spend one more minute around these people. But he couldn't leave her there.

He had to yell just to be heard over the storm. "You okay?"

She looked up, then straight at him—her face a mix of frustration, fatigue, leftover anger. She huddled a little tighter in her big gray puffy coat, but no answer.

It wasn't gonna work for him to sit in the car and yell at her. He climbed out and stepped inside the bus shelter. "Take a look." He pointed back out to the Sound. "In five minutes, it's gonna get way worse."

She craned her neck to see, then peered down the empty street. "I don't need to be rescued."

"Wouldn't think of it," he said and moved her huge suitcase so he could step a little further into the shelter. "But—and it's just a thought—it is warmer in the car."

Once he got her stuff loaded and had climbed in behind the wheel, he could see how pale she was. She must be running on empty. And maybe worse, she looked wet clear through. He found a clean towel in the backseat and handed it to her.

"You missed lunch." He mentioned a couple of his regular places.

"I'm not very good company."

"No problem. I've got the perfect place," he said. "And it's not a sports bar."

Fifteen minutes later, they made dash from the parking garage and ducked under the awning at the 5-Spot. Its windows were mostly steamed over, people inside more like ghosts than the usual trendy Queen

Anne crowd. Thanks to the weather, business looked slow. The 5-Spot's head man, Gib, met them at the door and showed them to Ben's table in the back corner. Mimi hung her coat and slid onto the banquette facing the street.

"So, what happened?" Ben said.

Her enormous brown eyes got even wider. "You were there."

"Your uncle said somebody tried to kill you."

Mimi pushed away her menu and, for a couple of seconds, just sat there. Then she ducked her head and slid a sideways glance at Gib. There it was, a bruise he hadn't noticed earlier, as big as the one on his dad, but lower, and maybe it spread down onto her shoulder, he couldn't tell.

Finally, she said, "You know, when you go to explain what happened, and it's something awful...talking about it just makes it worse."

"Right," he said.

She looked nostalgic, no, reflective, or...he couldn't put a name to it, how her eyes were sad, how she hadn't quite looked back at him but her mouth had tightened. Maybe she meant it to be a smile but if she had, it hadn't worked.

"My dad did not kill your father," she said.

"What makes you so certain?"

She slowly unfurled her napkin. "You think that because your father was going after Rex, that my dad is behind what happened. He's not." She looked up at him and blinked. "What happened to me and what happened to your dad are connected."

Ben tried to make sense of her, of the way she was looking at him, defiant, certain, but not angry. He said,

"Your dad's not behind it, and that's it?" *Wrong tactic.* The look on her face...he'd expected her to say *Are you nuts or just a jerk?* But all she did was stare him down.

"Sorry," he said, "I didn't mean to be snarky. But...okay, let's say it's not your dad. What about Ted? Or are you gonna say it's not your uncle either?"

She made a little popping sound with her lips. "Ted sees himself as a knight in shining armor. Ever since I can remember. He rescues people. What's legal—no, what's righteous—has always been more important than profit. His *doing the right thing* is what got him cross-wise with the Board at Rex. That's why he admired your dad—another man who did the honorable thing. Uncle Ted's pompous. I know that. But he would never murder anyone."

She folded her hands on the tabletop. "Here's what you don't know. Last Friday I uncovered a huge cache of stolen emails on a computer server at Rex. Your dad's emails were part of it, along with some other stuff. I reported what I found to Legal and asked the best man in IT to track down the hacker. I trust Raj, absolutely."

"So it is Rex."

She tilted her head to the side, like maybe. "It also could be somebody in Dubrovnik. Hackers use whatever computer system works for what they're doing. Sometimes it's a government system, sometimes a big corporation. They use big systems as a turnaround spot in order to lose somebody that's tracking them. Another thing they do is store what they don't want to get caught with on some gigantic server—chances are, it'll never get discovered because of the volume of activity. Maybe it is somebody at Rex. But it's equally possible that somebody has hacked their way into the Rex admin server and is using it. At this point, we just can't tell."

Their food showed up. She may have been tiny, but she ate like a linebacker. Make that a left tackle.

She didn't talk and eat. Once she finished, she carefully placed her knife and fork across her plate, leaned back and watched him consume the last of his cornbread. "Ted said you've set yourself up as a target."

He picked up his mug and—coffee was cold. "The police were saying home invasion. Which is wrong but they won't listen to me. Dad was working on this story—"

"About Rex, I know."

"I got his notes from his computer guy, but the fire destroyed his research." Okay, he was lying. But he wasn't about to tell her what he'd found at the lake house. "Thing is, I can't get at his emails and until I do—"

She was shaking her head like what? Like he was stupid? Like he'd crossed some invisible line? What was it about computer geeks?

"Assuming you know your dad's password—if you opened an email somebody sent to him, it would change the metadata. You'd lose the sender's identity, their real identity." And she launched into a mind-bending explanation.

It was the expert talking. Even if he couldn't follow most of it, it was fascinating to see how she blossomed as she talked him through the protocol she'd used to uncover the hacker's hidden file on the Rex system. Too bad he couldn't hire her to help with the stuff he'd discovered at the lake house. But he was not gonna be responsible for something happening to her when his dad's killer came after him.

Over peach cobbler and gallons of coffee, they talked it through again—detail by detail, the timing of everything that happened, including what they didn't know, but maybe could find out.

By four o'clock, he realized he was telling her about the documents in the lake house party room, and how he figured those documents, plus his dad's emails, were gonna lead him to the killer—exactly what he'd vowed not to discuss with anybody.

"That's why I did the TV interview," he said. "When I couldn't get what I needed without an expert, I figured, at least I could tempt Dad's killer into action."

Mimi pushed her bangs out of her eyes. "Might work, going it alone. You're pretty big. Big enough maybe you could fight him off. But maybe not. Maybe you need a sidekick. You know, even Batman had Robin."

She was smiling. It was an extraordinary smile. Wet hair and dumpy sweater aside, she was really beautiful. Tiny and not his type, but she could've been a knockout if she wanted.

"I'm the one who actually can help you," she said. "I know whatever you need to know about Rex and, trust me, I can take care of your email problem."

"It isn't your fight," he said.

"True. Your father's death is not my fight. But the killer is after me now."

It was still pouring outside. They ran the whole way to his car.

"Let me help," she said climbing in. "I'd rather be

252

hunting for whoever killed your father than jumping out of my skin every time I hear a strange noise."

"Too risky."

"More risky than getting knocked out and left to freeze to death at the bottom of a cliff?" She made her point by snapping her seatbelt into place.

He looked over. She had that wide-eyed stare going. He could feel himself giving in. But he couldn't be there every second. If something happened to her, it'd be on him. "I can't," he said.

"Yes, you can," she said. "If I had a safe place to work and the right tools, I could nail down whoever it was tried to kill me. And from there, I could prove they went after your Dad. Look—" she twisted herself around in the seat, pushed at his shoulder and waited until he gave her his full attention. "I don't know squat about football. My sport was gymnastics. Most of the time, when you're out there, you're on your own. But sometimes you need a spotter. I think it must be like that when you're hunting a killer too. So…let me be your spotter. You can be mine. Okay?"

Every damned day in rehab—*Stay away from entanglements.* But Mimi Fitzroy wasn't an entanglement, she was an expert. He started the car. "Where to?"

She turned on that smile again and he got who she looked like. Why hadn't he seen it earlier?

Chapter 40

Mimi piled out of Ben's car and glanced at her watch. Nearly 5:00 p.m. What on earth had possessed her to push her way into Ben Leit's business? She didn't really need his help to unravel what was going on in the Rex system. And she didn't need some big-time football hero to rescue her from a fight with her uncle.

She was exhausted and what she needed was to sleep. Since her escape at TK and Connie's, she'd slept on two planes, a few hours more where her aunt and uncle were staying, and now what he kept referring to as *the Laurelhurst House?* As if she had any idea, really, where she was. She should have said no to lunch, thanked Ben and asked for a ride to a hotel.

Instead, she was standing in the same kind of upscale neighborhood as her family lived in. She followed him inside and waited as he raced around— alarm, lights, apologies for the dust and cold. He stopped for a moment, called her into the living room, then pressed something that transformed the far wall.

She couldn't help but stare at the view. Forty feet, or maybe more, of glass doors opened onto a deck overlooking what Ben had already explained was Lake Washington. It was beautiful, even in the rainstorm; she could hardly think how it must be in the summer. For a second, she almost felt like she was back in the Bay Area.

Ben was rattling on about growing up in the house.

Suddenly, she was freezing. She couldn't stop shivering…anybody with a boat and binoculars could spot them. "Close the drapes," she said. "Or whatever they are."

She heard her voice break. Ben had too, judging by the fact he stopped talking and turned back to her. He gave her a look, like *where'd that come from?* She hadn't seen a double-take like that since her brother Jamie.

"Just…close them," she said and kept telling herself *you're safe, you're safe, they don't know where you are.*

Ben squeezed the control gadget again and the expanse of glass shifted back into what looked like a solid white wall.

"For anybody outside, we're targets," she said.

"Sorry. I should've thought." He motioned her over to a couple of mid-century modern chairs in front of the fireplace. He flopped into one, stretched his long legs out and nodded to the white panels that blocked out the view of the lake. "Better?"

Was she better? There hadn't been time to think about it really.

He stretched forward, put out an arm and patted the chair opposite him. The deep, wide seat reminded her of Robert Addison's over-sized furniture. Instead of joining him, she picked up a pillow, tossed it on the raised hearth of the fireplace and parked herself there.

She leaned forward, bracing her elbows on her knees. "I won't be a target again," she said.

"I don't want you to be one." He drew in his legs, then rotated his chair so he faced her. "If you were serious about helping... I was thinking we could work here. You could stay here, hide out." When she didn't answer right away, he flashed a grin—part *we can get through this,* and part *it'll be fun.*

She suspected he was good at that grin. It made him look younger than he was. A combination of sweet boy and badass that the other girls at her boarding school had always found irresistible.

"I'll be staying over at my condo," he said.

That stopped her for just a minute. Local TV had broadcast their interview with him just that morning. She shot him the kind of skeptical look she normally saved for Raj. "After your TV thing—that was over at your condo wasn't it? Pretty easy to stalk you, don't you think?"

He grinned again, but more like drawing his dad's killer out was going to be fun. That sure as heck wasn't how she saw it.

He said, "If you're thinking about how I'll get away, I may have been away from Seattle for ten years, but I can still drive these streets blindfolded." As if she knew Seattle, he rambled on about neighborhoods he knew, old watering holes, pizza parlors. In the end, she had to agree, anyone stalking him would have to be an expert to keep up with him.

As for staying there... If she stayed, and she wasn't sure she could, would it feel safer for him to be in the house, or for her to be there alone? She wished she had time and quiet to think whether his plan to lure the killer was as solid as he made it sound. Because it felt way too risky and she'd always avoided risk. And yet she'd jumped at the idea of helping him. In fact, over the past week she'd taken a whole lot of risks. And that scared the daylights out of her.

Ben stood out of his chair and headed for the foyer. "Come see what I found yesterday."

She followed him downstairs to what must've been a party room in the old days. And, wouldn't you know, there was another triple set of sliding glass that opened to the back yard. This time, though, Ben was quick to pull the drapes.

She squatted and opened a box marked *Internal*. For more than twenty minutes she pawed through the contents. Then she moved on, one by one, to the other cartons. Seventy-three of them had Rex corporate documents. Everything from email printouts to confidential memos.

At some point she shifted to sitting cross-legged on the floor.

Hovering over her, Ben fiddled with boxes and fetched and carried them whenever she asked. All the while, he kept up a running commentary on what he had gleaned from his dad's notes. Eventually she couldn't take in more and certainly couldn't look at more paper. She sat back on her heels and ended up staring at the pile of rumpus room furniture that'd been shoved to the back wall. The whole thing made her head spin. Her Uncle Ted had been the one person she could trust, and he'd turned out to be as nuts as the rest of her family. It wasn't like she could pick up a phone and call her Dad and say she'd seen the proof. But given all this, how could he claim that Rex was not breaking the law?

"What'd you find?" Ben had squatted down in front of her and obviously was trying to read upside-down.

She couldn't even put her worries into cogent sentences. So how could she synthesize what Ben Leit had in this basement? It was too much and her brain kept zinging from whether and how much her dad was involved, to what would happen to her Aunt and Uncle, to how safe Raj Banerjee might be with his little illegal family secret that he didn't know she knew about. The last thing she wanted was to ruin her family. Or Raj, or for that matter, the stupid company.

In the end, all she could come up with was that if helping Ben was what she had to do to trap the man who'd tried to kill her, if it meant proving that Rex was breaking the law...well, so be it.

Ben plopped another box in front of her. But she needed to stop.

She stood and dusted her gritty hands against her pants. "I get it you've been reading and summarizing. But there are ways to get all this into a database, you know. We could find what we need a lot faster if we did."

She needed to wash up. Was there paper? Something they could write on?

By the time she met Ben at the kitchen table, he'd closed the blinds, come up with pencils, a partly used pad of graph paper and made tea. She said something, really to herself, about the precipitating event.

Ben leaned across the table. His eyes looked alive, excited, like he couldn't wait. "The precipitating event... You mean, what happened that set everything in motion."

"Exactly," she said. A little surprised that, maybe, Ben Leit was smarter than she'd thought. Maybe she could work with him.

She picked up a pencil, doodling, making a list of what she knew about the ghost file, what she knew about Frank Leit.

Ben was tapping a finger on her list. "Maybe it's not *what had happened* but what was *about* to happen. What do you think? At least, that's where I keep going," he said. "I keep coming back to...if it's true that Dad was about to talk with the U.S. Attorney's office. And somebody found out. You heard your uncle. If it's not that, then I don't know. But it must be in the boxes, or his emails."

She looked up from her list. *U.S. Attorney, yes. Yes.*

He had gray eyes. She hadn't noticed before, not really.

He shifted in his chair. "Because Dad's killer was looking for something. He ransacked Dad's files. He dumped everything in Dad's office on the floor. He went through everything, even the DVDs and CDs." Ben scooted closer to the table and went over his story again. As he wrapped up his description, the sound of a car outside cut through the neighborhood. He peered out the blind, then turned back to her. "So, if I'm right, where does that put us?"

Mimi started a new list. Beginning with the rest of the equipment they would need if they were building a database that they could both work on.

"I can help with that," Ben said and pulled out his phone.

She took a breath then held it. Having everything they needed would get them going sooner, which was good. But involving somebody else? And coming up with equipment? It committed her. Did she really want to tie herself to Ben Leit?

Zack Berman must've answered on the first ring. Ben listened, then turned to Mimi. "Is tomorrow morning okay?"

Ben told Berman it was a go and pocketed the phone. He was halfway to the door, watching her expectantly. "Bringing the bags in then? Are you really okay with it?"

She must have hesitated because he launched into a spiel about how safe the house was, the security service, the neighborhood. Still, she couldn't help feeling like whatever she said there was too much hope loaded on her answer. Because of it, she almost said she wasn't. But in the end, she said yes, she was fine with staying there. And she was.

"Nobody knows I'm in Seattle. Let alone in some house on the lake. And the more I think about it...I think we can help each other. Besides, if push comes to shove, I'm pretty good with my Glock."

The news she had a pistol clearly startled him. "How'd you get a gun on the airplane?"

She considered lying, but no. "My lawyer has friends in very high places."

He blinked and gave her a second look. "Just don't shoot me," he said. And there was that grin again.

Chapter 41

Back at her South Lake Union hotel, Thorsen kicked off her shoes, sat down to the take-out dinner she'd picked up, and checked out the local news. By the time they got to the sports guy, she was ready to turn the TV off. But then, would you believe it? Ben Leit was giving an interview to some local sports reporter.

She caught the rest of 'Our Guy Ben Leit' on her phone and, once the show moved on to some basketball player, she replayed what she'd captured and focused on what she could see of the background.

Ben Leit had a pretty plush setup going, wherever he was living—what looked like a million-dollar view, and inside, high end granite and glass, a couple of big paintings. Two or three times, the interviewer said *condo,* so not the house on Laurelhurst. Or were they saying *condo* to hide Leit's location? Whatever...the background was water. And twice, she thought she saw a float plane. There hadn't been planes when she'd been over at the lake house.

That water...it could be Lake Washington or maybe Lake Union? There was too damned much water around to make sense of that and it didn't matter. Her gut said the key was that damned house. She took one more look at the Leit video, grabbed her jacket and headed down to her car. Back to Laurelhurst. With luck, there'd be a car in the driveway, or lights on, or whatever.

She fought commuter traffic to the closest bridge, then had to wait while it lifted for some boat, crossed through the University District and finally landed in Laurelhurst. A quick drive past the house…there was a Lexus parked in the driveway. In the low light, she couldn't make the color, but it was mid-tone for sure.

She whipped around the odd-shaped block and came back with her lights on high beam for the license plate and slowed as she came by the house. Once she got a couple of blocks past the place, she stopped to key the plate number into her phone.

She could've headed back to her hotel and traced the car just with what she had. But why miss the opportunity? Circling back, she found a parking spot off the intersection at 43rd. She checked the time thinking she'd give it an hour. It took less than half that for the Lexus to roll past her.

She tossed her phone into the passenger seat and pulled out. It had been a guy in the Lexus, she got that much. He turned left at 45th. She pulled out into traffic two cars behind and smiled. *Ben Leit.*

She was good tailing cars. She'd made a game of it with Jamie. When they were just getting to know one another, they ripped their way around Minneapolis tracking whoever. Sometimes Jamie in one car and she'd take the other. It scared the shit out of the natives.

That was part of the fun.

Through the University District, anyone else would've been trapped by a bus, but not Thorsen. She kept an eye on the Lexus, pushed her way into traffic, a quick left on Eleventh and down, ripping south and west, under the I-5 bridge, still west, down and west to the Fremont Bridge and across the Ship Canal. She almost lost him when he headed up into the curlicue streets of Queen Anne Hill. And did miss him on a turn but caught up as he disappeared down a side street. *Dead end. Christ.*

She blew past his street, hit the brake and shoehorned her car under a massive tree, hoping she didn't have to make a quick exit. After a couple of minutes scouting the area on foot, she climbed a steep embankment to a spot overlooking the condo parking area. Leit's car was right below her.

The bank was slick with old leaves and soaked with rain. But she settled herself on the ground anyway. Not exactly what she'd figured on for cover, but *see, don't be seen.* And other than wrecking her coat, this was more fun than she'd had in a long time. The cold air in her lungs left her feeling like she was waking up after a long sleep.

She was so ready for this guy.

She dragged her phone out of her coat pocket and re-read an AP story about Leit leaving the Giants. She thought she'd seen it before, and it was crap if you took it for the skinny. Nobody dumps their hot player mid-season because of an on-again, off-again shoulder. For damned sure, Maggie Kuykendahl would not be that hairbrained.

Thumbing farther down the string of stories, she spotted something she hadn't connected with earlier. Out of Houston. It implied that Ben Leit left football because of a concussion. Now that was more like it. When the time came, she'd keep concussions in mind.

Five or six cars pulled into the parking lot, but nobody seemed to be leaving. Thorsen shifted her browser through her international switchback protocol, moved on into the Rex server, to Mimi Fitzroy's company emails—nothing there, in fact, nothing outgoing for two days.

She was about to check the StarTrib for news that Mimi's body had been found when she spotted Ben Leit standing on a balcony. Condo or apartment, it was two stories up from the parking lot. He hesitated, went back inside, then reappeared carrying a bag. He started down the stairs and in seconds, she was off the hill and sprinting for her car. Once his Lexus slid past her, she eased out her own car onto the street and dropped a half-block behind him.

Leit was still waiting for a break in the traffic when she rolled up behind him at the stop sign at Aurora. *Too close.* In case he could spot her under the streetlights, she adjusted her rearview mirror and faked a lipstick repair. Leit shot away downhill toward Westlake. A minute later she dropped into traffic behind him. Just past Mercer, he pulled into a South Lake Union parking garage. She dogged the brake, pulled into the right lane and headed around the block. Two minutes later she pulled into the same garage. One look at the wall advertising and she was good. She knew this gym.

At the front desk, she dug out the alternate ID and credit card she'd used for Scottsdale and enrolled for a two-month guest membership.

Tom, the membership clerk, shot her a promising smile and entered the personal details for Merilee Dawson into their computer—details for a woman who lived in Lancaster County, Pennsylvania.

Tom handed Thorsen back her cards, said thanks, smiled again and added, "Merilee."

Thorsen pocketed her cards and returned the smile. "It's Lee," she said. "I've never been much of a Merilee."

Lee it was. She needed gear, she said. Her stuff was back in Pennsylvania. Tom was quick to say the guest shop could help her with that. And she needed a water. That too, he said.

Workout gear in hand, Thorsen headed for the changing rooms, stripped down, pulled on a snug little T-shirt, shorts, and slapped a support strap on her wrist. According to the wall clock, Ben Leit had been at it for eighteen minutes.

Beyond the changing rooms, a wide stairway led up to an open mezzanine. Just like Minneapolis, they'd located the weight paraphernalia on the ground floor. Spin rooms, yoga classes and the cardio setup were upstairs.

With the fluorescent lights all on high, a sound system blasting the usual pump-it-up music, and the thump and clank of weights—it was all just like home. And how convenient she could warm up, scout the main floor from above, and get a handle on where Ben Leit was working. She headed up and passed him on the stairwell landing—much better looking than the photos after the Giants dropped him, even freckles...not too many but...

What the hell? He hadn't noticed her? Now that was a first, she must be slipping.

She paused, looked after him like she knew his face from the papers, then continued on upstairs. Ben Leit was going to be fun.

She chose an elliptical trainer with the best view of the ground floor strength equipment where Leit was setting up. She boosted the resistance on the machine and hit her stride. It felt good to push. It felt even better watching him work his way through routines for his forearms and biceps.

Once he started shifting weights onto the carry pins for the leg press machine, she swung off the elliptical, toweled herself off and headed downstairs. The goal was to end up working next to him. *But let's take our time about it.* She started a few stations away from him on a hammer press. He shifted from leg presses to free weights, waved off the gym's spotter and went to work. It looked like eighty pounds on the bar. Not much for a man his size. But he went at it slow—all the better to do the work.

She had to respect that.

When he shifted from free weights to a weight machine, she headed over to the twenty-pound dumbbells and laid back on a work bench with her legs spread. Just as Ben had done, she worked the weights slow and steady 'til she could feel the stretch in her pecs.

One by one, the gym rats slowly walked by her. Two of them actually stopped to chat. She stuck with her routine, maybe letting the weights smack at the top of their arc. Enough that the guys found something else to do at the front desk.

But from Leit, not even a glance in her direction.

She finished two sets, sat up and stretched her neck. Once she replaced her free weights on the rack, she strolled over to the weight system where Leit was working and stopped next to his left knee, barely looking at him. No smile. No hostility. She was just another guy there to work.

"You mind?" She nodded toward the weight machine one over from his. He looked up, focused on her.

"No problem," he said. But his gaze slid away as if she were invisible.

Now that never happened to her.

She pushed into the click and shush of her routine but kept the poundage lower than her usual. No point in advertising she could bench press over 220. She was in the middle of her second set when Leit moved on. No *see ya,* no casual wave. What was it she'd read? Married for eight years, no kids. No mention of a woman. Was he queer? He wouldn't be the first one in the NFL that was for sure. If he was, that would certainly put a kink in her plan. But he hadn't given any of the men a look either.

Screw it. She knew where she could catch up with him. She moved through the rest of what would have been her regular routine, showered, changed and headed down to the parking garage.

When the elevator doors opened, that empty-garage shiver ran her arms—not a quarter full. And after the ultra-bright gym, the blue pools of light against the concrete emptiness felt like she was stepping onto the set for a thriller.

Safety first, she checked the shadows and listened. The scuff of her shoes echoed, then a car backed out. Not Leit's, it was a PT Cruiser rolling past her...the woman in the apparel shop. Then, across the garage, she heard a car start up.

She knew that car.

She headed over thinking how she had to play it and caught him just as he backed out of his parking space. She rapped on his window.

"Excuse me." She leaned in, softened her voice, and laid a hand on the open car window to keep him there.

His hand shifted on the steering wheel. He put his car into park and focused on her. And, once he smiled, she got it, he was beautiful. Beautiful in the way some male models she'd worked with were beautiful. Testosterone rolled off of them in waves—everything about them, about Leit, incredibly masculine but more perfect than any man you saw on the street. His dad had been handsome enough, but Ben Leit was something else entirely.

"I don't mean to bother you," she said. His skin was smooth as a trout's. "But aren't you Ben Leit?" She turned on the smile in her eyes, that was always what got the photographers. "You are, aren't you?" She took back her hand as if she hadn't realized she'd touched his car. She forced an obvious swallow. "I don't mean to be one of those *fans*, but I so loved watching you play. I still get to Giants games sometimes, but it's not the same without you." She took a step back from his car. "So…anyway, you were incredible."

He looked embarrassed. "Thank you," he said.

She delivered one more flash of her money smile and turned. A little wave at him and she started toward her car. Five steps and she dropped her car key and managed to kick it under a Jeep. "Damn!" She squatted and was reaching behind the tire when he showed up and snagged the key for her.

"Have time for a coffee?" he said.

Chapter 42

Ben was feeling pretty good by noon on Wednesday. Lee Dawson had been something to behold and then, thanks to Mimi, they'd completed a first pass-through of the document boxes in the downstairs party room. They'd piled what they'd reviewed onto every table, chair, the long sofa and most of the open floor space of the room. By one o'clock, they had made it out front and were handing off eight top-priority boxes to the company that would scan everything for the database.

They were figuring how to divide up the next chunk of work when Bobby Joe Jackson pulled up. He parked his truck out in front of the Laurelhurst house and strolled over to where Ben was standing on the driveway. Ben couldn't help thinking, it didn't matter that he liked Bobby Joe. Didn't matter Bobby Joe used to play in the NFL. When your AA sponsor shows up uninvited, it's never a good sign.

He glanced at Mimi, back to Bobby Joe and said, "Any other time, Bobby Joe. But I'm hip deep in a project. I can't explain except—"

"Right," Bobby Joe grinned. "Swamped. I know how that is." The big man raised his eyebrows like did Ben think he could sell that story. *Tied up* wasn't gonna cut it in the excuse department. "You know the drill, Ben. It's time to start working on Step Four. This is one of those meetings you need to be in on."

From the look on Mimi's face, she got it—he was gonna have to duck out for a while. "No problem," she said and patted her hip. "Zack's coming at five. There's plenty to read. I can hold the fort 'til you're back."

Once they got the big red pickup headed out of Laurelhurst, Bobby Joe glanced over at Ben. "Tiny Walker, you remember him? He's not doing so good these days."

Ben stayed focused on the road. Sometimes Bobby Joe could be a royal pain. Why couldn't Step Four wait a few days? And what was so important about meeting with Tiny Walker?

"Your dad used to come with me when he was up here. Visits from anybody who played ball mean a lot to Tiny. You okay?"

Ben nodded. Of course he remembered Tiny Walker. Tiny'd played nose tackle for the Giants while his dad was still a wide receiver. His dad had said Tiny was the perfect lineman. Over three hundred pounds— which was big in those days—six-foot-two, durable and quick. "I saw him play once. I must've been six or seven. After the game, Dad introduced me. I thought Tiny Walker was as big as the Kodiak bear I'd seen at the Brooklyn Zoo. They had the same almost-yellow eyes. But Tiny had that big friendly face."

Silence for blocks. Then a rain squall turned a low spot on Rainier Avenue into a swimming pool and traffic slowed to a crawl past a line of people waiting for the light rail. When they passed through the old Columbia City neighborhood, Bobby Joe glanced over. "He doesn't talk much anymore so we'll need to carry the load. Keep the conversation to stories about old games—the funnier the better."

Ten minutes later, an aide answered the door.

Bobby Joe stopped beside the aide. "Malik, this is Ben Leit. How's Tiny doing today?"

Malik stepped aside. "About the same. He's been waiting for you."

Bobby Joe gave Malik's shoulder a tap and headed straight for a big leather chair parked in front of a wall of sliding glass doors.

Ben followed Bobby Joe into what must've been a family room. He sure never would've recognized the man in the chair as Tiny Walker. Nobody would. Tiny's head drooped a little to the left. And shook like he had Parkinson's. He was nothing but bones and loose skin. It was like he'd collapsed inside his body and what was left of him had collapsed into that leather chair. He couldn't weigh more than one-fifty.

Ben sucked in a little breath. Right then, he would've booked it out of there if he could've. But Tiny had fixed his yellow eyes on them and kept lifting his trembling hands up, trying to stand. How many bad hits had Tiny taken? Three or four a year? And Tiny'd played, what, eight or nine years? Did they even know about CTE then?

Tiny's struggle stopped as the aide got behind the cumbersome chair and shifted it more upright.

"Hey Buddy." Bobby Joe took hold of one of Tiny's hands and motioned for Ben to come closer. "How you doing today? Look who I got here. It's Frank Leit's boy, Ben. You remember Ben Leit. You've been watching him play for the Giants. Remember he had that bad shoulder?"

Ben stepped up to Tiny, careful to look him square

in the eye. He caught Tiny's right hand mid-spasm—it felt like he was holding a bird, like the hand of an old, old man. And what was Tiny, fifty-five?

Taking his cue from Bobby Joe, Ben pulled up a chair and slid it close to where Bobby Joe had parked himself on the sofa. Bobby Joe talked about everything from the rain and the day's traffic to what he'd be doing that night. It was almost like listening to one of the guys doing the color commentary on a football broadcast—a few facts, a little news, a couple of lame jokes and carloads of memories.

Bobby Joe was great doing the visit. But Ben just couldn't think what to say. The doctors in Boston had told him they couldn't be sure about CTE. That was probably what they told all the guys that got sent to Boston. *We can't be sure. But you need to avoid blows to your head. We can't say for sure, but don't take chances. Oh, and can you please sign this agreement that your brain can go to our brain bank after you die?*

Nobody could be sure. But wasn't *he* gonna end up just like Tiny? And every time his dad had visited Tiny, wasn't his dad thinking the same thing?

Laughing...

Ben got it: he'd lost the thread of the conversation. He managed to pick it up as Bobby Joe launched into one more story about some game. Even before Bobby Joe got to the punch line, Tiny was hunched over making little heh-heh, heh-hehs, one side of his mouth up in a drunken grin. His face was wet with tears.

A lot of war stories got told, a lot of names got shared. Tiny nodded to every one of them, then did that drooling half smile. And Bobby Joe just kept it up, finally telling one about how Frank Leit had mowed down an official in the semi-finals.

Tiny mumbled a "Good...Frank." His voice was feather-soft, but the words were clear.

Ben could barely swallow. How the hell were they gonna leave this poor guy stuck here? He should've guessed.

The aide showed up in the doorway and Bobby Joe made a production of looking at his watch. Then he leaned forward and put his hand on Tiny's chest. "Gotta go buddy. But whatcha got goin' for supper tonight? Something good?"

Tiny looked up. First at Bobby Joe, then at the aide. "Barbecue pork, baked beans and salad," the aide said.

"Yeah?" Bobby Joe's face split with a grin. "Well, damned if that don't sound good. Wish I could swing it to come back for that." He stood and leaned over the recliner and gave Tiny's chest a couple of taps. "But I'll see you tomorrow if that's okay."

Tiny managed to lift his right arm like goodbye. Then he gave them both a look—*don't go.* It was as if something struck Ben in the chest and went on like waves out and out.

The whole way back to Ben's place, neither one of them spoke. For his part, Ben was too sick, too pissed at Bobby Joe, to say anything.

Bobby Joe pulled the truck up in front of the Laurelhurst house and turned in his seat to face Ben. "Okay... *We can't be sure.* They said something like that, didn't they? *We can't be sure* but no more football for you? They said maybe ten years, five of them good and then... That's what they told me."

Ben tried to get past the lump in his throat. He

looked down at his shoes.

"I'm on year eight," Bobby Joe said. "It still gives me a jolt when I can't think straight. But you move on."

Finally, Ben looked over. "You think—"

Bobby Joe shook his head. "I think nobody can be sure. We had a good run, both of us. All they said was don't get your head bashed, right? So, don't. I think it makes sense to buy a one-story house like Tiny's on the just-in-case. Set up a trust. But then live your life like you're good to a hundred. For all you know, you are."

Chapter 43

Ben wasn't ready to face Mimi. Not after Tiny. He let himself in the Laurelhurst House as quietly as he could. Then slipped down the stairs, dodged out the side door and headed down through the yard to the dock. Naturally, he slipped and nearly fell on his ass right as he stepped out on the old wood planking, but no way was a slick dock keeping him from walking on out to the end.

It was the best place on Lake Washington—the black shapes of the city to the south and west, the shadows coming off the bridge and crossing the lake, the trails of light. It was the time of day when the last of the sun drifted away on the kayakers' wakes.

He zipped his jacket against the cold and took in the view—Kirkland to Bellevue, Mercer Island to Madison Park, to the U… It never ceased to amaze him. How many times had he stood out there with his dad?

The sky to the west rolled up into cloud, making it too cold to stay out on the point. He headed in, re-locked the side door, and glanced into the family room—no Mimi. Stepping behind the bar… Did any of it really make a difference if he was gonna end up like Tiny? He leaned against the wall. He'd never guessed about Bobby Joe. His head felt like it was full of cheese.

It wasn't like he reached for the bottle, he was just

holding it—his mom's drink, Crown Royal Reserve Canadian whiskey. Never more than one, she always said. She always smelled like flowers. He never could decide what kind. At least she'd never know what happened.

He was looking for a glass when Mimi walked in and stared at him like an owl. He replaced the bottle on the shelf and stepped away.

"I saw you out at the dock," she said. "You okay?"

When he said he was fine, she motioned him over to a worktable and spread out a three-page chart. "I want you to look at something."

Pointing and explaining as she went, she tried to talk him through what she'd done, how far she'd gotten searching the first four thousand documents. He nodded, looking wherever her finger touched down, but all he could think was how much he still missed his mom, and how many things his dad had never told him, and his afternoon with Bobby Joe, and how it'd felt taking Tiny's hand in his own.

Mimi took a step back, knitting her eyebrows. "I thought you didn't drink."

"I don't. It was Mom's. I was just…" He licked his lower lip and it hit him, he was sweating. "Wanna help toss this stuff down the drain?"

As the last of his folks' liquor disappeared down the laundry room sink, Mimi rubbed the side of her nose. "Okey dokey." She pressed her lips together, then did that pop sound she did when she was cutting him off on something. "How long's it been since you hit the gym? Because…I could be wrong, but you look like you need to. Anyway, that's my antidote when I can't get it together. And if a workout isn't right, then a steam. Or a massage."

"No, I need you to show me how to work the database."

"Gimme a break," she said. "I can handle things here 'til Zack gets us the rest of our load files. Take a couple of hours. Hit the gym. Wear yourself out. Then pick up something to eat from Whole Foods. Cause if you don't get out of here, I'll have to fix something for you. And like I said before, I'm a terrible cook."

Chapter 44

Mimi watched Ben's car back out of the driveway. She closed the front door and re-set the alarm. Tomorrow she'd ask Ben to park the car in the garage. No point in advertising he was spending time there. She stepped into the kitchen, grabbed a Greek yogurt and ended up leaning her back against the refrigerator, staring at the chair where Ben usually sat.

Thirty minutes ago, she could have stripped herself naked and danced all around that family room. She very much doubted he would have noticed. He'd looked terrible. Unfocused and gray, like he'd had a full-on stress attack. Which didn't make sense given he'd been fine five hours earlier. Was it something that—what was his name? Bobby Joe had said? Or maybe it was just hitting him about his dad. How long had it been, a week since his dad died? She shook her head no; his father hadn't just died. He'd been murdered. What did something like *that* do to you?

She barely knew Ben. But it didn't make sense— that much change in one day? It had to be something more than losing his dad. She'd lost her mother. She knew that feeling. This felt different. Like something really bad happened. Like he was hiding something.

It was ridiculous, of course, to be psychoanalyzing him. And she tried to put it aside, tried to work. But she could not let it go. Something was wrong with him.

And as far as she could see, it had to be something big. Because she'd set her chart up so it was easy to make sense of. He should have gobbled it up, at least been interested. Yesterday he was chomping at the bit. Suddenly he doesn't ask one question? *Back to work!*

Once she set her own system loading documents, she parked herself in front of Ben's system and opened the internet browser. She typed *Ben Leit football.*

Two or three Seattle stories, all versions of *Ben's Back.* Then a bunch of AP items about Ben being dropped by the Giants; retiring because of his shoulder. He hadn't said anything about his shoulder when he was moving boxes.

Back to the browser. This time she typed, *Ben Leit football shoulder.*

Zillions of stories confirmed his shoulder injury. But that was almost two years ago, and he'd been playing well right up to when he retired. She wasn't buying it. Why wasn't Ben playing football anymore?

Back to the browser...*Ben Leit scandal...* Nothing.

Okey dokey. How about *Ben Leit drugs.* Nothing.

But he had looked at that bottle like it was the first meal he'd had in a month. But then he'd poured it all out? *Alcohol?* Nada.

What about an injury but not his shoulder? *Ben Leit injury.*

All those zillions of reports about his shoulder were there, but there were a couple of reports like *Ben Leit Out Cold.* One of them included a photo. Not only out cold, according to the article, he'd been carted off the field. And three weeks after the photo, a Houston reporter mentioned Ben Leit in a story on CTE.

Cripes. Why hadn't she put it together before?

Where had he gone with Bobby Joe? And how the heck was she going to talk to him about what really was wrong?

Chapter 45

Raj Banerjee pulled into the Rex administration building garage and parked in his usual spot. The half-lit gloom only added to the uneasy feeling in his gut. The General Counsel had called him. At home. On Thanksgiving morning. *I need you to come into my office.*

It had to be about Mimi.

General Counsel Addison met him in the atrium and escorted him into a small conference room. Rex Sports' Chief Executive Officer—the great David Fitzroy, himself—was standing next to a small conference table.

Raj had never met Mr. Fitzroy. But this man he was seeing was nothing like the man in the company's publicity photographs. This man needed a shower and shave. Better yet, a week's sleep. Was it possible that the publicity image was a product of Photoshop? Or perhaps Mr. Fitzroy also had been unprepared for the meeting.

Most certainly Raj was not pleased to be meeting the company's CEO while wearing a sweat-drenched undershirt. Perhaps Mr. Fitzroy was also.

Mr. Addison apologized for requesting him to come in on a holiday and pulled out a chair, asking him to join them at the small oval table. Raj sat.

Much too much courtesy. This had to be about

Mimi.

"I recommended to David that you join our discussions," Addison said and cleared his throat.

How was it Mr. Addison was speaking for them? Why was Mr. Fitzroy taking the back seat?

Addison leaned into the table. "You see, Mr. Banerjee, we have an emergency. There is every possibility that a lawsuit may be filed against the company. It represents the kind of conflict that could destroy everything we've built here at Rex. So, keep in mind that anything you say or hear in this meeting is covered by attorney-client privilege and should not be discussed with anyone other than us three. Understood?"

Raj nodded. Mimi would not be suing her father. At least he did not think so. If this was not about Mimi, it had to be the ghost file. And he had given his word to Mimi. If they spoke of the file, could he convince them of the lie she had given him?

Addison turned away to a credenza. "Then let's make sure our cell phones are off."

Raj did so and noticed that Mr. Fitzroy had not moved, that his face was tight as the head of a drum and the air around him looked gray and frozen. Was Mr. Fitzroy perhaps unwell?

Mr. Addison peered at Mr. Fitzroy, then distributed identical yellow tablets across the table and explained how their meeting should go. "At some point, Mr. Banerjee, we'll be asking you to coordinate our work with an outside law firm. But until that happens—"

"That will be in place by the end of next week," Mr. Fitzroy said.

"—Until the law firm is in place, I will be handling

matters. So, to business." Mr. Addison laid out his plan: nothing to be emailed, no electronic memo to the file, not even discussions by telephone except to confirm dates or times of meetings—and then, never mention the purpose of the meeting.

"And Mr. Banerjee, I need some answers. For a start, is there a way to tamper with a document that was created in the Rex system—tamper long after the document was created, I mean—is there a way to change, let's say, the author or the names of the people receiving the document... There is a way to do that, isn't there?"

No mention of hacking or the ghost file? For a moment Raj couldn't believe this man would ask such an obvious question. But then something in Mr. Addison's eyes...and Raj understood. Mr. Addison wanted him to educate Mr. Fitzroy.

Raj folded his hands on the tabletop and licked his lips. "I am answering you, *Yes.* Even if you were not the document's author. Unless the document was locked of course. But we in IT are probably the only ones who use that locking function."

"Lock documents? I didn't know I could do that." Mr. Addison raised an eyebrow at Mr. Fitzroy. "But, confirm for me if you would, if changes were made to a document, that would show in its history, wouldn't it? That someone had accessed the document and altered it?"

Raj fiddled with the top of his water bottle. "The document history would show that the document had been accessed, yes."

Addison leaned forward. "But wouldn't—"

And, that quickly, they dived into the intricacies of

the IT world. Mr. Addison peppered him with technical questions and during the back and forth, Mr. Fitzroy stirred, scrubbed at his hair, jotted something, then flipped the pen aside and stared as it rolled to a stop. At one point, Raj stopped mid-answer thinking Mr. Fitzroy had a question for him—but no, it was only that he needed to move around, first to the credenza, then the window.

Raj refocused himself on Mr. Addison and his questions, explaining again the challenge of proving that a document had been modified. Quite suddenly, Mr. Fitzroy returned to the table and planted his hands on its top. He glared first at Mr. Addison, but then also at Raj. "Are you saying that Anna Thorsen could have pulled up any damned document, changed it so I look like a criminal, and there'd be no way to prove that the memo had been messed with?"

Ms. Thorsen was altering documents?

Raj did manage to keep a serious face. But he could not help enjoying that they were seeing Ms. Thorsen for the creature she was. He took a deep breath and leaned his elbows on the table. "There would be a number of ways to show how a document looked. Either at the moment of distribution or any point in time that it had been edited." That should have closed the matter. But Addison's absurd questions continued as if Raj had said nothing. Obviously, for Raj the choice was to spend the entire day in that conference room and miss his mother's Thanksgiving dinner, or to reveal to Mr. Fitzroy and Mr. Addison what they clearly did not know about the level of IT's backup efforts.

Raj looked first at Mr. Fitzroy and then to Mr. Addison. "These documents you suspect have been altered…they are what, please?"

Addison squirmed. "Policy papers, marketing and growth strategy—I don't see why—"

"But surely you have working papers, yes?"

According to Addison, those could be discredited.

Raj couldn't see how, but if it was true, then it was time for him to come clean, as Mimi would have said. IT had a master backup server that did not show in the system description. For her own reasons Mimi had paid for it herself when she took over at IT. She'd set it up to retain the records of key employees. She even had built a special program to support it.

"Mimi did what?" Mr. Fitzroy caught himself. But his eyes clouded. "She tried telling me. Christ, why didn't I—"

"David," Mr. Addison said and patted the tabletop. "Then we have her. If Anna didn't know about that backup, she can't have gotten there. We'll pull everything together before she gets back. A load of work, but doable." He stood and offered his hand to Raj. "Mr. Banerjee, thank you. We're counting on your expertise."

Much more in command of himself, Mr. Fitzroy came around the table like the wheeler-dealer Raj had pictured.

"Mr. Banerjee, I won't forget your loyalty." Fitzroy offered his hand to Raj. "Of course our lawyers are going to talk about this with Mimi. Uh, once she's… If you talk with her, tell her how sorry I am. It's my fault. She was right. I see that now. Thank you. She was right. Sorry. Thank you."

During the long drive back to his house Raj kept thinking about Anna Thorsen. He considered whether he should call Mimi on the special phone he had given her. Where was she? And how safe was she? Then his thoughts would shift back to the evil thing he knew Ms. Thorsen to be, then to his mother's Thanksgiving dinner with all their guests and how important it was that he be there.

His mother was standing in the middle of the kitchen as he walked in. "Blessed." She beamed for one second, then her forehead crinkled up to her hairline. "All is well, yes?"

Well would not have been his word, but *yes,* he said, dreading the inquisition to come. But there was no inquisition thanks to the many women piling the dinner onto serving plates, hurrying the wine, the wheat tea, the juices and water to the tables that had overtaken his living room and dining room since he'd departed for Rex.

His mother was ushering the cousins and guests to the tables. With everyone in their place, she told the story of the American Thanksgiving and the pilgrims. And finally, they ate and talked and changed places to eat and talk with others. Because his mother had insisted, a huge turkey held the center of the serving table, along with its companion dressing and cranberry sauce. But most of the meal was much more familiar— his cousin's Malai Kofta curry, Gobi Pullao, and his favorite stuffed cabbage rolls in a spice gravy. Then with the main meal finished, an army of aunts, cousins, and friends brought in the desserts, including a blissful Galub Jamun.

So many people, the family and friends...he was nearly able to forget himself and Mimi and the troubles Mr. Addison had explained.

Chapter 46

Ben showed up at the Laurelhurst house before 7:30 a.m. and poked his head into the kitchen...nobody. So much for Thanksgiving—not that he liked turkey, but some pumpkin pie would've been good. He headed downstairs and joined Mimi and Zach, who were already hunched over their computers.

Around noon, Mimi pushed back from her computer and glanced at Zach. "Okey dokey, where's the turkey?" And, right on cue, Zach said he knew a dinner they could all drop in on. Mimi paused long enough to ask Ben was he coming.

"Think I'll pass," Ben said. A minute later, he was alone.

He put in another half hour on the database before it hit him what he wanted. He called Lee. "My team's taken off in search of turkey and cranberries," he said. "I was just thinking, you're new to Seattle...maybe you'd like to get together."

"I've been house hunting all morning," she said. "I was just going back to my place and crash. But...you wouldn't be interested in a walk, would you?"

"A walk sounds good," he said. "Except, you do know how cold it is."

"Tell you what. We're on the way back to my realtor's office. Queen Anne Real Estate? Meet me there? Fifteen minutes work for you?"

She was waiting out in front of the real estate office wearing a wool cap and a peacoat, looking cold but wonderful. With nobody much on the street and Ben driving, they made it through Ballard and out to Discovery Park in ten minutes. But then, as they turned into the parking lot, a foghorn cut through the wall of cloud.

Lee burst out laughing. Still laughing, she climbed out of his car. Her face was dazzling in the cold. "Great view," she said and turned up her collar. "What are we looking at?"

Ben pointed in the direction of what, on a clear day, they would have seen. "Well, there's the Sound. Bainbridge Island, Vashon Island. The Space Needle's back to your left and then, well you can't see it because of the weather, but way out there...is Japan. And if you have more questions regarding the sites of greater Seattle, I will have to charge the usual fee." He caught her elbow and they headed down the path agreeing that at least they could get in a walk.

After a while, their shoulders bumped, and she glanced over. "What was the best thing about the NFL? And don't say the cheerleaders."

"The beer," he said. "What was the best thing about being a model?"

"The travel. And I didn't have to go to school."

"You had a tutor though."

"Lessons after runways, shooting sessions, whenever they could fit them in."

"Okay," he said. "What was the best thing about the tutor?"

She stopped and unbuttoned her coat collar. "You're thinking I'm going to say the sex." She shot him a wicked grin. "*She* was a wonderful tutor."

Turned out the tutor had stepped in after her dad died. She'd just turned twelve. A year later, she'd started a T-shirt business. "Kaput," she said and laughed.

He motioned her on down the path. "At thirteen you had a failed business?"

She shrugged like who cares—incredible how beautiful she was.

"At *fourteen* I had a T-shirt business. Six months of success and it pancaked two weeks short of my fifteenth birthday. I was devasted. Magali, she's French, helped me work through it."

He glanced over. "So you speak French like a native and went to Paris and—"

"I was a runway model in Paris. Magali saved my butt academically *and* got me into Columbia." She put a hand on his sleeve. "What was the best thing about quarterbacking a Super Bowl?"

Embarrassing to say. And he was saved by a downpour. They booked it back to the car, both of them soaked through and shivering. They stripped off their coats, he dealt with defogging the windshield, and pushed the heater to high. Maybe it was the suffocating smell of the wet wool, or the pounding rain, or her legs. He heard himself saying he had a fireplace. Next thing he knew, she had her phone out and was telling some dinner delivery guy she wanted a double order of her usual and giving them Ben's address.

Twenty minutes later, they raced up two flights of stairs from the parking lot to his condo. Their dinner box, which it turned out included wine—had she said anything about wine? It was waiting on his front door balcony. He hoisted the box to his shoulder and motioned her inside.

He was still thinking what to do about the wine when she tossed her coat on the entry tile floor saying she was soaked clear through and did he have anything she could change into? He found some clean sweats and said she was welcome to a shower if that might warm her up. Meantime, he stowed their dinner in the kitchen, pulled on an old sweater and dry jeans, then parked himself on the huge granite fireplace hearth. He had a fire going in no time.

When he'd called her, he'd been thinking a coffee at Starbucks and then heading back to his project at Laurelhurst. Dinner and a fire felt like he'd started down that slippery slope they'd warned everybody about in rehab.

He was staring into the fire and thinking what was he going to do about the wine when she showed up barefoot and wearing his bathrobe, carrying two full wine glasses and a bottle stashed in the crook of her arm. He'd never been a wine drinker. But after rehab, yeesh...

"Yes, I spilled," she said. "But just a little. And on me. Not on your precious carpet."

He could get the carpet cleaned. How had he missed that she ordered wine with dinner? Two feet away and the musky scent of it filled his throat and sent his head spinning—and not in a good way.

She handed him a glass and padded around the huge living room, swirling her wine like an expert... Sipping, swirling again. Her fingers played on the glass. Sip. Her thumb stroked the rim. The curve above her hip under his robe. The way it cupped beneath her ass.

Sip. She stopped in front of a pair of paintings his folks had given him. Her bare toes worked against the floor like a cat. She said something he didn't hear, then she glanced at him over her shoulder and raised an eyebrow. She finished her wine and took a sudden detour down the back hall.

It was almost a relief she'd disappeared. He could relax. There was nothing to see there but his office, and a couple of empty bedrooms—one with a partly completed California closet if that impressed her.

She returned. "Your decorator missed those last two rooms. You know that don't you?" She sat on the fireplace hearth and set her wine glass aside. Suddenly she was amazed by the one-of-a-kind wrought iron tools. Did he have someone forge them?

"Decorator," he said and watched as her eyes continued to take in the room.

"Wish my realtor could find me a place like this." She shot him a knowing look. "Honey trap. The sofas, mood lighting, fireplace—and like you said, the view."

"Check it out." He grabbed his glass and headed for the cold air of the balcony.

A watery haze obscured most of the view beyond the I-5 bridge. She walked out to the railing anyway and stared. A smattering of rain made it under the roof. She blinked and took a step back, bumping into him. "Amazing on a clear day, right?"

He would have said something. But as he glanced at her, she was looking down. There was a pulse on the side of her throat, then it disappeared.

"How far down is it?"

"That's Aurora down there," he said. "Ten stories."

She stepped back, "Not so good with heights. And

I'm hungry. How about you?"

As she headed inside, he dumped his wine. By the time he closed the sliding doors, she was kneeling in front of the fireplace unloading their takeout dinner.

She looked up. "I thought a picnic. You mind?" She stretched a long arm over to the sofa and pulled a bunch of pillows down. "M-m-mm, Moroccan," she said and pried open a big paper container which immediately overflowed onto her hand. Quick, into her mouth, she sucked the red sauce off the end of her thumb. "So good." She patted the floor beside her.

As she filled their plates, she told him about Morocco. Her first trip there at age thirteen, a photo shoot.

He listened, nodded, and tried to focus on the food instead of the way she looked and the smell of the wine. The lamb was unbelievable. One bite, and, to his relief, the spices in the lamb were not only delicious, they helped mask the smell of the open wine bottle. And the lemons—they were cooked some way. She said something about sitting on a camel but he couldn't concentrate. Her voice was so low. The sound left him with the feel of stretching out on a summer day, letting the sound of water wash over him. The tie to her robe had slipped. She glanced down and re-tied the thick belt.

Trouble. Definitely trouble. He resettled himself, moving a little away from her and leaned his back against the sofa. She recovered his wine glass from where he'd abandoned it. Refilled it, placed it next to his knee, then refilled her own. A toast, she said.

He should just tell her, right? But he wasn't ready to go there.

He picked up his glass, raised it, pretended to drink. He agreed the wine was excellent, then set his glass aside in favor of his plate. For a while, they both concentrated on the food and, by the time they got to the honey and orange dessert, his red-alert about the alcohol had slipped away almost entirely.

Thing was, it still felt like she was settling in for the evening. She was lovely. And a few weeks later, maybe that would've been fine—more than fine—but not yet. He wasn't gonna let himself get off track. He glanced over at her. She was staring into the fire…with that creamy skin. The robe had come open again. Without looking, her hand drifted down and snugged the belt tight.

What he should do…was…something. Coffee. Motioning she should stay put, he stood, bussed his wine and their empty plates. He had the espresso machine going when he felt her hand on his back.

"It's been lovely," she said.

The next thing he knew, though he wasn't quite sure how it worked, she was dressed and standing with her back to the front door, her still-wet coat open. He had his car keys in his right hand so he must've been figuring he'd take her back to her car. But his left hand was inside her coat, under her shirt and—bad idea, bad idea—he kissed her. She tasted of cinnamon and salt and honey and wine.

"Coat's wet," he said.

She shrugged it onto the floor, slid her arms inside his jacket and kissed him back. Then, stepping away, she said, "I should go."

"No," he said. "Not yet."

Chapter 47

Nearly midnight. Thorsen stared at Ben Leit's computer screen while her cloning program went through its paces. Even with the door shut, she could hear him down the hall, snoring.

Roofies do that, leave you in that beyond-dead, on-your-back, unconscious hole. Same drug as she'd used on his daddy. But bigger man, bigger dose. And this time, not in the wine. This time would be nothing like Phoenix. There'd be no *wake-ee, wake-ee*. No *what the fuck.*

She just needed to check out his office. She would take care of his evidence later. There'd be another accidental fire. But nothing to connect Ben's suicide to his dad's death. Once she had what she needed, she would head back to Minneapolis with her Triathlon contracts lined up and her position at Rex secured.

Something in the cloning report caught her eye and she leaned in—no, nothing of any value. She returned the crap on Ben's desk to where he'd left it. That house on the lake, it shouldn't be difficult to wrangle another invitation. Maybe a little note...

Sorry for leaving you in dreamland but I have an early morning meeting. Call me, Lee.

She carried the note to the kitchen, stuck it on the fridge and padded back to Ben's office thinking, as a practical matter, the whole night had been a bust. Even the sex. No problem, she wasn't in it for the sex. As far as Ben was concerned, she'd been begging for more.

Once the hard drive cloning finished, Thorsen retrieved her thumb drive, stuffed it in her coat pocket and took a last look around the room. Fifteen moving boxes, every one open, and not one of them worth the time it'd taken her to check them out. The man had moved pens and paper, paperclips, a tape dispenser, a load of books. Probably cost him more to move than it would have to replace.

Who does that? Ben Leit, nice guy.

It wouldn't take long to ferret out what was really behind that aw-shucks grin. Ten to one, whatever it was wouldn't be *nice*.

Her old man had been a nice guy. People always said so. Wife disappearing, saddling him with a kid not his own, a kid he could've turned over to grandparents who would have given her a normal life. He'd have been a free man. But not her dad—he loved his little sweetie too much to give her up. He used to whisper that in her ear. He used to say it to other people. And they admired him for it.

Shows how tuned in they were.

One last look, then she grabbed her stuff, opened the front door and listened. Still snoring.

Chapter 48

Mimi was still working on the database when her phone pinged. The only people who had her number were Zach Berman, Ben, her Minneapolis lawyer and her Uncle Ted. And they'd all agreed, *No texting.*

She leaned forward, elbow on the table, and looked at the little icon with its check mark. The app she'd planted on the Rex file had done its job. Somebody—the hacker, it had to be—had accessed the pirated file. She straightened up. She could track the guy from the trail he left. She'd have the guy in a few keystrokes.

Except that it made no sense for the hacker to access a file he knew had been compromised. Anybody savvy enough to set up that file, plant the software, hide the file itself and keep the whole thing going for way more than a year. Anybody who could do that would have copied what they needed long before now.

No. It had nothing to do with copying. The hacker opened the file because he needed to change something. *Or delete it.* That's why he was hunting for a copy of the file in the first place, he wanted to be rid of the evidence. Her hand lifted away from the keyboard and closed over her mouth.

The hacker *knew her.* Or he knew enough about her to know her protocols—he knew she would never delete the file. He knew that without fail, she would have made a copy of the file the instant she found it. He had searched her office and her house and come up empty. The only reason he'd hadn't found her copy was, she'd left it with her lawyer.

She gave her smart phone a weary stare. What she wouldn't give to use one of the computers in the house to access that ghost file. But that would mean leaving a footprint in the ghost file that would lead right back to her and she sure as heck couldn't risk that.

What she could do was use her phone. Anybody tracking it would land in Minnesota, wouldn't they? Naturally, hacking into the Rex system by phone was like running in mud, but she managed it. Administration to operating programs and on and on. Once she confirmed the app, she'd set up hadn't been messed with, she took a look at the pirated file's programming and virtually tripped over an app that hadn't been there when she first cracked the hidden file.

If she was lucky, the hacker's app would contain the hacker's URL, or contain something to help her locate him. A few minutes studying the app's programming and she concluded it was more or less a duplicate of the one she'd planted...

Suddenly, the ground under her shifted. She tried to swallow her panic and couldn't... The hacker knew she'd cracked the ghost file because the hacker's app had just sent him the warning.

She took a deep breath. She willed her heart rate to settle down.

Okey dokey. Since you're already screwed, get what you can. Where were the hacker's alerts being sent? It didn't take her long to land in somebody's system in Wolfsburg, Germany. Messages to Volkswagen? No. The hacker was not in Germany. A message to Germany meant that the hacker was bouncing his signal all over the place.

It felt like she had mittens on, using the miserable phone. *You can do this.*

Agonizing how slow it was. But she managed to modify the hacker's warning app so the thing would fail. That was fine for the future, but what was she gonna do about the alert that had already been sent?

Because, with the power of the Rex system behind it, that blasted alert had gone out to the hacker less than one nanosecond after she'd opened the file. And whoever the hacker was, he might be sleeping right now, but sooner or later, he'd get the message.

And what if he could track the signal to her phone and not just the identity of it?

Cripes. How much time did she have before he came looking for her? She reached back and touched her pistol where she'd snugged it in her waistband. It had been almost twelve years since she'd bought it. Her instructor had been clear right from the beginning.

Don't draw your pistol unless you're prepared to use it. If you aren't ready to shoot somebody, get yourself some Mace. If you are going to shoot, use both hands on the pistol and plant your feet. Eyes open. And don't talk. Talk and he'll know you're afraid. Don't give him a warning—you have a gun aimed at him, you think that isn't plenty of warning? And don't think you can shoot to wing him. Your target's right here.

And he'd pointed at himself, right at the center of his chest.

With what felt like a fire alarm going on in her body, it took her two minutes to check that every door and window in the Laurelhurst house was locked and the security system was, yes, on alert status.

How long would it take for the hacker to track her down? A day at least wouldn't it? She was thinking how far away from Seattle could she get when it hit her: *she* didn't need to be somewhere else. She needed the *phone* to be somewhere else. And to hold the hacker's attention, the phone would have to make calls or send emails after it got where it was going.

First things first, she set up an email to Rex Security, innocuous but the content didn't matter. She just needed her phone to broadcast that email starting in five hours, and keep sending it every forty-three minutes until the battery died. To get the phone as far from her as possible, she put in a call to Ben, she needed his car...no answer. She glanced at the time. Where was he at 1:23 a.m.? She tried him again. And again.

And he'd promised to keep her safe. Right then, she could've kicked him. Who else was there?

Her Uncle Ted. Even if he had tried to ruin the company, he'd help her. And he picked up on the first ring. But before she could explain what she needed, he launched into a thing about her father needing them back, that everything had changed. He sounded on top of the world. And sober. He and Madge were on their way to Boeing Field, right then. One of the Rex jets was waiting.

"I'll give you a ring once I know more," he said. "Meantime, honey, watch your back."

Mimi stared at the phone. He'd hung up. He hadn't even asked why she'd called.

For a moment she wanted to blame her uncle for everything. But what good would it do to go off about him when what she needed was to get rid of the darned phone?

She could rent a car... She called Hertz. They weren't open until 6:00 a.m. Not good enough. She tried Ben again and let it ring. Hopeless. She wasted more time trying to convince herself it would be okay to wait for Ben to show up in the morning. No. Waiting five hours for Ben to show up was a really, really stupid idea.

That stairway up to the main floor haunted her. That's how he'd be coming, whoever he was. Deep breath—okay, she was in serious trouble. She took another deep breath. Another. And she got who to call. It was humiliating, and he barely knew her, but what about Zach Berman?

Zack showed up twenty minutes later. He took the compromised phone and promised to check back once he'd dumped it north of Bellingham. They agreed that if she was right about the hacker, having the phone traveling up the I-5 corridor would definitely lead whoever it was away from her and maybe to Canada. She actually hugged him.

Zack took off and she locked herself in, hoping she'd be safe enough for the night at least. Sleep was out of the question, so she headed downstairs to the computer setup. One more thing before she went back to work on the database... She slipped the Glock out of her belt, flicked off the safety and laid it on the table next to her mouse pad.

Three weeks ago, she couldn't have shot anyone. But things had changed. After what happened in Minneapolis, nobody would ever do that to her again.

Chapter 49

Thorsen pulled her car into the hotel garage and glanced in the rearview mirror. Fucking storm. Just getting from Leit's place to her car, she was soaked through and her left leg was cramping. On top of the physical misery, she was now three hours behind schedule and she'd come up empty at Ben Leit's condo. Of course, that did mean the 'proof' Ben was blathering about on his dad's blog had to be in the house on the lake. And she'd take care of that soon enough.

Back in her room, she stripped, took a steaming shower and wrapped herself in one of the hotel's robes. Out of habit, she checked her email.

The redrafted 10K report she'd been expecting had arrived. She'd have to get it back to Addison ASAP—damned annoying that Addison wanted her to sign off on that 10K, but nobody said it would be easy. And if that wasn't enough, there was a pile of emails full of news she didn't need to bother with and...what the? Her alarm for the hidden file had sent up a flare.

Who else but Mimi Fitzroy? Thorsen opened the alert and checked out the visitor metadata. Of course, Minnesota. That's where Mimi had bought her phone. But by now, Mimi Fitzroy could be anywhere. Time for a little insurance.

"Specialty Dining."

"Your catering manager please. I need to arrange

an out-of-town picnic. Can you handle that?"

"Of course, madam. One moment."

And she was dropped into the middle of a soft-rock mish-mash...boring...boring... Then just as abruptly, once again, she was among the living.

"This is Karla. How may I help you?"

Thorsen launched into a long-winded explanation of the picnic she was planning. The woman interrupted her. "That would be Special Services. May I have them call you back?"

"Of course," Thorsen said, ended the call and waited. Less than a minute later, her phone rang— terrible reverberation on the line this time.

"Yes, madam. You are requesting luncheon sur l'herbe?"

"Not precisely." She used the requisite food-jargon and ordered tracking for a certain phone number, which *might* include an on-the-ground search. While she was at it, she asked them to hand deliver an invitation to the Guerneville address and to provide the usual paraphernalia for outdoor picnic games—horseshoes, badminton, whatever. Equipment requests always meant she needed another passport, credit cards and ID. And *hand deliver*...she wasn't kidding: boots on the ground. If Mimi was in Guerneville, she needed to know it now.

Order complete, she raised her arms over her head, stretched and felt something in her neck slip back into place. On to payment... She logged into her own numbered account and transferred fourteen thousand dollars from Switzerland to an account in the Caymans. The memo, confirming receipt of the transfer, gave her the entry code for a drop box located on Rainier

Avenue. She could pick up her new ID in twenty-four hours.

She retrieved an energy drink from her mini-fridge, downed it, and returned to her desk. With the search for the phone under way and a fresh ID in the offing, she had most of a day before she could strike at the lake house. She pulled up the revised 10K report and for a moment stared at the computer screen. She absolutely needed the trace on that phone. As for whether the passport was necessary, every woman in business knows you're a fool not to watch your back. And you're a bigger one not to preserve your options.

Chapter 50

Three and a half hours later, Specialty Dining woke Thorsen out of a sound sleep. Bottom line, the cell phone that accessed her pirated email file had been initialized in Minneapolis on Monday, November 25 at 8:43 a.m. It had pinged towers between downtown Minneapolis and the Minneapolis-St. Paul International Airport where it called an unlisted number, part of a block of numbers they believed was assigned to a secured service. Where it also had been used. It subsequently pinged towers from San Francisco International Airport north to Guerneville, California. Cell tower records reflected a return, the same day, along the same path to SFO where the phone was turned off. It turned on again at SeaTac airport and subsequently pinged towers between SeaTac and Seattle proper. While it was near the University District, it made several connections to Rex Sports, the most recent near 1:00 a.m. PST. It also made six telephone calls to a local Seattle number, one call of four minutes to a Minneapolis cell phone number and one local call. The signal shut down at 1:24 a.m. PST and has not resumed.

The name registered to the phone was Mary Wilson.

Mary Wilson my ass. So, Mimi was in Seattle. Wasn't that convenient. "Stay with it," Thorsen yawned. "Include the ground tracking. Use your best judgment and keep me informed of any change in location."

Her eyes were too tired to work on reports. But no way could she go back to sleep. She swung her feet out of bed, retrieved a coverlet from the bed and shrugged it around her shoulders.

At the window, she tugged back the draperies enough she could unlock the slider. As she opened it, a wall of water from the deck soaked her feet and the carpet. She hopped back and slammed the door shut. Did it *never* stop raining? Maybe setting the Triathlon in Seattle was a mistake. On the street below, for the first time since she'd arrived, not one car in sight.

She loathed the middle of the night. It left her feeling old. She wasn't, of course. She wasn't forty. Not yet. But the year had been a grind. And now that she was so close to the finish, she was impatient to be done with it. Seemed like there was always some annoying element that refused to slide into place. Frank Leit had been one. And more than one business deal had threatened to go off the track. But the real problem was Mimi Fitzroy.

Who pulled the strings to get Mimi a government-issued false ID? Ms. Wilson? Really? No wonder she hadn't found Mimi on the flight passenger lists. Who could come up with a security phone and ID that passed Mimi through TSA like she was the President?

Thorsen dumped an armload of towels on the soaked carpet then stopped, truly stopped, to consider her chances for making her scheme work. She decided she was too tired to think. She stretched her long frame out on the bed.

Two hours later, Specialty Dining reported in. The subject phone had turned on at 3:30 a.m. Cell tower activity suggested it was on its way north along the I-5 corridor. Could she trust that Mimi had split for parts Canadian? Or had the little bitch tossed the thing onto a garbage truck like that movie?

Finally, the rain sloughed away. At the balcony windows, she could almost make out Queen Anne Hill. She opened the door, stepped over the soggy towels and out onto her dripping hotel balcony. The air was dead still, the sky had lightened to gray, and the insane traffic below her proceeded in a stately crawl, leaving great swirls in the standing water.

Another glance over to the condo. Ben Leit—one more way-too-gentlemanly player. Just like his Daddy.

She returned to her desk and was only half-listening to a parade of voicemails from her Minneapolis assistant when she caught what JR was saying. Legal wanted something. She speed-dialed him back.

She loathed his subservience. But she trusted his instincts. He answered immediately. "You alone?" Then *sotto voce,* "Fitzroy has cancelled his run for the Senate."

"Where'd you get this?" she said.

"His Number Two texted me," JR said. "It's all hush-hush. Her last word was 'Delete if you ever want anything else from me.' I can't get anything else out of anybody. *And,* there's been nothing on the internet or in the papers. That's not all—"

Thorsen swore and pitched her phone across the room. It shattered against the marble floor of the bathroom. For a moment she stared at the shards of plastic and metal. When she checked, the phone's SIM card had cracked all the way through. She turned on her heel, dug the other phone out of her bag and dialed.

JR picked up the conversation as though it hadn't been interrupted. Legal had asked for Thorsen's work papers. "They want everything on your last key deals—including Indonesia-05 and -06. Everything—notes, work papers, even your day timers."

Thorsen counted ten even breaths. Then spoke with absolute calm. "Thank you, JR. There's nothing at all for you to be concerned about. Give them anything they want. Of course, my day timers have been shredded. You might remind Legal that it's their policy we've been following." She ended the call.

She had a picture of Addison's face when he heard that one.

Item by item she re-shuffled her to-do list. She'd have to break off her Seattle meeting schedule and get back to Minneapolis—a task for Maya. If Robert Addison thought he could screw her with her own papers, he was sorely mistaken. She'd seen to virtually everything already. The only thing left, the only thing that really would put her at risk was Frank Leit's papers. If Ben Leit had more of the same... Well, that was one more reason for wrapping things up pronto. And, as far as that fool Addison went, before she was through with him, he'd wish he was in jail.

Gradually her breathing and heart rate returned almost to normal. She called the hotel concierge. She needed someone to clean up, she'd broken—no, she was not injured—just send someone to deal with the mess. Oh, and the carpet by the balcony door was wet. She needed new towels. And could they arrange to have her usual breakfast sent up.

Other than letting them in, Thorsen ignored the hotel crew, returned to the window and stared across the lake to the condominium perched on the side of Queen Anne Hill.

Bob Addison's paper hunt was all about David Fitzroy staying on as CEO.

Not for long he wasn't. She'd blow the whistle on Rex herself. She could easily 'discover' the illegal business deals that David and Bob Addison had been putting together. She'd be shocked. She'd be mortified. She'd do the only thing she could—bring in the State Attorney General. Or better yet, the U.S. Attorney. She'd give the prosecution proof that the entire Fitzroy clan was tainted—why else would Fitzroy's own daughter have jumped ship? Mimi Fitzroy knew what was going on. She just didn't want to get caught. If it cost the company a couple of years' profits, that would hardly be a catastrophe.

David Fitzroy would be lucky if he didn't spend the next ten years in the slammer along with his buddy Bob Addison. A tight smile leaked across her lips.

She took a deep, cleansing breath, she could feel the energy flooding her back and shoulders. She could make it work. The Triathlon contracts were all in place, they just needed signing and she could handle that long-distance. Other schmoozing in Puget Sound, she could handle that down the line. She fired off an email to *her* Board members calling a meeting at 10:00 a.m. Tuesday. She would bring down the Fitzroy family and Bob Addison in a single stroke.

Chapter 51

Friday morning, Raj Banerjee's cell phone rang—
brother to the one he had given Mimi. He answered
saying *one moment.* Then he hit the DND button on his
office phone and locked himself in, "Yes? Mimi? You
are well?" His wretched voice gave him away, he knew.
Worry makes such a terrible sound.

She was well, she said. In Seattle, but he should not
tell anyone.

He could hear a breathless panic in her voice and
was wishing he could ask what it was. But also, he was
thinking he should tell her about her father, what her
father had said. Because family holds together, and he
wanted to believe this was true for her family as well.
But in spite of all his beliefs of family and wishes for
her, he could only think *restrain yourself Banerjee.* She
would tell him what she could.

"I've done something really stupid," she said and
explained about checking the ghost file. "I'm sure the
tripwire wasn't there the first time. And I'm sure that
by now she knows I was looking at the file again. But
here's the thing: It's Anna Thorsen behind the ghost
file. I can prove it."

His belly lurched and for a moment he could not
get his breath. He must convince Mimi to get away
from there. But even as he was trying to speak, she was
saying Ms. Thorsen was in Seattle pretending to be

someone else, that it was all tied to Frank Leit's murder.

"Get it?"

He wasn't quick enough to stop his groan—she must have heard.

"I know I sound scared. Well, I am scared. But I'm safe. Really," she said and explained what she'd set up.

Did it make sense she was safe because she had a gun and knew how to use it? That she was safe because some man named Zach Berman was driving the cellphone north to lure Ms. Thorsen away from Seattle? The whole idea was wishful thinking. He told her she should not be staying there. Not hiding by a lake with her gun.

Had he known she had a gun? He could not think of her shooting anything. Gun or not, it was crazy for her to think of staying in Seattle.

"One moment," he said and calmed himself. In truth, there was but one thing to be done.

In spite of Mr. Addison's instructions, he told Mimi of his Thanksgiving meeting at Rex. He told her all of it. The investigation of Ms. Thorsen, Mr. Addison's plan. Most importantly, he told her about her father and what he had said.

Chapter 52

Late. He was late. Ben opened his eyes, shut them and untangled his arm from the sheets. His head was killing him, his tinnitus the worst it'd been in months. His hand flailed toward the bedside table. He grabbed his phone. Ten o'clock? And Mimi'd called in the middle of the night. Six times and he didn't wake up? Christ. He rang her back—voicemail. He threw on sweats. She was probably on the phone with Zach. He called again. No answer and no voicemail, his gut wrenched. She was in trouble.

He pounded down his stairs to the parking lot. The hillside lot was flooded, with leaves and tree branches everywhere; by the time he piled into his car, his shoes were soaked. He fought his way up 5th Avenue, made it around a downed tree, and switched over to 6th, then jammed the Lexus downhill and made the switch-back onto Aurora. Through Wallingford, then the U District—everywhere he looked: upended news boxes and trash blowing on the wide streets.

At the lake house, he sprinted for the front door, stepped into the foyer...

Snick.

All he could see was the barrel of the gun. Right at the edge of the bannister, an unwavering black hole.

"Mimi, don't shoot."

She shaded the gun up and away, but he couldn't

keep from yelling. "Jesus Christ, Mimi. You could've shot me."

"I'm sorry." Her face crumpled and she disappeared down the stairs.

He'd made her cry. He dumped his dripping jacket on the bannister and headed after her. He could barely hear for the leaf blowers in his head. And, right under his left eye, it was like something had stabbed him. She'd aimed that gun right at him. He hated guns. He hated that gun. He hated what it did to him. He wanted to shake her until she understood.

She was wiping her eyes when he walked into the family room. "I shouldn't have yelled, I'm sorry," he said and slid onto the sofa. "Migraine."

She found a towel, ice, and handed it over. "I called because I've IDed the hacker. It's Anna Thorsen, a key player at Rex. I've known her most of my life. I've tied her phone and computers to everything. It's complicated but I've even figured how she could've been in Phoenix."

She explained about the trap she'd set and the other one that she'd sprung when she accessed the email file eight hours earlier. That was why she'd called. "But it *is* Anna," she said. "It has to be. She had thousands of your dad's emails, and his friends', she must've followed me to the park—"

"Dad wasn't killed by some woman. I've been through that already with Al Baldwin."

Her eyes went wide. "You really think because Anna's a woman, it couldn't be her? Listen to me. Anna Thorsen's a martial arts master. She picked me up and threw me off a cliff."

He didn't want to talk about it. He pushed the

towel off his head and pressed that place above his left eye. His dad was still on that table, the overhead lights still buzzed into the air, the bones in his dad's right arm, his skin all waxy.

Finally, he sat up and stared at her. "And what do you weigh, Mimi? A hundred pounds with your backpack loaded? Knocking you out and tossing you in the river does not compare with what was done to Dad."

"Just stay there," she huffed. In seconds she'd picked up a box and thrown it aside. It hit the wall next to the sofa, the sound ratcheted through his head as if she'd hit him. Then another box. And another.

She broke open the bottom box of the stack, parked a handful of files on the floor and turned back for more. "I know I saw it yesterday." More pawing and she came up with what looked like a magazine. She waved it at him. "She's as big as you are or nearly. See for yourself."

He glanced at the slick cover. *A Bold Future.* A man and a woman. Same cheekbones, same... His gut dropped to the middle of the earth. "It's Lee. Lee Dawson. Except for the hair."

"No, it's Anna Thorsen, and ignore the hair color. She changes it all the time."

"But—"

"Tell me how you know her," she said.

He wanted Mimi to shut up, to be out of the house. He wanted to drink until he floated away. No. He wanted to call Lee or Anna or whatever her name was really. He wanted to see her again. He wanted her to think he didn't know about her. He wanted for her to think she was in charge, to think that she was safe being with him. Then he would take that lovely face in his hands and smash it, smash it until it was as ugly as what she'd done to his dad. Christ. He lurched off the sofa and headed out into the yard.

When he came back, Mimi was staring at her computer screen. She asked if he was okay and, in spite of the roar in his head, he told her everything or nearly—the gym, coffee, Discovery Park, the take-out dinner they'd shared at his condo.

Mimi pushed herself back from her computer. Her lips had compressed to a little line...not like she was mad, like he'd let her down. "You slept with her, right?"

He pressed the pain-radiating knot at back of his neck and closed his eyes just so he couldn't see the expression on her face.

"Oh, grow up," she growled. "You're still alive. She probably wanted to check out your condo. You bought into her con. You're not the first one, I think you can count on that."

She dropped her gaze to her keyboard. "Anna Thorsen is a monster. She has this way of working, coming at you like she's just going the same direction as you, as if you had all these things in common. And you're alone and she's alone, and you're convinced she thinks you're this wonderful person and she's, well, she's just doing whatever comes her way, and you go along talking and all of a sudden, you're carrying her suitcase and paying the way and your dog has died but it's not her fault and on and on. You get it. She's conned my dad, conned the Rex board, most of my family, my brother. She was engaged to my brother. Did I tell you that? That I had a brother?" She shot him a wide-eyed look but then went quiet for a while.

He went back to the couch and stretched out. His headache was beginning to back off, but then she thumped something on the floor.

"You're sure you didn't tell her anything else? Growing up in Seattle, your time here? Because but I'm thinking she must know where we are. Maybe she doesn't know that *I'm* here but—"

He shifted the cold towel. "I never mentioned you, or what we're working on, or Laurelhurst. She has my phone number but not my email. She knows I have a project going. Okay, I get it, she must've gone through the condo. So she knows I'm not working there. But I give you my word, I did *not* mention this place."

It took her less than five minutes to crack the King County tax records and find his dad's name and the address for the Laurelhurst house. One more search, she had street and the overhead photos. He called the security service. Could they station somebody at the Laurelhurst house for a couple of days? They were sorry, but not on such short notice, not with the holiday weekend. They could put the house on their short turnaround list; somebody would be by every half hour.

Ben looked over at Mimi. "So it's up to us," he said. "And we can do it. We can. We've got you and that gun. And I'm no slouch with a baseball bat."

They checked the house, inside and out. There were no signs of anybody, no prints in the grass, the flower beds. They went over the alarm system, including its battery backup. They decided Ben would move in. They'd stick together, keep working, nap if they had to on the family room sofa. Zach could bring them whatever they needed. Once they pulled their proof together, they'd get hold of a U.S. Attorney. Mimi's uncle would know who to talk with.

They were laughing, toasting their decision with orange juice when it hit him.

"You said Rex wasn't even willing to sue Dad. You're saying whoever set up that file—" He got it, he was pissing her off. "You're certain it's her."

A quick shake of her head. "Of course I'm certain. I could prove it in court if I had to. Anna Thorsen built the ghost file. She started the file setup using her own system, her own cell phones. She's been accessing the file using other employees' IDs. But it started with her, just her. And she was in Houston when your Dad was killed. How hard would it be to get from Houston to Phoenix, and that's a rhetorical question."

He had his dad's bankcard report. There were charges the night before. If Mimi was right, somebody at the Scottsdale hotel had to recognize Anna Thorsen's photograph. His head was throbbing. He needed to talk with Detective Baldwin, but Mimi was still talking and if she would just shut up, he could think, if she would only shut up, shut up, shut up.

She was looking at him like he'd told her. Had he actually said to shut up?

"Sorry," he said. "I was thinking what if she's covering her ass… What if she's after her own stuff? What if she wrote something that was…? What if most of this paper doesn't matter? What if it's only her stuff? We could pull her stuff together easily, couldn't we? How long would take? A couple of days?"

"One," Mimi said, triumphant. "If we're lucky, less."

It felt like he was about to play the game of his life.

The good news, his wingman had more grit than anybody he'd ever known. He took a deep breath and set to work. His computer was still searching away when his phone rang, a Minnesota number. Less than a minute later, he let out a whoop. "Touchdown," he shouted. "That was the Deputy U.S. Attorney Dad was talking to. His name's Teach Esparza. He's headed out here."

Chapter 53

Thorsen could barely contain herself waiting for end of the day. Rain or not, once the light went, she'd be going in. At 4:30, she ditched her business suit in favor of rowing gear and grabbed her pack. Down the hotel elevator, out the front door. What she hadn't considered, once she was out on the street, the wind nearly knocked her down. Rain coming at her sideways and a wicked chop on the lake.

No fucking rainstorm was getting in her way. So what if the row was risky? She headed down the block and across Eastlake to Duke's, put the scull in the water, climbed in and pushed away. Twenty yards from the dock, she had to face facts. The scull would be swamped long before she made it to that damned house. Her entire future depended on finishing things with Ben Leit. But she was not willing to drown trying. She'd go tomorrow.

She barely made it back to the dock. As for hauling the scull out of the water, stowing it, tying it down. Jesus. She boosted it up onto the dock and tied it down; that was the best she could do.

Back to her hotel, she stripped and dried off. She paced the suite. She forced herself to sit at the damned too-small desk and focus on the shit work she needed to finish before she got back to Minneapolis. She spent the night plowing through reports, projections, Legal's analysis of proposed trade regs, more reports, until finally, she had to crash. And then, she couldn't sleep.

Her cure for insomnia: she reminded herself of all the ways she had made herself safe. From her father, from the woman at the modeling agency, her b-school mentor, from Jamie. She told herself the plan would work. She'd be fine. The files at Rex—they'd prove Fitzroy was behind the deals. She'd cleaned everything on the Rex system all the way back to 1999. Not that she'd deleted files, that would've been too much of a flag to an auditor. She'd just massaged things a bit. No one would notice.

Chapter 54

Teach Esparza didn't get to Laurelhurst until late Saturday afternoon. And then he was not what they expected. He was short, for one thing, and way younger than either of them had guessed. Though it did look like what he'd told them over the phone was true, that he'd done his share of intercollegiate wrestling. Ben's guess, Esparza could definitely hold his own in a fight. And given their situation, that was good news. The bad news was, Esparza's bosses didn't know what he was planning, his office didn't have an official investigation going, and there was no grand jury looking at Rex.

Did that mean this guy was just looking for a way to promote himself? Ben glanced over at Mimi—she was thinking the same thing. He said, "Did my dad know you didn't have an investigation going?"

"That's why he came to Minneapolis in June, to get one going," Esparza said. "The plan was for Frank to pull the facts together, then hand it off so I could take the case to my superiors, and by then it'd be air-tight."

Stone-faced, Mimi said, "And Rex wouldn't get the chance to make it go away."

Esparza regarded her for a moment as if he recognized her, but then turned back to Ben. "Your dad protected everybody by keeping the focus on the story. There was always the risk that sooner or later somebody would do something—last June I asked him if he was keeping himself and his evidence safe. He just laughed."

They headed downstairs. Esparza dumped his coat on the family room sofa. "You need to understand, a case like this is like a forest fire. When it starts, chances are, nobody knows it's there. But once it gets going, it will make its own weather. And it'll cost a bundle to put out...or prosecute. The other thing: cases like this take time, time to put them together, time to sort out the parties. Sometimes it's ten or fifteen years."

As if he were on to bigger things, Esparza parked himself at Ben's computer, shoved his sleeves up and scrolled through the memo Ben and Mimi had put together earlier.

"Another thing you should understand." Esparza didn't even bother looking up. "Cases like this usually don't go to trial. People enter pleas. The court imposes fines and the companies either go under or turn around. Point being, you need to be patient." He made a sudden adjustment to Ben's chair and bent closer to the screen.

Ben kept looking from Esparza to Mimi. This was not how he'd imagined it going. "You mean, what happened to Dad doesn't come into this at all? We're sure Dad was killed because he was about to expose what was going on at Rex."

Esparza's left hand lifted off the keyboard long enough to adjust his glasses. "Your dad's murder is Arizona's deal, not ours. I'll have my hands full developing the case he brought us. And, believe me, the last thing I want is to let him down."

Mimi's eyes flew wide, wide open. "Ben's dad was murdered and it's no concern of yours?"

Esparza kept working, scrolling down the computer

screen: "It kills me. But it's not our jurisdiction."

Ben nodded. Not that he agreed with the guy, but he was not gonna argue about the law. The main thing was, Esparza wasn't getting it—they were, right here and right now, at risk. That was the first thing they'd written in their memo...in all caps. "I get it about Arizona," he said and stepped a little closer to Esparza. "Do *you* get it about Anna Thorsen, from what you're reading there?"

Esparza looked up. His ears were red. "Do I get it? From what I've heard, Anna Thorsen is a witch, a bitch or a business genius. It all depends on who you talk to. Have I met her? No. But I've lived in Minneapolis five years. I heard all about her the first year I was there."

"You just read our memo," Mimi said. "And you don't get it? She'll do anything to protect herself. She's not going to stop."

Esparza leaned back in his chair and turned to Ben.

"Look, I need to do this. And I need to concentrate. Why don't you guys go upstairs or something... I gave my word to your dad I'd take this on. I can't help what happened to your dad. I can help finish what your dad started. As far as Anna Thorsen goes... What I didn't say on the phone: believe it or not, I grew up in an L.A. ghetto. Ninety percent of the guys I started school with ended up in knife fights, prison, or they're dead from drugs or drive-bys. Anna Thorsen doesn't scare me. I got over being scared a long time ago."

Esparza replaced one thumb drive with another and moved on to copying the computer's picture file. "Look, I appreciate everything you've done here. My job is to sell this thing to my boss. And I only have the rest of the day and tomorrow morning to pull it together. It's time I got to work on the documents."

"C'mon." Ben wrapped an arm around Mimi. They headed upstairs where he pulled a couple of the big living room chairs close together and found a box of tissues for Mimi.

"He doesn't get it," she said.

"I know."

"No. You don't," she said. "She didn't just kill your father. She killed my brother."

Did he know her brother was dead? Her skin was ashen, her eyes glassy.

"They were all saying it was an accident," she said. "The newspapers, the rangers, everybody. But Jamie climbing at Yosemite? It didn't make sense that he was there. He was afraid of heights. He'd never climbed before. And suddenly he was climbing with Anna? Besides, he was breaking up with Anna." She blinked. She took one tissue, then another. "They were going up one of those granite cliffs. On the ladder part. It's not really a ladder. It's steel cables. It swings partly free. The rangers said people do it all the time, that climb. But there'd been a storm. After Anna came back, she said Jamie slipped on the ice, that he couldn't hold on, that he fell. I went over there—I was still finishing my PhD at Cal. I talked with people. I found one man who was there that day. He said something was wrong with what happened, like it wasn't really an accident, like Anna had stepped on Jamie or made him lose his balance or something. The park rangers said they couldn't be sure what happened, except that he fell four hundred feet. And there was nothing to stop him."

Chapter 55

Saturday morning, Thorsen was up at dawn. The TV news was saying the storm had shifted south. If it was cold and right on the edge of rain, so what? She would get in that house. She would finish the job.

After four hours of trying to not think about the Laurelhurst house, she decided she'd do another drive-by. If Ben's car wasn't there, if the lights weren't on, she'd go in from the street.

The whole way over, the streets were clotted with blow-down from the storm, and the lights were out at University Village. She turned into Laurelhurst, followed the winding street, and, as she came up to the lake house, her cell phone pinged—Specialty Dining was confirming, her new ID awaited pickup. She looked up just in time to spot a security car parked in front of Leit's house.

She tapped the brakes, closed her eyes and centered herself, finally pressing three fingers into the right side of the base of her skull...wait for it...the pain vanished. With those bozos out front, she'd be going in from the water, and weather be damned.

Five hours later and confident it would be dark by the time she made it through the Montlake Cut, she loaded everything she would need (including everything she might need if the break-in went sideways) into the scull and pushed off. There was still plenty of chop on the lake, but it was manageable. A week ago, she'd thought she'd taken care of the problem... She dug an oar and recovered and refocused on the rowing job. Christ, here she was, dealing with another set of Frank Leit's shit when she should be back in Minneapolis taking care of David Fitzroy.

She stroked her way up the east side of Lake Union. It felt good to put her body to a speed test against the chop. Through the Montlake Cut, she raced north, crossing Union Bay and bypassing the low marsh that lay between the university and the beginning of Laurelhurst. Ahead of her, she could just make out Leit's house at the tip of the peninsula.

She'd screwed the pooch in Phoenix when she'd failed to check out the house first. This time she'd done the reconnaissance. This time, she would wrap the whole thing down. This time, there would be no surprises.

As she pulled even with the house, she leaned forward in the scull, fished out her night-vision binoculars and wedged them between her thighs. She tucked her oars and scanned the lake—nobody else on the water—then she settled back, perpendicular to her target. The car lights crossing the Montlake Bridge moved at a glacial pace. But no problem with being spotted, she was black on black with nothing to pick up the ambient light.

She checked the house again and fine-tuned the boat's angle. It must be a lot like being a cop doing surveillance—don't get noticed, don't get distracted, stay flexible, and don't get bored.

It started raining, again. But at least this time it was what the locals called drizzle, a suffocating mist that fogged the binoculars and drove the cold through her. A quick check…all three floors of the house were dark. She wouldn't miss this time. She had four canisters… She couldn't imagine the size of the fire that would take the house down. Too bad she wouldn't be there to see it, but for damned certain it would mean one less thing to worry about.

She checked her pulse—too high. She spent a few minutes bringing it down and pulled the scull up to the bank. In the end, she swung the scull around under an old-fashioned willow tree next to the rotting boathouse. The air smelled wet and green. The tree's canopy would keep the scull secure. She stepped ashore and tightened the line.

After a quick sprint up the side of the yard, she dumped her pack at her feet, fished out a pen light, and checked the masonry at the basement side door. A Rhyymtek alarm? She gave a little snort. Back to the bag, she pulled out her black box, the same one she'd used on Mimi Fitzroy's place. In seconds, she shut down Ben's security system as if he'd turned it off himself.

At the door, she clenched the pen light between her teeth and went to work with her picks. He'd made it way too easy. *Why bother locking the place up at all?* She dropped her picks back in their case and stowed them in her pack.

One last piece of prep: she exchanged her rowing gloves for surgical ones, then strung her bag across her chest bandolier style to prevent it bumping against anything. Once she palmed the pen light, she closed the side door and stepped quietly inside.

Chapter 56

Thorsen slipped past a laundry room, a mudroom/bath, and a storage room. Up ahead on the left were open stairs, to the right, a big archway. A chair scraped and she shut down her penlight. A man said something… Not Ben.

Her whole body threaded with electricity, enough she paused and took a long silent breath to get hold of herself. She had two options. She could leave the way she came in, head back to the hotel and try again later, or…

A thump, much heavier this time, and she stripped off her latex gloves. She stuffed them in a pocket, pushed back her hood and stepped around the corner.

"Ben around?" she said softly and stepped on into what obviously had been a family room. Now, equally obviously, it was a war room for Ben's project.

Big smile, her curious face on, "Hello," she said. The man was standing knee-deep in stacks of paper. Trim, dark-haired, he seemed surprised. He wiped his hands on a yellow cloth and smiled.

On closer evaluation, he was late twenties, with brown or black eyes, five-foot-eight at best. Slim wrists and hands, narrow feet. A swimmer or…he was thick enough through the shoulders, maybe he'd wrestled. There were creases ironed in his jeans. And he was wearing a dress shirt under a V-neck sweater, and loafers. She guessed he was the one who'd left the portfolio, and a carry-on bag on a folding table. She'd put money on it, she was looking at Esparza. Well, well.

She turned her smile up twenty degrees and took a couple of steps toward him. "I just had some trouble with my kayak. I hope I didn't startle you." She apologized for dropping in uninvited. "I was hoping I could catch Ben and—" She let the rest of the sentence go, smiled again and took another step forward, offering her hand. "I'm Lee," she said.

He smiled. It was a beautiful smile. He came forward to where she stood, his hand ready to take hers. "Everybody calls me Teach," he said. "Good to meet you."

She gripped his hand firmly. But instead of letting go, she jerked him toward her, spinning him around. He tripped. She caught him against her. Her right arm clenched his body rigid against her own. He tried slipping down and away from her. Fool. With her free hand, she gripped the right side of his head, wrapping him up like so much butcher paper. The meat of her forearm jammed into his mouth, and her fingers dug into the soft indentation at the base of his skull. As if it would do any good, he tried to fight her. He might have tried saying something, she wasn't sure. She wasn't listening.

The rest was as easy as unscrewing a jar—a quick yank. His head snapped toward her left shoulder. His legs trembled and he went limp against her. She held her breath, slowed her own heartbeat and probed under his jaw for a pulse.

She rolled the body to the side of the landing and

stared for a moment. So much for improvisation. First things first, she stepped over to the curtain and pushed it back... There were the French doors she'd seen that led out to the terrace. It took some time to wrangle the security bolts but once the doors opened, she braced them wide.

She made a quick survey of the boxes. It was the Arizona stuff all right. Christ, had it multiplied like rabbits? She parked her backpack on a partly-empty box and unloaded the prepaid cell phone, fuses and powder packs. The incendiary assembly had been tricky to formulate, and a damned sight more complicated to assemble than what she'd used in Arizona. But this stuff was better—more explosion, more fire, more reliable. Four packages.

Big breath. Her fingers trembled a little as she clipped the firebombs together. By the time she tucked the last of the little cuties among the boxes, she only had to arrange the papers to get the best burn. She'd set everything off once she was back on the water. And the phosphorous would keep any heroes out 'til the fire had done its work.

She took a last look around—all good to go—and was just stuffing the contents of the dead man's portfolio into her backpack, when she heard voices at the top of the stairs.

"Teach?"

Ben. She grabbed her pack and took off across the patio.

Chapter 57

Ben made it to the bottom of the stairs two jumps ahead of Mimi. He tossed his phone at her.

"Alarm first," he shouted and sprinted into the yard.

He caught a flash of a white shoe booking it down the left side of the yard, heading for the water, and took off after her. Past the Lebanese cedar, he hurdled one flower bed, then the other. Even with his shoes slipping on the wet grass, he was gaining on her.

But then, right at the dock, shit, she was waiting for him. He hit the brakes. She whirled. Her left foot whipped around just as he slipped. He went down on his ass, sliding for miles across the deck. Up again, he charged her. She whirled, her shoe passed over him, skimming his hair. And she disappeared.

Yard Lights—and for a second, he couldn't see. Then the kick was coming, a bomb to his shoulder. And before he recovered, she planted her feet, ready for another go at him. The look on her face, he was a dead man. She was whirling, the kick headed straight for his knee. He dodged and got it: she wasn't trying to get away. This was how she'd killed his dad. Now she was gonna kill him.

She angled around the grass, striking, driving him out on the dock, stalling for a better shot with…Christ, she had an oar. He backed away, slipped on the deck…

She slammed the oar into the water. The spray blinded him. And she was swinging again... He threw an arm up as cover. The oar clipped the top of his head and light screamed through him. He must've yelled.

Gunshot.

"Mimi... Don't shoot me!"

A second shot. A third.

He came to under water, the oar was pounding his neck, his head, his shoulder. He kept trying to dodge away but the water sucked at his clothes, slowing everything, and the oar just kept coming. The oar was bad enough, but the cold made it hard to pull in a breath. Worse, the security alarm was splitting his head. His eyes burned and there was no way to touch bottom. If he could just stay out of her way, stall her, the cops would be there...

She was standing right above him.

He thrashed his arm across the water, back flipped and frog kicked down, praying he was under the dock. He surfaced, gasping, but getting some control. *Where was he?* Way closer to the bank than he'd thought. There was maybe a foot and a half between the water and the underside of the old planks. Except for a thin horizon of night sky, it was completely black. The air reeked of mold, mildew and the stink of whatever had died in the rock embankment. He couldn't touch bottom, but for the moment at least, he was safe.

Safe, but he was freezing. He tried yelling but nobody was gonna hear him over the sound of the alarm and he gave it up.

His clothes and shoes kept dragging on him like weights. He struggled clear of them and lay back into the water. His head felt like a balloon. *How long had it been?* The cold was eating at what energy he had, and he was struggling just to keep above water. His left eye wouldn't open. The only thing he could make out to hold onto was the rotten stringers under the deck—too slick to grip. Where in hell were the cops?

The Gardners'—if he could make it underwater to the Gardners', he could climb up on the bank unseen. They had a tool shed. There'd be something he could use.

Then, footsteps. She was right above him. And she stopped... He pressed his fingertips against the planks. It seemed like she was going away. But she'd never quit. Christ, was she going after Mimi?

A sudden thud, then a crack, and the whole deck shook. What, he was seeing sky, then a plank landed in the water. As a second plank gave way, he filled his lungs again and again building an oxygen reserve and dived as deep as he could manage. He torpedoed into the cold of the lake. Heading anywhere away from her.

He surfaced maybe twenty feet out from the dock. Lights from the traffic crossing Montlake Bridge danced across the water. He scrubbed his eyes, then started a breast-stroke back toward the Gardners' yard.

Suddenly, flashlights. Big ones. And voices. Had to be cops or at least Security. For a second, he treaded water. She had to be somewhere.

Then he spotted her blasting out from behind the boathouse. She was building speed, her back to him. Not a rowboat...a scull. He waited—low enough, the water slapped in his ears and at his mouth. He watched as she bent low, working the oars. If she capsized, her clothes would slow her down, he'd have the advantage. He timed his dive and surfaced right as the scull came alongside. He gripped her craft and jammed with all his weight on the starboard side, praying the scull would capsize.

It could have worked. But she counterbalanced, took a club to his head, and once he dropped away, she put everything she had into making her escape.

He floated there, trying to breathe, watching her—Anna Thorsen, with her hood thrown back, her face shining in patches of light. She headed north-east across the lake. She'd be gone by the time any police boat could get under way.

His shoulder and head throbbed. He thought he'd be sick. He needed to get warm and dry. Most of all, he needed to see Mimi. And Doc Abrams. And soon.

Chapter 58

The police had a firm grip on Mimi even before they dragged Ben out of the water.

They were very upset about her Glock. She got it: Option One, they could arrest her for discharging a firearm blah, blah, blah; Option Two, she could cooperate fully, be a fount of information, and give up the pistol cheerfully. Either way, there was no chance she'd be talking with Ben, not for a while.

All she could do was watch as they pulled him out of the water. He was almost naked, and filthy. He was shivering so hard she could see it from twenty feet away. Blood was running from his head, his shoulder, his hands and arms. He was dead pale. But he was alive, thank God. They loaded him into an ambulance, and he was off to the hospital.

She kept telling herself that was good. Ben would get the care he needed. At the hospital, he'd be safe. But—a big but—that meant she was stuck with explaining to the cops what she knew and what had happened.

The questions started with what she'd *seen,* then what she knew about the dead man, Teach Esparza, which wasn't much. But she had plenty to say about Anna Thorsen. She identified Anna as the woman who'd broken into the house and killed Esparza. She told them everything, even about the attack at

Minnehaha Park. She offered to show them the same photos she'd shown to Ben. But they said she couldn't go back in the house.

Whether they believed her about Anna, who knew?

Once Detective Larson showed up, she hoped things would get better. But no, he went back to the beginning about her gun, firing it in the city, no license. A couple of times she had to sit on herself to keep from losing her temper. Finally, she said, "But really, what was I supposed to do? Let Anna beat him to death?"

"Well, Ms. Fitzroy, that hardly seems likely, does it?"

Clearly Detective Larson hadn't gotten a good look at Ben.

She ended up suggesting that the Seattle police talk with the Arizona detective who was handling the Frank Leit case. Al Baldwin could put them straight on what kind of damage Anna Thorsen was capable of inflicting.

Finally, it was her turn. "What are you going to do to protect Ben? Because Anna Thorsen tried to kill me, and now she's almost killed Ben. You'll assign someone, right?"

He was sorry but no. He lacked the authority. He explained about their limited resources and budget, saying that the police weren't in the security business, they had their hands full as it was. "I'll give Hospital Security a heads up when I stop by to talk with Mr. Leit," he said. He looked sympathetic enough, but looks didn't feel very helpful.

Nearly two hours after they dragged Ben out of the water, Detective Larson handed Mimi over to a man from the Fire Department who said they suspected there was phosphorous in the firebombs, what could Mimi tell them? She hadn't noticed any firebombs. No, she hadn't touched the packages, she hadn't seen them. Ben had run through the room, but he hadn't touched anything but the floor. One look at the fireman's face though, clearly, they wouldn't be going back to the lake house 'til the hazmat people had done whatever they do.

When she finally caught up with Ben, he was swaddled in warm blankets and about a zillion bandages. He had a cluster of bruises blooming on his head and neck, and a cast on his left forearm. He was talking his head off to a nurse and not making much sense.

Mimi stopped just inside his door.

"Mimi," he said and beamed at her.

He looked stoned to the eyeballs. But it was so good to see him. She was right on the edge of crying. Ridiculous, but she was so relieved they both were okay. She hauled a chair up by his bed and cupped her hand on his good arm. Yes, she knew, Anna had gotten away. But everyone in Seattle knew who Anna was and what she'd done. By now, her picture must be on the local news. The police would find her.

"We're safe now," she said. "I talked with Detective Larson. He's taking care of everything. Including, he's put Hospital Security on notice." A lie—she wasn't at all sure they should rely on the hospital's security crew. But for the moment, she needed Ben to believe her.

He blinked, suddenly serious. "You coulda shot me, you know."

"Not unless you were under that flower bed."

"Well you nearly gave me a heart attack."

She apologized. She hadn't meant to scare him. But the sound of shooting might've stopped Anna, or forced her to make a mistake, or run for it. Truth was, though she certainly didn't say so, she'd have done anything to stop Anna beating him.

"But you called the police." He had blood on his teeth.

"That's where I've been. With the police."

"The house?" he said. He looked so out of it.

"The police and fire department were still there when I left. They'd promised to lock it up." No need to fill him in on the firebombs in the family room. He'd hear about that soon enough.

The nurse came around his bed fiddling with his IV. "Teach," he said, "I shouldn't have left him. My fault."

Mimi tapped his arm to draw his attention back to her. "No, it isn't. Remember? Teach wanted us out of there. And we were right upstairs."

Ben's talk rambled and she kept stroking the place on his arm and reassuring him until, eventually, he nodded off.

Assured the nurse would be there a few minutes, Mimi went in search of a phone zone with no press hanging around. She ended up at a side exit with a rain shelter.

The cold night air felt good and to tell the truth, she was grateful for the quiet.

Ben was right. They had dropped the ball for Teach. It left her sick at heart. If she'd been alone out on that porch, she would have sat down on the curb and had a good cry. As it was though, crying might have upset the smokers. She pulled out Ben's phone, scrolled down his contacts list and found Al Baldwin's name.

Detective Baldwin sounded old. He asked about Ben. She said Ben was doing okay, considering. She explained about the break-in and Anna Thorsen. Baldwin listened. He asked the name of the Seattle Detective, then said he'd get back to her tomorrow.

She was tempted to stay outside and call her uncle. But every time the door opened, she felt another wave of residual panic. Anna Thorsen was still out there somewhere. She headed back.

When she got to Ben's room, he had a doctor with him so she started to leave. But Ben wanted her to hear what Dr. Abrams had to say, which was, yes, Ben had a concussion.

"If you're lucky, this one won't aggravate the situation," Dr. Abrams said. He was using a pen light to peer into Ben's left eye. "But we need to keep a close watch on you for a couple of days. As for the other injuries, I'd call a broken arm and twelve stitches significant, wouldn't you?" According to Dr. Abrams, the cuts to Ben's hands, shoulder and head would all heal but they needed special attention because of being in the lake. The good news, it wasn't a separated shoulder, it was a bone bruise.

Just as the doctor headed for the door, Detective Larson poked his head in. Hospital Security had promised to look after them. For the long run though, he was working on setting them up in witness protection until Anna Thorsen was apprehended. He'd see them tomorrow.

Mimi followed Larson out and got it: down the hallway, a man in a security uniform was watching them. The guard nodded her direction and crossed his arms—he looked big enough to do some damage, but he also looked way too nice. And there was no sign of a sidearm.

Once the nurse left, Mimi stepped back into Ben's room, quietly closed the door, then leaned against it. Hospital security probably was better than nothing. But it sure seemed like, for the next couple of days at least, their safety was going to be up to her. Because she didn't for a minute believe that a citywide search would stop Anna Thorsen from trying to kill them. The Anna Thorsen she knew would never give up.

She bullied the recliner closer to Ben and looped the call button so she could send out the alarm if she had to. Next, she retrieved a plastic cup from the trash and carefully balanced it over the door's handle. Not much, but it would rattle down if somebody came in, and that would get her attention.

She stood for a moment and studied him, his deep even breathing. She'd done what she could.

She slid into the big chair beside him and settled herself with the phone and a book from her bag. The glow from the night light was enough she'd be able to read. One more thing. She leaned forward, wrestled off a shoe, and tucked it under her shoulder blades so she wouldn't sleep. Then, blessed quiet.

She opened her book and found where she'd left off reading.

"Mimi?

The book dropped to her lap. She glanced at the door—still closed, cup still there.

Doing her best to sound normal, she said, "Can I get you something?"

"No," Ben said. It was a far-away voice. "Just, you okay?"

She was now.

"Yes," she said and listened for his breathing. Once it slowed into sleep, she cradled his phone in her left hand and found her place again in Tracy Kidder's masterpiece, *Strength in What Remains*.

She read until morning.

Chapter 59

Fighting the wind and the pounding water, Thorsen powered her scull around the Laurelhurst peninsula and straight for the Magnusson Boat Launch at the north end of Lake Washington. Once she hit calmer water, she made the call activating the phosphorous bombs at the Laurelhurst house and dumped the contents of Teach Esparza's briefcase overboard. Then, as she got close enough to grab onto the dock, she punched holes in the bottom of the scull and pushed it away.

She checked her watch, then endured hours of bus rides to get back to her car in the UW parking lot. There'd be no more Rex Sports for her and no more Anna Thorsen anywhere. She'd be traveling light for a while. But she had what she'd need in her car.

She would've been great. But she'd be great again. Just not on this continent. Meantime, she had two things to take care of before she went off the grid entirely. Ben Leit and that Fitzroy bitch had ruined everything. She owed them a big finish.

Sunday and Monday, she hacked the admissions lists for every hospital in King County, she monitored Ben's condo and haunted the email of the usual suspects at Rex Sports, including that damned football website. There was no sign of Ben or Mimi. But she was not giving up, not yet.

By Tuesday morning, she figured she had a few

hours before she'd have to take off.

Just after dawn, she took the stairs from the crest of Queen Anne Hill down to a spot near Ben's third floor condo. She stashed her pack almost exactly where she'd sat days ago and waited. Unless the Seattle Fire Department was completely incompetent, that house on the lake would be a hazardous waste site for months. So, sooner or later, Ben would show up back at the condo. And he would not be in top form. All she had to do was blast one boot square in his chest, let him back into that cave of a living room to get away, then she'd finish him. Just like she'd done with Daddy.

It was nearly noon Tuesday when the Lexus finally rolled into the parking lot. Thorsen flattened herself against the brushy hillside. She gave him thirty minutes, then took the stairs up.

As the door opened, she took a step back to make room for her best kick.

Mimi Fitzroy opened the door, froze, then opened her mouth like a parrot.

"Well hello honey," Thorsen said, shot Mimi a cheesy smile and latched onto a tiny wrist.

"Ben!" Mimi grabbed frantically at the door. "Ben! It's Anna!"

Thorsen jerked Mimi off her feet and up into the air—swinging the little body out, over the balcony railing like a soggy bath towel. Then she stepped into the condo and locked Ben's front door behind her. Smoke. Ben burning his breakfast? Oh-o-o-o-o, somebody call the fire department. For that matter, call in the army. She'd take on God himself, but she was gonna shot-putt that stupid fuck off his ten-stories-down-view-of-the-lake balcony.

Now, where was he?

****

Ben stepped into the entrance hallway just as Thorsen locked the front door. *Mimi.* He couldn't go there. The key always was staying calm. He had to stay calm.

Anna Thorsen was standing on the carpet runner that ran the full length of the long entry hall. Her clothes were filthy, her hair wild. She looked poisonous.

He'd faced that look probably twenty weeks a year for fourteen years on dozens of linemen and linebackers. It was how those guys got themselves up for the kill, with that mad-dog eat-you-alive shit. He was ready, and he knew how she'd come at him. The trick was to keep her occupied 'til she went for that spin move. Just like on the dock, it would come three steps forward, then she'd plant that foot, her weight would shift, and her heel would lift.

"Where's Mimi?"

Her glare disappeared and her mouth shifted to a tight line. She glanced past him to the lakeside balcony, then looked straight through him, waiting, watching him. She shifted her foot...

Dropping flat to the floor, he grabbed the runner she was standing on and yanked.

She went sprawling on her back. But too fast, she was on her feet.

Concentrate. Trust that Mimi is still alive.

A man with a cast on his arm—Anna would think she had him and over-reach in the fight. He shifted his stance and angled away, first for the balcony. She countered and blocked him, pressuring him back into the long living room. To where he couldn't escape her kicks. She sailed a dining chair at him, and he dodged. It broke against the raised hearth of the granite fireplace.

From the way she focused, she was looking for a tell. So...tempt her, give her a little frantic. "Give it up," he said. "Mimi's already gone for help." He winced as if he were hurting, then glanced at the fireplace tools. She angled closer.

"I don't want to hurt you," he said and kept going on with more inane shit he knew she wouldn't answer. Anything to divide her attention. He glanced toward the hall, then at the fireplace tools...

She bought it and went for keeping him away from the fireplace. She shifted two side-steps. *Come on, one more...* As if he were trying to reason with her, he dropped his shoulders and stepped forward almost within her striking range... "Can't we—" he said, and she took the bait, shifted her weight back, that heel lifted...

He exploded at her, pads down, dropping low. He connected like a battering ram, square on her hip, driving her backward, taking out the leg she was balanced on. He rammed his cast up, under her jaw, his left shoulder drove square into her pelvis. And her ass slammed into the granite corner of the hearth. She went down like a tree. She full-out screamed, then caught a breath and rolled onto her belly, panting, swearing. She braced herself up with her arms and got her left knee under her. She tried pushing up and standing, but her right leg wouldn't hold, and she fell trying to walk.

He'd seen it before—something broken, pelvis, femur. Whatever it was, she wasn't going anywhere. He jammed a hand into his pocket—Mimi still had his phone—then the land line in the kitchen... He dialed 9-1-1 and was heading back to Thorsen, making his report, when he got it: she'd made it to the balcony.

She picked up the dining chair she'd been using as a crutch, tossed it away, and shifted her hip up on the railing. For a second, she looked around, like she was taking it all in: the wrecked furniture, the hall runner. She lifted her bad leg up, over, and balanced there.

For a split-second, she turned away from him and her shoulders dropped. Her fingers gripped white on the railing, then she straightened her body. The rain, like glitter on her hair.

She looked down at the hillside below, then back to him, like she'd never seen him before.

He started for her. "Don't—" he shouted.

She smiled at him. "You lose," she said. And she was gone.

Chapter 60

Mimi... Ben had raced out his front door shouting. But then he spotted her little body pinwheeled on the garage roof below his front door. "Mimi. Do not move." He pounded down the stairs. "Coming." With his good hand, he grabbed the top of the six-foot parking lot fence, jack-knifed his legs up and hooked an ankle across the fence cap. From there, even with the cast, he could boost himself up. Her arm moved. Only slightly, but he saw it move.

"Hold on," he whispered.

He couldn't think how she'd survived. Falling two stories down from his front door. There was blood all over her face, her shirt, even in her hair. No wonder. She'd landed on gravel. "I know it hurts," he said. "But don't move." He knelt beside her trying not to freak at how she looked. Her jeans were shredded, her shirt destroyed. The worst of it, her right shoulder and thigh had ground-in gravel. She was shivering, holding her breath.

He stripped his sweatshirt off and wrapped it around her. He'd called 911 before, because of Anna. It couldn't take all that long, but what else could he do? He took her hand. She winced and pulled away. Shit, her hand looked broken.

"You," she caught a breath. "Drive."

"The ambulance is coming."

Her eyes tracked back to the balcony. He fingered a strand of her hair away.

"Anna's gone now," he said. "What happened to your hand?"

"Missed. Grip."

Sirens. He guessed they'd be coming up from Aurora. But where were his neighbors?

"Drive." She closed her eyes.

The pain in her voice made him ache. She sounded so desperate. Should he try taking her? That's what she wanted, but could he get her down off the roof by himself? Stupid idea. Who knew what else she'd hurt?

"Just a little longer," he said.

By the time the police cruiser rolled into the condo parking lot, she was shaking all over. At least they had blankets. They tucked one under her head for support, the other around her.

Her face was grim against the pain. "Please."

He got that she was in shock. How long could they wait? There were three of them now. The older cop, Nathan, was almost as big as he was and pretty-boy Brian not much smaller. How about it? Could they get her down?

Brian pulled the phone off his belt and checked on the ambulance. "Almost here," he reported. For two minutes, Ben answered every question the cops had for him.

It took Ben, the two officers, and both EMTs to get Mimi and the backboard off the roof. Once they had her loaded in the ambulance, Ben motioned to the EMT to wait a second and turned back to Nate and Brian. "I'm going with her. You can follow me or call. Or you can talk with Detective Larson. But if you want me to stay here, you're gonna have to arrest me."

He climbed into the ambulance. "Let's roll," he said. And they did. Four minutes later, ER cut what was left of Mimi's clothes off of her, wrapped her in warm blankets, and stashed her in a cubicle. She was still shaking, eyes closed, stretched out on the exam table.

"We'd usually clean you up first," the resident said as he swabbed the blood and gravel from her shoulder. "But you'll feel a whole lot better once we do this. Then we can take care of the rest of you." He positioned his hands, "Deep breath," he said and popped her dislocated shoulder back into place.

Four hours later, Ben took her back to the condo, adjusted the sling for her arm and helped her settle on the sofa. He made a fire for her. She slept there nearly twenty-four hours. Next day, after a serious talk about modesty and how important it was to change her bandages, Ben turned out to be a reasonably competent nurse.

To get their minds off the fact he was staring at her mostly-bare ass, she told him about her years at Stanford. In return, he told her about his stint in rehab and the times he'd spent in Arizona with his mom. Mimi said she'd lost her mom to cancer. It sounded a lot like his mom's story, but not.

After two or three days of old movies, grilled cheese sandwiches and chicken soup, they fit in the condo as if they'd lived there for years. They got together each evening to talk over the day, even though they'd just spent it together. Usually they stood out on the balcony and watched the traffic on South Lake Union.

One night, out of nowhere she said, "I would've

liked your dad. He was funny, what I read. It must've been great growing up with him."

Ben couldn't help thinking how his dad would've liked Mimi.

He said for years he'd thought every kid had a home like his. He rambled on about how it'd been growing up in Seattle. She was staring off, squinting into the distance. He thought she was listening.

A red float plane scooped past them, up, and circled around to the west.

"My father wished he'd lost me," she said. "Instead of Jamie."

As he tried to think what to say, she went inside for tea.

A couple more planes lifted off.

When she came back, she said, "That story about why you left football? Pretty much bunk I think." She handed him some cookies. "You got a concussion in the Eagles' game. That's what Dr. Abrams is about."

He hadn't talked about that game for nearly a year. But there, with her, he didn't feel so—exposed. More like he was trading up to a new team.

She stretched her good arm up across his back and rested her hand between his shoulder blades. In an echo, he put his arm around her; careful not to hurt her shoulder.

They were still standing there when she said, "Hypothetically. If a player had been diagnosed with something serious, it would be important, wouldn't it? For him to take care of himself." They stood there a long time like that. Leaning together. Just listening to the traffic.

A word about the author...

B. Davis Kroon fell in love with football watching games with her father. During her university years, she wrote the book and lyrics to the musical comedy, *The Lady's Game*, and subsequently spent several years acting and working in theatre as a producer/director. To support her theatrical life, she worked in law (where she did technical writing, trial work, and designed and built databases to support complex litigation).

She has published numerous poems in literary journals, as well as one section of the book of poetry, *Millennial Spring*.

She and her husband remain dedicated football fans and travel extensively to support their favorite college team. *Trap Play* is her first suspense novel.

CPSIA information can be obtained
at www.ICGtesting.com
Printed in the USA
LVHW021520230720
661378LV00015B/1210